TEMPTED...

Wendi straightened, moving back from the bed and licking her dry lips.

"I—I believe that's about all I can do."

"That's not even close to what you could do if you wanted to," Nick growled in a voice laden with unmistakable want and need. "And you better get the hell out of here before I decide to make you admit it."

Wendi rushed toward the door, stopping as though she'd run into a barrier when Nick almost silently murmured her name.

"What?" she asked, refusing to turn around.

"Thank you," he said.

The simple acknowledgment did what his carnal comments couldn't. She turned to face him again, losing herself in his eyes for a yearlong moment. She glanced at his mouth, finding his lips pursed in a pout . . .

What would happen if she actually walked back to that bed? Touched his lips with her fingertip? Bent down and kissed him?

Spellbound

TRANA MAE SIMMONS

JOVE BOOKS, NEW YORK

SPELLBOUND

A Jove Book / published by arrangement with
the author

PRINTING HISTORY
Jove edition / November 1998

The Penguin Putnam Inc. World Wide Web site address is
http://www.penguinputnam.com

ISBN: 0-515-12390-0

A JOVE BOOK®
Jove Books are published by The Berkley Publishing Group, a member
of Penguin Putnam Inc.,
375 Hudson Street, New York, New York 10014.
JOVE and the "J" design are trademarks belonging to
Jove Publications, Inc.

PRINTED IN THE UNITED STATES OF AMERICA

10 9 8 7 6 5 4 3 2 1

*To Belle, who taught me what the goose bumps
mean and who loves to prowl the same
graveyards and haunted houses
and
To Mary and Shari, for their fudge
and
To Samantha, fellow ghostbuster-ette
and special friend
and
To Barney, who protects me from the
bumps in the night . . . sometimes!*

*"An' [If] it harm none,
do what ye will."*

—The Wiccan Rede,
the supreme law of the Craft

Spellbound

One

New Orleans. Damn, it still stinks after ten years.

Nick Bardou steadied himself against the deck railing, staring at the activity on shore as the combined passenger and cargo ship *The Lady Rachelle* nudged the bulwark. Shipping company employees in salt-stiff clothing scrambled around, grabbing ropes tossed from the sailors on board and securing them to the pilings. On the dock, stacks of goods in huge crates and boxes waited to be loaded as soon as the passengers departed and the hold was cleared of the incoming cargo.

As Nick watched, the pain in his leg increased. He'd rested on his stateroom bunk until the last possible moment before he came on deck in response to the captain's message that they were getting ready to dock. The pain always heightened under stress. It had been a long time since he first left New Orleans, and he had no desire to make his first appearance with a limp announcing his physical weakness. Gritting his teeth, he concentrated on the scurrying mass of people on the shoreline and the piles of waiting cargo.

Wrong move. Foreboding nudged him. Memories hid and demons waited to pounce among the stacks of cargo. If he hadn't already known the stifling heat was typical for this time of year, he'd think it came from the bowels of hell, carried here by those concealed demons.

Hell would be easier to handle than coming back here, he mused.

"Mr. Bernard! Yoo-hoo! Mr. Bernard!"

Nick stiffened. How long would he be able to keep his identity hidden here? Not long, for sure, too many people were likely to remember the Bardou name. He turned to see what the heck Miz Thibedeau wanted this time.

"I've taken care of getting the luggage unloaded and given them the address to send it to—the one you gave me so I could telegraph my son and let him know where we'd be staying," the portly woman said between huffs as she hurried up to him. "And the purser said the company's got carriages waiting to take the first-class passengers wherever they're going. All we have to do is look for the carriages with the shipping company logo on the side of them waiting on the dock."

Despite Miz Thibedeau's harried voice, which still carried a southern lilt after many years spent far from New Orleans, not a hair on her head risked moving out of place in the stiff gulf breeze. Nor did a wrinkle dare mar her starched dress. A multitude of creases lined her face, but Nick barely noticed them anymore.

Nick had never intended to find a servant from New Orleans—someone who might know his true identity. But damn, could she cook up a mess of red beans and rice, along with an iron skillet of cornbread that would make a sinner repent. Even Nick couldn't resist good old Cajun cooking.

Nick had gained a taste for crawfish and other foods his Creole class disdained as a kid while prowling the swamps with a friend his father didn't approve of. He hadn't had any in over ten years, and he was sure Miz Thibedeau would know exactly how much red pepper to put in to raise blisters on his fingertips after he broke off several dozen of those delicious tails. . . .

"I could have handled taking care of the luggage," he said.

She flapped a negligent hand. "Oh, you probably could have, but since you didn't bring a manservant with you, who really ought to be the one to do it, I took care of it myself. Now, out in that wild California country we just left, no one would have thought twice about a gentleman handling his own minor inconveniences. But we're back home now. It just isn't done. You know that."

Home, hell. And he bit back telling Miz Thibedeau that people in New Orleans had long ago denied him the title of gentleman. Let her foster her illusions for a while longer. He hoped that after she found out who he really was, she'd still want to return to California with him. But if not, so be it. He'd had plenty of practice the last ten years at dealing with the pain of losing people from his life. He handled that suffering the same as the physical pain in his leg—by accepting the inevitability and controlling the ache any way he could.

Bringing her with him had been a chance he had to take, because he doubted he'd be able to employ any other servants in this city—not when they learned who wanted to hire them. And he didn't much care to be subjected to the stares and behind-the-hand speculations he'd encounter if he dined out while he was stuck here.

The salt-encrusted gangplank gears squeaked and squalled as a nearby sailor cranked the mechanism to lower it, and Nick glanced over his shoulder to see the captain approaching. Two more sailors behind them shouted at the steerage passengers, warning them to wait until their betters disembarked before they sullied the deck with their dirty bodies. The sailors interspersed their orders with only mild curses, in deference to the ladies flooding onto deck from the upper staterooms, but Nick knew what they'd rather be saying.

Miz Thibedeau clenched her jaw, and as though reading her mind, Nick knew she found it as hard to tolerate the class distinctions here as they both did in California. Out there bigotry was directed at a different class of people, mostly the Chinese and other foreign immigrants who filled the railroad and construction jobs. But the separations were every bit as defined as in this centuries-old city.

During the war, he'd shared possum and snake with swamp rats and generals alike, and he didn't much care for snobbery any longer.

Ah, N'awlins. After the horror of the war, no wonder I prefer California. Out there a man makes his own reputation rather than feeding on his lineage.

Better not let that thought take effect, either. He could feel the relentless strain on the door shutting off the memories in his mind.

"I hope you had a pleasant journey, Mr. Bernard," the captain said with exactly the proper measure of deference.

"Very pleasant," Miz Thibedeau answered for them both. The captain's brows climbed up his forehead in surprise, just like they had every time Nick's servant had dared address him. Servants just didn't do that.

Mine do in California . . . Nick started to say, but instead he decided to treat the class-conscious captain to a dose of his own medicine. Casting a disdainful look down his nose at the shorter man, an admonishment of his audacity in thinking Nick gave a shit whether he had made the journey pleasant for him or not, he took Miz Thibedeau's arm and strolled toward the gangplank. Thankfully, he managed the walk without utilizing his cane; hopefully people would think he carried it for style rather than assistance.

Miz Thibedeau's plump body shook with repressed laughter, and Nick almost joined her when he looked down and saw her supercilious look and pursed lips. Damn, he would miss her if she turned on him when she found out his true identity. Only Miz Thibedeau could lighten the darkness clinging to him in an unshakable cloud of despair. Only Miz Thibedeau would he tolerate doing that.

How the hell he noticed it amid all the other activity on shore, he never understood. But for some reason, as he and Miz Thibedeau strolled down the gangplank, Nick's head unerringly swiveled to get a better look at a disturbance toward the end of the pier.

He zeroed in on the figure of a slender woman in a pale green dress. There were a dozen or more women in the crowd, most of them waiting for husbands, sons, or other relatives to disembark, and several of them weren't exactly ugly. None of them except this one, however, drew his gaze—or made him feel a faint stir of male appreciation with only seeing a feminine back.

While weaving her way through the multitude of street vendors meeting the ship and hoping for a few coins' profit, the woman bumped into a pushcart filled with flowers. She was in such a hurry, she failed to notice what she'd done until a huge pile of flowers started sliding out of the cart and the pushcart vendor shouted in alarm. Not really interested in the outcome of the spectacle, Nick kept walking.

Suddenly he froze.

The woman turned, and the entire mass of flowers hung in the air, waiting for her to scramble back and catch them.

They couldn't do that.

But they did.

One side of his mind told him that she'd been too far past the cart to make it back in time to catch the bouquet in her arms. The other side informed him, in no uncertain terms, that's exactly what she'd done—with the flowers waiting for her! She returned the flowers to the cart, then caught his eye from across the crowd.

"Ouch!" A long minute later—or maybe only a short second, he had no idea—Miz Thibedeau slapped his hand and tugged against his hold. "Ow, Mr. Bernard! You're squeezing my arm off. Let go. Please!"

Nick released her, but he couldn't tear his gaze away from the woman by the flower cart. If her actions were any indication, she was apologizing profusely to the vendor, her strawberry-blond hair on her un-bonneted head shining in the sunshine and her delicate hands arranging the flowers securely on the cart. If he thought his eyes were playing tricks on him before, this time he had to be going crazy.

That woman had been dead for ten years. He'd killed her himself.

As though sensing his intense preoccupation in her, she lifted her gaze once more and stared across the distance separating them. From here he couldn't tell if her eyes were blue or not, but she had the same familiar petite figure, which shouldn't have stirred a man as much as a more voluptuous one would, but did. The gulf breeze blew her skirt against slender legs, endlessly long, given her short stature. For a man who wanted a woman he could easily handle and adjust for his own pleasure beneath the sheets, she'd be perfect. And she was exactly the proportion and coloring he'd avoided with a distaste bordering on fear.

Nick watched as an older woman entered the picture, stepping between him and the strawberry-blonde. Then the crowd encroached, shutting off the sight of them both.

Leaving Miz Thibedeau standing there, Nick strode down the gangplank and pushed his way through the crowd on the dock, using his cane when necessary to both lean on and clear his path. Angry shouts and muttered curses fell in his wake; a corner of his mind wished someone would confront him and let him vent the furious anger boiling inside him. Had he been wearing the more casual attire he preferred in California, rather than the proper clothing of the Creole gentlemen in New Orleans, no doubt someone would have satisfied his need for a confrontation. As it was, only verbal discontent followed him, since the crowd mistook him for one of their betters.

It couldn't be her, he reassured himself sternly. But if it were, he'd haul her ass over to the Bardou mansion on St. Charles Avenue and keep her there until she told him how she'd escaped death. How she'd managed to survive a five-inch knife wound in her heart and a slit throat. Survived being buried in a coffin, looking every bit as beautiful through her death pallor as in life. He'd only glimpsed her briefly at the burial—an attempt to confirm what he'd seen two nights before—and he'd had no qualms she was dead.

When he arrived at the flower cart, panting and gritting his teeth against the horrible pain in his leg, the only person there was the vendor and an elegantly attired gentleman purchasing a bouquet of roses. The strawberry-blonde was gone, disappeared without a trace.

"Where'd she go?" he demanded of the vendor.

"Who?" he asked.

"Sir," the gentleman waiting for the vendor to wrap his

flowers said, "wait your turn. I'm buying flowers for my wife right now. It's our anniversary today."

Nick ignored the man. "The woman who was just here," he insisted. "The one who knocked the flowers off your cart. Where did she go?"

The vendor shrugged and turned his attention back to the gentleman. "That will be ten cents, sir."

"Damn it . . ." Nick began. Suddenly a flash of strawberry-blonde a few yards to his right caught his attention, and he headed for it. When he seized the woman's arm and jerked her around, watery eyes in an aged face topped with obviously dyed hair met his gaze. She couldn't have gotten that rare color naturally.

"Ye don't havta get nasty, mister," the whore said. Her foul breath whooshed past a mouthful of rotten teeth and knocked him backward a step. He released her arm as though it were as odious as her breath. "We kin takes care of bidness right over there, 'mong the crates. Won't nobody catch us, 'cause me friend Biddy'll keep a watchout for us."

Nick limped away, but she grabbed the back of his frock coat. "Wait, mister. I ain't et for a couple days, so's I'd be willin' to give it to ya cheap. I ain't got no diseases—"

Nick distastefully freed himself from her hold. The easiest way to get rid of her and keep from making a more conspicuous display of himself would be to pay her off. Digging in his pocket, he pulled out a gold piece without paying any heed to the value of it and thrust it into her hand. Then he shoved her aside, disregarding her babbled "God bless ye, sir."

Miz Thibedeau met him halfway back to the gangplank. "I don't blame you for wanting to see for yourself if that really happened, Mister Bernard," she said in a breathless voice. "Why, that looked like magic when that pretty woman kept those flowers from hitting the ground. And didn't she look a lot like Sa—"

"Come on," Nick snarled before she could utter the hated name. "The ship's carriages will all be full, and we'll have to try to find a hansom ourselves. I'm not inclined to wait around in this heat to get transportation to the house."

"Nick!" another voice called. "Hey, Nick! Nick Bardou! Is that you?"

Nick closed his eyes for a brief moment and shook his head. When he opened them again, he saw Chet Emilie hurrying toward him. Damn it to hell, the two of them had shared dozens of hangovers, so there was no chance of convincing Chet that he'd mistaken Nick's identity.

Funny. When he glanced down at Miz Thibedeau while he waited for Chet to reach them, she looked completely unfazed at hearing someone hail him with a different name than she knew him by.

"Wendi Chastain!" Sybilla pulled Wendi through the crowd. "You shouldn't have done that. You should have let those flowers fall. What if someone saw you?"

"Aunt, I'm appalled," Wendi said. "I'd think you'd be glad to see my magic work so easily after all the trouble I've had with it. Besides, I did it instinctively. At least half of that vendor's flowers would have been ruined in the filthy street because I knocked them off the cart, and his family might have gone to bed hungry tonight. Did you see how not even one single flower slipped out of the bunch and hit the ground?"

"I saw," Sybilla said in a grudging voice. "But I'd much prefer you practice at home instead of in front of a hundred people."

"Hmmmmm. Then why did you turn that woman's hair

the color of mine? What do you think she's going to do when she looks in a mirror and finds out she's no longer gray?''

''She won't. The spell lasts only ten minutes, and then the color will change back. But we'll discuss this when we get home, not here. Not where someone might overhear us.''

Aunt Sybilla's obvious agitation silenced Wendi as they continued away from the docks. Had they known a ship was arriving, they probably would have put off their shopping trip rather than fight the crowds of people. But the bare cupboards couldn't be filled with magic. Well, they could be, but the food wouldn't be nearly as delicious as real food. For some reason, food conjured from and cooked with magic lacked something intangible.

That the Fates had decreed the trip this morning wasn't beyond the realm of possibility. Aunt Sybilla's uneasiness was triggered seemingly out of thin air, as though something had been waiting for just the proper moment. The confusion and distress in Sybilla now were a different type of bewilderment than she'd seen in her since her aunt's magic started giving her difficulties.

Wendi shifted her shopping bag to the other hand, glad she hadn't forgotten it at the flower cart. The okra, corn, potatoes, and tomatoes in it wouldn't make a flavorful soup without some type of meat or seafood to season it, but Aunt Sybilla had turned them toward home before they reached the fish stall. Wendi followed her rather than call attention to them both any further by arguing with her aunt. Maybe they could pick up some crawfish or shrimp at Stefan's bayou stand near their house.

The farther they got from the docks, the more the crowds thinned. Unfortunately the smells didn't abate in the same proportion. Thank the Goddess they'd been able to grow multitudes of flowers around their house, encasing their yard in a cocoon of sweetness nearly year round. She especially loved the honeysuckle, which the upper-class neighborhoods considered a weed. The poverty of her neighborhood couldn't be completely hidden, and the small house on Canal Street was a far cry from the manor house where she'd spent her first four years, but most of the owners of the houses in her neighborhood tried their best to keep their dwellings in repair. They were too close to the docks and factories to completely escape the odors, but growing flowers helped.

A familiar face caught her attention. Doc Meneur stumbled down the sidewalk, deep in his cups even this early in the day. Wendi winced at the grating sound of his drunken jollity.

"I'll eat when I'm hungry!" he jolted out. "I'll drink when I'm dry! And if women don't kill me, I'll live till I die!"

Suddenly he saw her and grabbed his decrepit hat from his head, holding it across his chest.

"G'mornin', Mish Wendi." He staggered against the building wall, thumping to a halt with a silly grin on his face. "An' Mish Shybilla."

Sybilla shook her head at him, but Wendi paused a second and said, "Good morning, Doc. And how's Mary Jo?"

"Mish Wendi!" he said enthusiastically. "She's real happy, now thet we kin..." He snickered and winked sloppily. "You know. I sure do 'preciate that there potion."

"You keep drinking all day and all night, it'll take more than a potion to help you the next time, Doc," she warned halfheartedly. Doc wouldn't see next spring, with the insidious damage from tuberculosis already claiming his lungs, let alone the damage years of drinking had done.

She didn't know if his finding Mary Jo a couple years

ago had been good or bad, since the homely spinster owner of the local hat shop had fallen in love with him so solidly. Mary Jo kept him fed when he'd eat and gave him a place to sleep when he made it home at night, prolonging his life and giving them both a short span of happiness. But she couldn't reverse the disease's progress. Nor could Wendi's magic. It seemed the Fates had decreed Doc a short life.

"Tell Mary Jo that I said hello," she said with a sad smile before she hurried after her aunt.

She tried another tentative thrust into Aunt Sybilla's mind, but her aunt had effectively closed off the psychic communications between them. Even at twenty-two and having endured two failed love affairs, it would be years before Wendi's magic would be as strong as Sybilla's. Anyhow, as strong as Aunt Sybilla's had been until recently.

She didn't need magic, however, to know whatever had upset her aunt back there had nothing to do with someone noticing Wendi's successful spell. And she'd bet her next week's success at magic that Sybilla's distress had to do with the man walking off the ship with Thalia Thibedeau. Despite the length of time this former client had been gone from New Orleans, Wendi recognized Thalia Thibedeau on the gangplank. She would have waved, but the man beside Miz Thibedeau flagged her feminine attention, as well as her appreciation.

Devastatingly handsome, he'd caused a definite stir of awareness in her. Tall, dark, and with a fitted frock coat outlining very adequate shoulders, he stood out from the crowd as though absolutely no one else at all on the dock even mattered—at least, to Wendi's mind. The black aura surrounding his body was almost the same shade as his hair, though, and it immediately filled her with unease. The color reflected deep pressure and tension, while the extension of it over his head meant physical injury. She knew at once that he carried the cane on his arm for aid with an injury rather than fashion.

She also noticed orange in his aura, an indication of his courage. He needed that, according to what she sensed. She'd only had time to briefly touch his mind before Sybilla stepped between them, and the depths had been so filled with shadows and pain she rebounded from them in distress.

As soon as they arrived home, she'd ask Aunt Sybilla if she knew the man. Something had sent her aunt hurrying away from the ship—something strong enough to overcome Sybilla's hunger, which she'd been griping about all during their walk to the docks. Wendi couldn't shake the strong suspicion that their flight had to do with the wondrously attractive man with the black aura.

Aunt Sybilla hurried on past the turnoff to Stefan's bayou stand, strengthening Wendi's suspicions. There hadn't been a scrap of food left in the house after breakfast, since they'd both been too busy to shop the past few days—perhaps also decreed by the Fates. Of course, there was that sweet potato pie their neighbor had brought over to pay for her tarot card reading—the neighbor who thought vinegar enhanced everything. Even the Afghan hound Aunt Sybilla had befriended, which kept the neighborhood cats at bay, wouldn't touch that.

Wendi stopped at the turnoff. "Aunt!" she called when Sybilla didn't notice she'd halted. "At least let me get us some shrimp from Stefan's!"

Sybilla turned and motioned to her. "No. I'll ask Little Bob or Tangie to get us some after we get home. Come on."

"It'll just take me a few minutes, Aunt. What on earth's your hurry?"

"Please come with me, Wendi. We need to get home and talk."

Wendi glanced down the intersecting path leading to the bayou, and her stomach growled. There hadn't been any flour to make biscuits or gravy that morning, either, and grits never satisfied her hunger for long. It wouldn't take Stefan more than five minutes to throw out his net and retrieve enough fresh shrimp for a meal. This time of year the bayou teemed with both shrimp and crawfish.

When Wendi continued to hesitate, Sybilla walked closer to her. "Remember when I told you that I'd seen something in my scrying speculum yesterday evening, child? Something foretelling a major change coming into our lives?"

"I remember, Aunt."

"Well, that change just walked off that ship beside Thalia Thibedeau!"

Two

"It's always been a lovely house," Miz Thibedeau murmured as the carriage pulled up outside the Bardou mansion. "But I suppose it'll be quite the mess after being closed up all these years."

The carriage driver climbed from his seat, then pulled down a set of steps on the side of the vehicle for his passengers to dismount. Ten years ago Nick would have disdained the steps, but now he used them grudgingly. Turning, he held up his hand for Miz Thibedeau. A look of surprise crossed the carriage driver's face, but Nick didn't bother to explain himself. Miz Thibedeau more than repaid his little courtesies. In fact, he wondered sometimes if she wasn't the only person on earth who thought him worthy of her care.

Not that he would ever let her far enough inside the barrier to his emotions to recognize his gratitude.

Miz Thibedeau climbed down and smoothed some nonwrinkles from her dress. "Shall I wait out here for our baggage to come in the wagon?" she asked. "Or should I go get started on the dust inside?"

"Right now, just wait," Nick murmured. He pulled a

coin from his pocket and handed it to the carriage driver. The man glanced at it and his mouth dropped open.

"Oh, sir, thank you," he said gratefully. Tugging his hat in a leavetaking, he climbed aboard and set his horse in motion.

"Now," Nick said sternly to his housekeeper and cook. "Before we go inside, I want to know how long you've been aware of who I am."

"Oh, lordy, for ages," Miz Thibedeau said breezily, waving a hand in the air, but with a suppressed twinkle in her eyes. "Even before I come to work for you. Why, you don't think that newspaper telling about the tax sale on this beautiful mansion just accidentally found its way open so you'd see the piece, do you?"

"Damn it, Miz Thibedeau—"

She patted his arm and walked past. "You look a lot like your father, Monsieur Bardou," she said, addressing him for the first time by his French Creole title. "And I've always wanted to see inside this beautiful place. Though I do wish it wasn't going to be covered in dust the first time I see it."

Nick limped after her. "I wired my attorney, Justin Rabbonir, and asked him to have the house readied for us," he said with a sigh of resignation. "He was also supposed to see if he could find any servants to assist you for the few days we'll be here, but he wired back and said he couldn't. They did at least clean the place, and they damned well better have done a good job for what I had to pay them. But none of them would agree to work here permanently, even for a few days."

"No, probably not," she agreed. "I'll get some servants, don't you worry, Monsieur Bardou. Do you suppose Monsieur Rabbonir is waiting for us with the key?"

Nick shook his head and picked up a flowerpot filled

with bright-blooming red geraniums on the landing wall. He frowned down at Miz Thibedeau. "Didn't you notice the grounds were kept up when we pulled up at the curb? And it looks like Justin brought over some flowers."

"I assumed your neighbors wouldn't put up with a neglected house beside theirs. The estate probably set up funds for a groundskeeper. Or maybe your hired help at Belle Chene, outside of town, took care of it."

It shouldn't still surprise him that she knew things about him—things he'd thought secret from his previous life—but it did. Shoulders heaving in defeat, he shoved the key in the lock and opened the door. Holding out a hand and giving her a wry look, he allowed her to proceed him.

She stopped just inside the marble-floored entranceway, mouth dropping in awe. "It's every bit as beautiful as I'd heard," she said after a few seconds. "Oh, I'm so glad you wired ahead and had it cleaned."

"I asked Justin to make sure the larder was stocked, too."

She giggled like a young girl. "You and your belly, Monsieur Bardou. Did you by any chance think of transportation?"

"There's a small barn out back, and I believe you might find a buggy and horse there, as well as a mount, should you decide you wanted to try to ride that way. Use the mare, though, not the stallion I asked Justin to have sent in from Belle Chene."

"Oh, Monsieur Bardou, you made a joke," she said with a laugh. "Maybe it will do you good to be home."

Invisible weight fell on his shoulders, heavy in its nonexistence, and Miz Thibedeau's face changed immediately. "Well, maybe you just don't know it yet," she murmured. "Will you show me around, or would you rather I familiarize myself with the house?"

"We've probably got time for a tour before the wagon with our baggage arrives."

The Bardou mansion wasn't the largest house on St. Charles Avenue, but Nick would rate its opulence beside any other mansion in New Orleans without question. Justin had evidently overseen the work, because the place smelled just like it did right before the times his mother had entertained. And she'd entertained several times a week in the earlier period of her marriage, but he didn't want to let that memory out yet, either.

He motioned Miz Thibedeau through the door on the right, which led into the ladies' parlor. Through the room was another room, a mirroring one, but decorated in more masculine style—the men's parlor, where he'd drunk more liquor than he cared to recall and puked his guts out one night. He checked the bar as they passed through, finding it fully stocked. Justin had even remembered the brand of brandy he preferred.

They passed through the game room and out onto the back veranda. Though still somewhat overgrown, an effort had been made to tame the profusion of roses, wisteria, and azaleas in the garden back there. Several marble statues stood cleared of vines, though they still needed to be scrubbed free of bird droppings. The small barn demanded a coat of paint, and beyond that, the rear wall was covered in ivy. Sun sparkled on the pieces of sharp glass imbedded in the top of the wall to help keep intruders from invading the family's privacy.

Over and above the other flower scents, honeysuckle mixed with jasmine drifted in the air.

"My mother always loved the smell of honeysuckle and jasmine," Nick told Miz Thibedeau. "See where it's planted over there?" When she nodded, he continued. "Up above that area is the master bedroom. She liked the windows open at night so she could smell her garden."

"I knew your mother," she told him, not expanding on her statement.

He didn't ask her to. "Come on, we'll finish the tour."

They walked across the veranda and entered another door, which the same key opened. He bypassed the oak stairwell for now, leading her to the front entranceway again, then to the other side of the stairwell. Here, another parlor was used for less formal visitors, and just past it was the library/study his father had called his own. He only muttered an identifying comment to her for now, then led the way up the stairwell.

There were six bedrooms upstairs, and it didn't take him long to show them to her. Three had attached dressing rooms, but only the master suite had a sitting room and wash closet.

As they started back downstairs, Nick said, "There's another small building off the back veranda that you probably saw. It's used for the kitchen. I want you to feel free to do anything necessary to make that room usable for yourself. And there's a small living quarters above that, which you may use if you wish. Or you can have any of the bedrooms upstairs."

"Other than the master suite, I assume," she said, quirking her eyebrow.

"Other than the master suite," he agreed, knowing it would look like he couldn't handle the memories if he didn't use the room designated for the mansion's owner.

"First thing I'd like you to do for me," Miz Thibedeau said as soon as they got to the bottom of the stairwell, "is hitch up that buggy. My sister's expecting me, and I'll drive over there and see what sort of servants she can round up for us. With all her children and our various cousins, I believe we'll find a very adequate staff."

"Just remember, it's only for a few days. But tell them I'll pay them for at least a month, if they're good at their jobs. I don't like to have to worry about the house running itself while I deal with other matters."

"As you wish." Cocking her head, she gazed at him with the merry look he didn't like to admit he enjoyed thoroughly. "I seem to recall a bayou stand run by a Cajun named Stefan near where my sister lives. Would you by any chance be interested in some crawfish for the evening meal?"

He had to swallow the sudden moisture in his mouth before he could answer her with any degree of nonchalance. "Whatever *you* wish. Your meals are always delightful."

"Hmmmmm. Etouffe, then? Or jambalya?"

"We're tired from the trip. Just boil them."

"Ah, yes, with lots of spices and hot peppers," she mused. "Some new potatoes and corn cooked in the pot with them. And I'll bet my sister made some pralines, knowing I was coming. That will do for dessert this evening, if you agree."

Damn it, moisture would run down his chin if he opened his mouth! Instead, he jerked his head "yes" in agreement and headed for the rear of the mansion. A few minutes later he had the buggy hitched, Miz Thibedeau on her way down the back alley, and was closing the gate. Now he could give in to the pain and strong desire for the taste of brandy tantalizing his senses.

Leaning on his walking stick more heavily now that no one could see him and judge his depth of misery, he made his way up the flagstone-lined pathway and onto the veranda. The door jammed for a second when he pulled on the knob, and he jerked it loose with a curse. He didn't have to put on a front for anyone now, and the dam against the pain crumbled as though it were a levy giving way in a flood.

He didn't bother with the men's parlor—he headed straight for the library. Knowing Justin, that bar would be stocked as adequately as the other one, perhaps even more so. He flung the door open and hurried over to the sideboard, where cut-glass decanters and heavy crystal glasses sparkled invitingly.

When the unrelenting pain sent a tear sliding down his face, he grimaced in anger and grabbed the brandy decanter. Shakily, he leaned on the walking stick, pulled the stopper out with his teeth and spit it away. It landed soundlessly on the carpeted floor. He took several long swallows, then closed his eyes and waited for the relief the bottle held.

Brandy never made the pain disappear completely, but it helped him bear it. Over the years, however, it took more and more brandy to help—and longer and longer for it to work. He stood there a full five minutes before he felt confident enough to stagger to one of the overstuffed armchairs in front of the huge teakwood desk without collapsing along the way. The fight with the agony in his leg took all his energy, but instead of dropping immediately into the chair, as he would have ten years ago, he eased himself down. One of the things he would miss the most here in this harshly humid land was the specially designed furniture in his house in San Francisco. After another swallow of brandy, he leaned his head back against the chair.

Still he withheld the thought threatening to escape, focusing on another direction, hoping the memories frothing for notice like pounding waves at high tide would recede.

Why the hell had he even bothered to come back to New Orleans? Seemed like some twisted Fate had started it all. Hiring Thalia Thibedeau. Her son sending her periodic New

Orleans newspapers all the way to California. Her knowing who he was all along.

He could have ignored the notice of the tax sale on his family home and the outlying plantation of Belle Chene. Pretended he hadn't seen it, even though Miz Thibedeau had left it open beside his breakfast plate that morning. At the time he didn't realize that had Miz Thibedeau seen it, she would recognize it as having anything to do with him. He hadn't used the Bardou name in years.

For that matter, why the hell did he even hire Miz Thibedeau that day? Surely his longing for the taste of the spicy Creole and Cajun dishes from his childhood hadn't been that bad. His stomach growled and his mouth watered. He snorted a sound of disgust at the lie crowding his mind, recalling the day he'd found Thalia Thibedeau so far from her New Orleans home.

He'd been interviewing prospective servants and thought it provident to find a widow who had traveled from New Orleans to California with her husband before he died. But look at the twisted path that turn of Fate had led him on. He'd vowed never to set foot in New Orleans again, and here he was—not only in this hellacious city but in his family mansion. And Miz Thibedeau had set the wheels in motion.

He'd sworn never even to travel any farther east than the Rocky Mountains again. Too many memories lay beyond those craggy peaks. Too many nightmares waited in the wings for release.

He was right in the middle of those nightmares now. Try as he would, he couldn't keep his thoughts focused on California, not with the walls of the Bardou mansion surrounding him. Not with the memory of the wind-blown strawberry-blond hair on the woman peering at him across the dockside crowd. Peering at him with a gaze that some-how connected to him.

And her petite but voluptuous body could have belonged to the dead body he remembered.

Oh, he'd had time now to realize who she was. Sabine's daughter. She could be no one else.

Nick opened his eyes and stared at the portrait he'd caught sight of as he made his pain-fogged way to the side-board. He'd avoided acknowledging it since he entered the library, but he knew damned well who that was, too. Sabine herself.

Where the hell had the portrait come from? Had those spiritual Fates moved it here from some unknown dimen-sion? It hadn't been here when he left ten years ago, and he probably should get up right now and burn it. It taunted him, as she had in real life.

He tilted the brandy bottle at it.

"Sabine," he whispered in a mocking voice.

Sabine. The woman at the dock, her daughter, could be her twin at that age. He would never forget the tint in those blue eyes or the look of that silky, tousled hair. Or that drop-at-my-feet-fool beauty, which had entrapped his father and resulted in his mother's broken heart—her death. The last time he had seen the girl's mother, though, Sabine had been lying in a pool of blood at *his* feet, dead beyond a doubt, her blue eyes closed forever.

He didn't remember the girl's name, but he damned sure remembered her mother's name. Sabine. Such a parody on the martyr Saint Sabine of church history.

"Sabine." He sneered at the portrait, lifting the brandy bottle in a caustic salute once more. "Sabine. Bitch. Whore. Adulteress. *Witch*." The last word stretched out in a snake-like hiss.

Her curse had proved true. He could still hear her words

ringing in his memory. Hidden in the stable at Belle Chene plantation, miles from this St. Charles mansion his mother occupied, he had listened to the curse his father's mistress screamed. Then he'd drawn his knife from his boot and stepped out from the shadows to confront the woman who had caused his mother so much pain—and confront the man with her, whose voice was obviously disguised.

When he next remembered anything, he woke up beside Sabine's dead body. Heard footsteps approaching and scrambled to his feet and into the dark recesses of the barn again. A moment later he watched his father bow his head over Sabine's dead body, keening and sobbing desperately, and realized he held a blood-stained knife in his hand.

He had sense enough to drop the knife before he stepped out to confront his father, and pretend later the real killer had dropped it. But someone had spread the rumor that it was Nick who killed Sabine, although nothing could be proved. That, on top of the exposure of Sabine as Dominic Bardou's mistress, had driven his mother to suicide.

He curled his lip in a savage grin. The curse didn't matter any longer, even though he'd never forgotten the words. Nick had no desire to bring children into a world so filled with pain.

"Sabine," he whispered, unable to keep from repeating the name. "Have you returned in the form of your very sensual daughter to taunt another Bardou male?"

He knew where she lived, if she still lived there, which she probably did. He'd been to more than one of the whorehouses on Canal Street, and he'd actually seen the house more than once—had it pointed out to him by a friend as drunk as he was the first time, and been unable to ignore it whenever his path took him close to it after that.

If I co'ld find me a piece as pretty as the one your father keeps over there, his friend had slurred that initial time, *I'd set her up and keep her for myself. Wouldn't have to worry 'bout who'd been in the bed before me. Whether this is the time I'd walk out with the pox—or somethin' worse.*

He could go outside right now. Saddle up the stallion Justin had left in the barn. Be there in fifteen minutes of a painful ride, given the way his leg hated to be astride a horse.

But Miz Thibedeau had mentioned going to the bayou stand, and the stand wasn't far from the house. Besides, he'd pay for it for days if he rode a horse instead of using a buggy. But he didn't feel much pain right now.

He glanced at the brandy decanter. Hadn't it been nearly full when he started? A good half of it was gone now.

He took another long swallow, set the decanter on the floor, then lurched to his feet. He started out of the room, then paused and looked back at the bottle. Even through his clouded mind, he knew what sort of nagging he would have to put up with if Miz Thibedeau came back and found that bottle on the shining floor.

Using the cane, he staggered back to the chair. He had to sit down to be able to reach the bottle, and it took everything he could find in his reserve strength to get back to his feet. He stepped toward the sideboard, then glanced down at the bottle with a speculative look.

He could feel the eyes in the portrait on his back. His skin crawled, as though a hundred spiders crept across his shirt. Turning, he slung the bottle at the portrait.

Three

By the Goddess, when Aunt Sybilla gets back, I'm going to sit her down until she talks to me, even if it means pitting my own magic against hers!

Fuming, Wendi paced around the kitchen. How dare Aunt Sybilla act like she had at the docks—make the remark she had at the path to Stefan's—then escape to visit a friend with that ragged hound that followed her nearly everywhere before explaining anything. She'd been gone over an hour, and just a few minutes ago, not one, but three customers arrived on the porch.

She finished the tomato she'd taken from her shopping bag, wiping at a bit of juice sliding down her chin. Salted, it was palatable, and at least it kept the hunger pangs in her stomach from being audible. It would have been much more satisfying sliced and between two pieces of bread, but there wasn't a scrap of bread in the breadbox.

She glanced at the uncut vinegar-laced sweet potato pie and shivered. She wasn't *that* hungry yet.

After washing her hands and smoothing her skirt, she turned toward the doorway leading into the parlor. Closing her eyes for a brief moment, she called on the spirits to help her make the readings she was about to give accurate. Accurate readings brought repeat customers, but she felt bound beyond that. She genuinely wanted to help her customers, who sometimes became her friends.

She and Aunt Sybilla had far too few friends in this town, due partly to their practice of witchcraft—partly to the old scandal. Neither of them could possibly give up their witchcraft, and nothing could be done about the scandal now. It was ten years past.

They performed their readings in the parlor and kept that room as bright and cheery as the rest of the house. Funny how some people walked into it the first time and stared in confusion. She'd finally asked one of her repeat customers why she'd acted so strangely the first visit, and the customer explained:

"I expected a dark, dreary place, and for you to come out from behind a beaded curtain in a cloud of smoke. Instead I found a bright and sunny room, filled with plants and frilly white curtains on the open windows. The only thing to remind me I'd come to a witch's house was the smell of incense burning."

"The humidity makes the house dank at times, so we like to burn some jasmine-scented incense, which we make ourselves," Wendi had told her. "And the spirits like brightness and cheeriness, too. At least, ours do."

Shaking her head as she remembered how the woman's eyes had widened at her casual familiarity with their guiding spirits, Wendi walked into the parlor to find Cherie Bonheur standing at the reading table. The other two women would be waiting on the porch, probably sitting behind the rush shade hanging down one side. None of her customers would sit out in plain sight at a witch's house. Once inside, they could be friends, but not in public.

"Hello, Cherie," Wendi greeted. "Are you here to ask about your coming little one?"

"Oh!" Cherie's eyes rounded. "You could tell I was with child just by looking at me? But that shouldn't surprise me, I guess."

Wendi laughed. "Either by that or by your *enfant* gown and lack of corset. I'm so glad to see you're one of those women who agrees you shouldn't subject your body to a corset when you're with child. They're torture enough the rest of the time."

Cherie blushed a becoming pink. "It's Henri, as much as me. He wants this child so badly. He doesn't care whether it's a boy or girl, but I'd like so much to please him and present him with an heir the first time. Then I can have my girl next."

With the door open, Wendi easily heard the sound of a horse stopping at her gate. She started to look out and see who it was, but no doubt the new customer would join the others waiting on the porch, and Cherie deserved her attention at the moment. Darn Aunt Sybilla for not getting back to be courteous to the waiting customers or help with the readings.

"Well, sit down and let's see what we can find out," she told the young woman across the table, married barely six months and already excited about her first child.

A set of heavy footsteps climbed the porch steps, and Wendi frowned. Either her new customer was a man, or an elderly lady was being helped onto the porch by her footman, since the footsteps had a strange cadence. She hesitated for a moment, but as she anticipated, whoever it was didn't enter the door. She could have tuned in her psychic senses to see who it was, but she guessed it didn't matter.

Shrugging, Wendi sat across from Cherie and took her scrying speculum from the shelf beside the table. At times her customers wanted card readings; at other times they were fascinated with what she saw in the speculum for them. She'd found her speculum—an old, glass fisherman's lure—while walking along the beach one day. When it had information to impart, it glowed with just enough light to fascinate her customers.

It didn't disappoint Cherie today. Wendi cupped the lure and murmured a request. The glow began immediately, and within the circle of light, Wendi saw a tiny child laughing and playing with his father. The short knee pants gave her the sex of the child.

"It will be a boy," she told Cherie, who clapped her hands in delight. "Uh—" Another tiny child ran into the circle of light inside the lure. "And a girl."

Cherie covered her mouth with her hands briefly, then dropped them. "Twins?" she whispered. "Oh, I shouldn't be surprised. My *grandmère* was a twin."

Wendi peered closer at the speculum, hoping against hope what she wasn't seeing was a trick of the light. But no matter how hard she looked, she didn't see Cherie in the picture. And when Henri turned his face so she could study it, she read the sadness there.

Her heart lurched. She hated this part of her abilities. She could never tell beforehand whether the future would be good or bad for her clients. She also never told them the bad news, unless they somehow sensed it themselves and demanded to know. Today, Cherie's delight didn't allow for any misgivings.

She stood quickly and said, "I must tell Mama. We'll have to surprise Henri in six months, though, because he wouldn't like me coming here to—"

She caught her bottom lip between her teeth briefly, then glanced away from Wendi. "I'm sorry. I didn't mean—"

"It's all right, Cherie," Wendi assured her. "Just be happy with your Henri while you wait for your precious babies to be born."

"I will," Cherie said. "Thank you so much."

She took a coin from her reticule and laid it on the table before she turned and hurried onto the porch. Wendi thought for sure she would hear Cherie tell the other women out there about her coming twins, but Cherie's steps hesitated for only a second. Then she went on down the steps.

Madame Burneau came in the door next, frowning over her shoulder toward the porch before she took the seat across from Wendi. Wendi started to ask her who else was waiting, then didn't. She'd learned the first time she did a reading that her customers at times played a game of not recognizing each other.

"How are you today, Madame Burneau?" she asked the older woman.

"Restless," Madame Burneau replied. "My Thomas has been dead now for over three years, Wendi, and my bed's awfully lonely. Why is it society thinks only men have itches that need scratched?"

Wendi blushed, and Madame threw back her head, laughing so uproariously the waiting customers were sure to hear. Her double chin quivered with merriment, and Wendi couldn't keep from joining her. At last Madame wiped a tear from the corner of her eye and studied Wendi shrewdly.

"You aren't exactly a stranger to relationships, my dear," she said. "Why, one of my dear cousin's sons was courting you for a while, if I recall. You would have made a delicious addition to our family circle, and he still won't tell his mother why he dropped the courtship. And there was another man—"

"Did you want a card reading or wish me to use the scrying speculum?" Wendi interrupted firmly. She didn't need those old wounds opened, even by a customer she enjoyed as much as Madame Burneau. One of the two men in her past had already left behind irreparable damage.

Madame agreeably allowed the focus to return to her own visit. "The cards, if you will, Wendi. They appear to give more accurate timeframe readings than the speculum. And I do want to know how long it will be before I can end this frustration over the dreams I have at night that leave me drooling in the morning—and aching for a man's arms around me."

Wendi shook her head tolerantly and reached for the cards on the shelf. She handled them reverently, as they were a legacy, owned by no one, but there to serve any woman in the line with the gift for prophecy. She took her time with Madame, knowing there would be a huge tip at the end of the reading, but vastly interested herself in the congenial woman's future. Madame had been devastated when her Thomas died so suddenly in the carriage accident, but had been satisfied when Sybilla contacted the man at a séance and told Madame that he indeed was at peace.

Twenty minutes later Madame left, content she would find another husband within the year. The next customer was someone new to Wendi, and she realized immediately why the young woman had come. Beautiful in an angelic way, there was something sad and heart-tugging about her. Wendi smiled at her, but let her mind's eye pick up the woman's aura as she introduced herself as Anna Martinique.

Deep blue, her aura indicated a desperate need for healing. Although at times this color aura could mean a physical problem, Wendi sensed both physical and emotional needs in Anna. The large, vivid birthmark marring the entire side of her left cheek accounted for both needs. She could only imagine what the poor young woman had gone through thus far in her life, with the birthmark ruining her beauty.

"They tell me it's from the veil over my face when I was born," Anna whispered after she sat. "And that the veil was because my mother looked in the face of someone with the evil eye while she carried me." She lifted her gaze, desperation swimming in the azure pools of her eyes and her hands twisting together on the tabletop. "Can you take it away? Oh, can you? If you can't, I truly fear I will not be able to keep from taking my own life. I cannot live with this even one more day."

"I can take it away," Wendi assured her, and Anna's joy was palpable. "But it will take me a little time here today. And I need you to sit quietly while I study you for a few moments. Also, I will need you to answer any questions I ask you truthfully."

"Anything," Anna said. "Anything." Then she fell quiet, her face lit with anticipation.

Wendi studied her, allowing her intuitiveness full rein. She saw much sadness in Anna, as the aura and her initial mood indicated, but there were sparks of something else in the young woman's life.

"There's someone who doesn't seem to care that your face is marred," Wendi murmured. "Who is he?"

"He's the reason I'm here," Anna answered in an honest tone. "John. He's a friend of my brother's. He says it doesn't matter—that he loves me for who I am, not what I look like. But he's so handsome and so gentle and kind. He deserves a wife he can be proud to have on his arm."

Wendi smiled as a picture of John formed in her mind. He was slight of stature and would go bald early. But his eyes were deep brown and comforting, his manner outgoing yet caring toward others. He loved Anna with the deep, abiding love of two soulmates finding each other after many previous star-crossed lives.

Yes, her magic would be aided by the spirits here today. The Fates meant for Anna to finally have her happy life.

"Wait here," she said. She went into the kitchen, hoping Aunt Sybilla hadn't taken out the garbage. She hadn't. Digging in the paper sack, she found the dried-up lemon she'd tossed in there that morning. Closing her hand around it, she shut her eyes.

> "Goddess and god, set my magic free.
> Do it for Anna, not for me.
> So mote it be."

All right, so she wasn't a poet, she thought not for the first time. But the spirits knew her heart was true and that she deeply desired to use her magic to help the people who came to her.

She opened her eyes, found a knife, and split the lemon in half. Squeezing the juice into a bowl, she then took the baking powder from a shelf and mixed a tablespoonful with the lemon. Closing her eyes again, she called upon the spirits once more, then wet a washcloth under the pump and wrung it out. Carrying the bowl and washcloth, she returned to the parlor.

"I want to put this on your face, Anna. Please stand up and close your eyes."

Anna complied, and Wendi murmured further praise to the spirits and pleas for assistance as she dipped her finger over and over again into the paste and gently wiped it on Anna's face. The spirits liked to be catered to and shown respect for their powers, she reminded herself, recalling Aunt Sybilla's training. She continued to whisper incantations and praise until the birthmark was completely covered.

"It's tingling!" Anna gasped as the paste covered the last tiny spot. "Oh, it feels . . . strange."

Wendi only smiled, although Anna couldn't see her with her eyes closed. She truly didn't want Anna to look into the mirror behind her chair just then anyway. The young woman might be a little afraid when she saw the smoke rising from her cheek, but it reassured Wendi the spirits were aiding her today. Just then a tear slid from the corner of Anna's eye, and Wendi hastened to catch it on her thumb before it hit the paste. A tear would raise a hiss of steam, one which Anna wouldn't be able to ignore.

After a long two minutes, Wendi quietly said to Anna, "I'm going to wipe your face with a damp cloth."

She cleaned off the paste, joy filling her at the new turn Anna's life could now take. Her clear, soft skin was unmarred, an even, smooth peach like the rest of her face. When she opened her eyes at Wendi's behest, her beauty was incomparable. Wendi stepped aside so Anna could see in the mirror behind her.

"Sweet Mother of God," Anna whispered. "It worked."

She slowly stepped over to the mirror. Disbelief on her face, she stared at her countenance, turning her head, examining what wasn't there any longer. With a twist, she grabbed Wendi, flung her arms around her, and buried her face on Wendi's shoulder.

As Anna sobbed her heart out, Wendi wrapped her arms around her in return and let the emotions run their course. Her own joy at what her magic had done—despite the problems she'd had with it in the past—was truly satisfying.

A shadow loomed in the doorway, and Wendi's gaze flew toward it. She gasped, although she continued to pat Anna on the back as the woman controlled her sobs.

Wendi's own feelings did an about-face so sharp she could have easily lost her balance and missed the chair on her side of the table if she fell.

The man from the ship stood in her doorway, and if anything, his aura was darker. The stir her emotions experienced was enough to make her want to fan her face. Which she would have, had Anna not filled her arms and needed her comfort. Anna seemed to sense some change, however, and she drew a deep breath and straightened. Instead of looking behind her, she stared into the mirror again.

"Oh, I can't believe it," she murmured.

"Believe it," Wendi said at the same moment the man in the doorway said, "Neither can I."

Anna whirled, her delicate chin tilting up when she saw who stood in the door. "Monsieur, you made your views well known when we waited on the porch. Now, how do you explain this?"

She turned her face so he had an unobstructed view of her flawless cheek, and the man shrugged.

"I don't have to," he growled. "You do. Now, if you'll excuse us, I have business with . . ." He let his gaze travel over Wendi, and she felt every inch of the scan, a mixture of disgust and something she couldn't quite understand. ". . . with this person here."

With a decided limp, he stepped to the side of the doorway. Anna glanced at his leg and pointed a finger at his walking cane, which dangled from his forearm.

"You won't need that when you leave here, and I'll thank you to promise to apologize to Mistress Chastain for your rudeness and disbelief after she heals your leg!"

"I didn't come here for healing, madame," he said in a tightly polite voice. "Please. Excuse us."

Anna gave him a supercilious glare, then took her good,

sweet time removing some coins from her reticule and laying them on the table. Wendi divided her attention between Anna and the man, recalling that her aunt had said this man was trouble. Still, instead of feeling afraid of him when his impatience increased and his aura neared ebony, her amusement grew to the point where she had to bite her bottom lip to prevent her laughter.

Anna held out a hand and thanked Wendi profusely yet again, then pattered on for a few more minutes. The man's face darkened, the deep red of tension and irritation tingeing the aura's outer boundaries.

Finally Anna pulled her gloves on and headed for the doorway. She paused beside the man, tilting her head so her cheek was toward him and patting it with a gloved index finger to draw his attention to her newly unmarred skin. With a haughty sniff, she swept out the door.

At the flustered look on the man's face, Wendi dissolved in silent laughter. She sank into her chair, dropping her head and trying to hide her face. When the man *clump-thumped* across the floor to the table and stood opposite her, though, she giggled aloud. Looking up, she wiped at her face, realizing too late she still held the baking soda-lemon juice soiled washcloth in her hand.

The mixture landed in her mouth, and Wendi spit and sputtered, standing abruptly. "Excuse me, I need to go in the kitchen—"

"Sit down!" he roared. "I'm not waiting one more minute to talk to you!"

"Well, snippity, snip to you, too, monsieur," she flung at him. "You can leave right now, or—"

"Or what? You'll turn me into a frog?"

She gave him a calculating look. "No, not a frog. A toad. An ugly, repulsive toad, to match your aura and manners."

She strode toward the kitchen, hearing him start after her.

Whirling, she pointed her finger at him, a stab of fear at last penetrating her exasperation when she noticed the angry glower on his face. He could be so handsome if he would only smile—

"I told you to leave," she said.

All at once a tingling surge swept along her arm, out through her finger. Sparks crackled in the air around her fingernail, and a violent wind swirled through the room. The man stopped as abruptly as though he'd run into a wall, then staggered backward. At the very moment Wendi thought he would fall, the chair sidled over beneath his rump, and he sat in it rather slowly, almost as though the wind floated him downward. His rear met the seat, and he uttered a disbelieving "oomph."

The wind died for a second, but when the man moved as though to stand, it heightened again. He sat back in the chair.

"What the hell do you think you're doing?" he snarled.

Wendi looked at her finger in surprise, then curled it to her palm. The wind died once more, but when she uncurled her finger, another spark flew and the wind grew.

Huh. She flexed her finger, and the wind played a here-I-am, here-I'm-not tune a couple times.

"Damn it—" the man said.

She gave him a warning look. "If you're still here when I come back from the kitchen, you better plan on spending the rest of you life on hinged legs."

With a satisfied twist to her lips, she lifted her head and scurried into the kitchen, slamming the door behind her this time. Halting as soon as she had privacy, she held her hand out in front of her. She worked her index finger up and down, curled and uncurled, but nothing happened.

Glancing at the ceiling to send her words speeding to the spirits, she said, "What on earth are you doing? Is this my magic, or yours? Or does it have something to do with him being here?''

No one answered. A fine time for them to leave her to her own devices once again!

She crossed to the dry sink and rinsed out the washcloth, then wiped her face. Suddenly a well-rehearsed clamor filled the backyard, and Wendi shook her head as she hurried over to the back door. She got there just as the neighbor's mottled tomcat raced up the trunk of the magnolia tree and sat hissing on the branch it knew was just a couple inches beyond what Aunt Sybilla's hound, Alphie, could reach, even with his highest leap.

Sure enough the ragged red-and-white Afghan, which walked around with a tattered coat no matter how many times a week Sybilla brushed it, set up his usual roar of frustration at the cat's escape. Leaping and twisting beneath the branch, the hound roared its fury and demanded the tom leave his territory. The tom casually sat in a corner where the branch met the tree, lifted a leg, and took a bath.

For once, Sybilla ignored the fray, rather than joining the hound and yelling at the cat—something she hadn't the courage to do without the dog's backup. She hurried onto the porch.

"He's here, isn't he?" she demanded. "I can sense it. His aura's inside the house."

Alphie, his game not following the normal routine, sat down beneath the tree and looked over his shoulder. Whining, he gave his mistress a puzzled look.

"If you mean the man who was on the ship—the one you warned me about, then took off and refused to explain to me what you meant—" She cocked a fist on her hip. "*That* man's inside. And yes, he does have a very nasty aura."

"Has he hurt you?"

Sybilla stepped close and ran her palms down Wendi's arms. Shorter by inches, she peered up into Wendi's face, and some of Wendi's irritation left her as she realized exactly how worried her aunt was.

"He didn't get close enough to hurt me—" she began.

"He tried?" Sybilla interrupted. "Oh, no! What did he try to do?"

"I'm fine, Aunt," Wendi told her in exasperation.

Alphie trotted over to the porch, up the steps, then plopped at Sybilla's feet, while the tom eyed them balefully from the tree branch. Evidently disgusted that the game was over so quickly this time, the tom stood, stretched, and sauntered along the limb. Jumping over the fence dividing their yard from the neighbor's, it disappeared.

Wendi sighed in resignation when the hound looked up at her with mournful eyes. "You should give this animal a bath so he's not smelling up your bedcovers when he sleeps with you," she said to Sybilla.

Sybilla bristled. "I just bathed Alphie last week. He—" She shut her mouth and studied Wendi. "You're trying to get me off the subject here. Tell me what Nick wants."

"Is that his name? He didn't introduce himself."

"I don't imagine he did. Nick. Nick Bardou is his name."

Wendi stared at her. "My mother's lover's son? He doesn't look that much like Dominic."

"The other son, Pierre—the one who was killed in the war—looked more like his father. Nick got his mother's Creole coloring."

Wendi whirled and shoved through the door, muttering, "I'll turn him into something a hell of a lot worse than a toad! What does he think he's doing—coming here bothering our clients and trying to order me around?"

Sybilla shouldn't have been able to move so fast at her

age, but she did. Surprising the fool out of Wendi, she caught her and yanked her back into the kitchen before she even touched the door to the parlor. Pushing her ahead of her, Sybilla didn't stop until they were back on the far side of the kitchen—well out of danger of being overheard in the parlor.

"You listen to me, missy," she hissed. "We can both be in a world of trouble karma-wise if we don't find out what's going on here before we start messing with whatever the Fates have set up! I should have known something was up when we found Sabine's first Book of Shadows a month ago. We've walked across that piece of floor thousands of times and never suspected it was rotten."

The hound shoved through the door, whining and sidling up to Sybilla. Wendi caught the concern in Alphie's manner and noticed the strain and beaded sweat on Sybilla's upper lip. Carefully she took her aunt's arm and urged her toward the kitchen table.

"He's probably not even still here, Aunt," she said as she gently pushed Sybilla into a chair. At fifty-five, her aunt should have many years ahead of her, but she didn't need this sort of worry, especially with her own magical powers failing for some reason. "I told him to leave."

Relief filled Sybilla's face, but only for an instant. "Then we've got time to—"

The door between the rooms opened, and Sybilla's face whitened when she glanced over her shoulder.

"You should come out here, I think," Nick said in a weird voice. "That thing you left on the table is glowing. Does it get hot? I doubt you want your house to burn down if it starts a fire."

Four

Nick stepped back, holding the door and expecting the two women to barrel into their parlor. Instead, the older one clasped her throat and stared at him in horror. Sabine's daughter speared him with the knife thrust of her blue gaze, and he quickly glanced at her right hand, relieved to see her fingers curled into her skirt instead of pointing at him.

"I thought I told you what would happen if you didn't leave," the daughter said.

"Hush, Wendi," the woman said. Nick mentally noted the name once more, so different than anything he'd ever heard before. Maybe short for Gwendolyn?

The daughter turned her attention to the woman. "Aunt Sybilla—"

"I said hush."

Sybilla. He was right. She was Sabine's sister. She stood, laying her hand on the head of a hound that crawled out from under the table and growled at Nick.

"You, too," she murmured to the animal, then said to Nick, "You are definitely entwined in our Fate if you're making the scrying speculum glow without either one of us in the room. Do you have the courage to face what it might tell you?''

He snorted a quick sound of disbelief. ''I don't for one damned minute think there's anything illogical about that lure making it glow. And I've never been faulted for my courage.''

''Oh, but you're wrong, Monsieur Bardou,'' Sybilla said. ''You ran away ten years ago, didn't you?''

''Damn you,'' he snarled at her. ''There wasn't any reason for me not to leave.''

''Only in your own mind, monsieur.'' She turned to Wendi. ''I want you to give him a reading.''

''No!'' she said. ''I want him out of here. I've already told him to leave once.''

''It's not possible yet,'' Sybilla said in a troubled voice. ''I don't think he can.'' She looked back at Nick. ''Have you tried?''

After staring at her for a few seconds, wondering how she knew, he nodded curtly. ''The door appears stuck. But believe me, if I want out of here, I'll go. If I have to, I'll bash that door down.''

He didn't bother telling them the door had closed virtually in his face when he gave up waiting for Wendi to return to the parlor. The only reason he hadn't forced it right then was because that stupid glass fishing lure started glowing on the table. Whatever he might have done in the past, he couldn't walk out when there was a possibility the house might catch fire.

''Do you want to leave?''

This time Sabine's daughter spoke, and he couldn't decide if the tone of her voice dared him to stay or not. Sultry as a bayou summer night, it taunted him, making him realize how much lower than her mother's it was. But then, he'd been listening to that voice for an hour on the porch before he confronted her, thinking the brandy clouding his mind must be what was making him so aware of the distinctive nuances in it. Thinking how much it reminded him of the dead one just by being so different.

"I want to know if the two of you have been in my house," he said grudgingly, at that very moment realizing why he had indeed come here. "There's a portrait of . . ." He curled his lip, reluctant to speak her name out loud. "Of . . ." He nodded his head at Sybilla. ". . . your sister hanging in my study. I've never seen it before, and I'm going to find out where the hell it came from."

"It must be the one your father had commissioned," Sybilla said, and Wendi looked at her in surprise. "But I thought it was still out at Belle Chene. As far as I know, it was never uncrated after it was finished and packed for shipping."

"Have you seen it?"

Sybilla shrugged. "Only once, when it was nearly done. Two weeks before she died."

Nick flinched as though her words had struck him. It didn't help that the daughter stood there taking in every word, quiet but more noticeable that way than if she had butted into the conversation.

She'd removed her hands from the folds of her skirt. She wore several rings on her fingers, almost as though in the middle of dressing for a ball and having yet to don the rest of her jewels. All the rings were unadorned except one, which caught the light now and then when she moved her hand. The plain green gown was a far cry from anything more than just a cover for that body, which rivaled her mother's and then some. Sabine had been able to do the same—turn cotton into feigned silk just by wearing it.

"You didn't answer my other question. Have you been in my house?"

Sybilla evaded his gaze, patting the hound and then glancing at Wendi. The look passing between them seemed as though they were communicating without words. He'd heard married people could do that after years together, so an aunt and niece should have no trouble with it. Yet it made him uneasy—and irritated him.

"The truth shouldn't take you ten minutes to say," he growled. "It's lies that take planning to tell."

"Not necessarily." Wendi stepped forward, shielding her aunt whether or not it was her intention. It brought her close enough to him to smell a tantalizing mixture of jasmine and honeysuckle on her skin. "If you'll take a seat in the parlor, I'll be right there."

"And if I don't?"

Blue didn't really describe her eyes, but then, it hadn't described Sabine's, either. Had he believed in magic, he might think they were capable of toying with his will. They were smaller versions of clear blue crystal, depthless yet filled with secrets better left to unfold in the night—preferably between a set of satin sheets.

But then, that's exactly what his father had done with her mother.

The fury and aching agony for the pain his mother suffered, never far from the surface no matter now deeply he buried it, rose in him. Before he could spew it at her, however, she spoke.

"We haven't been in your house. However, we did search the garden one evening. Aunt Sybilla saw a vision, and we thought that's where it wanted us to go. We didn't think it would matter to anyone, since the house was empty."

"It probably wouldn't have mattered—had it been anyone else trespassing on my land. And just what the hell were you searching for?"

She looked at Sybilla again, that communicating look passing between them. Evidently, Sybilla gave her permission to explain.

"My mother's second Book of Shadows. It's a type of journal witches keep. Look, I don't intend to discuss this with you unless you quit towering over us like you're going to pounce any minute. I could force you to leave, but my aunt seems to think we have more to talk about with you."

Hell, he couldn't fault her nerve. Or perhaps it was stupidity. She seemed to think just because whatever little trick she pulled on him when she sent that wind through the room and sparks from her fingers caught him by surprise, she could protect herself from his displeasure. His gaze wandered to her fingers again, and he jerked it away.

He'd be better prepared for their next face-off. For now, it would be easier to let her keep her false conception that he was wary of her so-called powers, at least until he found out what he wanted to know. He hadn't made his fortune in California by not knowing when to attack, when to make a false retreat.

After a quick scan of them both, he nodded and limped back into the parlor. The brandy was wearing off—had worn off while he waited on the porch. He'd known it would and filled a silver flask before he left the house. Filled it in the parlor, because he wasn't about to go back into the study and face the destruction he'd done to the portrait.

He left the kitchen door open behind him, and after he eased himself into one of the chairs at the table, he was surprised to see they hadn't shut it after him. Wendi stood with her back to him, her slender figure taller than her aunt's, but her aunt's wider hips and skirts flaring from where she stood in front of her niece.

He took the flask out of his trouser pocket and uncapped

it, swallowing a satisfying amount without taking his eyes from them. They were either communicating in that wordless way again, or in whispers, as the only thing he could hear was a mockingbird in a wisteria bush out by the street.

After a few seconds Wendi turned and came toward the table. She closed the door behind her, leaving her aunt in the kitchen, and he raised an eyebrow in inquiry.

"Aunt Sybilla is going to start supper," she said. "She expects Tangie to show up with some shrimp any minute, but she can start the gumbo without that."

Somehow he kept his stomach from growling in reaction. By the time he got home, Miz Thibedeau should have his own meal ready.

Wendi took her seat and cupped the lure in her hands. Nick hadn't paid much attention, but now he realized the glow had died until she touched it. She closed her eyes for a moment, then opened them and looked at him in intense concentration, although her gaze skittered away from his eyes. Instead, she looked up and down his body, and when she spoke, her voice was feathery and indistinct, but clearly understandable.

"You've been living by the ocean, but it's not like our Gulf here. You like the water, and you prefer traveling that way instead of on horseback."

He leaned back in his chair and crossed his arms. Hell, it didn't take a witch to figure that out. With his injured leg, ship travel was a hundred times more comfortable than either horseback or an uncushioned stagecoach seat.

"It's not only because of your leg," she said, and he clenched his fingers to control the start of surprise that maybe she'd read his mind. She frowned in concentration. "Your business out West is in shipping."

"I thought we were going to talk about here and now. I

already know what my past life has been like and what I do for a living."

She met his eyes this time. "Here and now is mixed with the past. As is the future. Your future has been coming to this since you were born, monsieur."

"You can talk in all the riddles you want, but it won't make any difference. You fortune-tellers never make a clear statement. That way you can interpret your *readings* according to what happens later on."

"You think you killed my mother," Wendi said in a ringing voice. "Is that clear enough for you?"

The pain filling his eyes hit Wendi like a blow to the stomach, and only rigid control kept her from dropping the scrying speculum and curling her arms around herself. She clearly heard him mentally howl with the pain, like a lobo wolf finding its life mate dead and cold. The silence of the rending sound made it all that much more ghastly, and it showed in his eyes. Deep blue and endless, the attempt at coldness was shattered by his mental agony, and his jaws clenched too tightly for him to respond to the truth of her words.

Those full lips would be beautiful if he ever smiled, she mused. He'd worn down-turned grooves in the corners of his mouth, though, and it would take a miracle to smooth those out.

Pain.

She sensed so very much pain in him. She wanted to soothe him more than she'd ever wanted anything in her life, but something told her she would make his pain much worse before it got better.

She gazed down at the speculum, desperately wanting to see his future, as she'd seen the future of plenty of others. The glow had died, though, and no matter how many pleas she sent to her guiding spirits, the speculum remained dark

and cold. Trepidation filled her. The nonresponsive blackness in his future could mean different things, one of them
being his death. She needed to talk to Aunt Sybilla.

Standing, she said, "I think you should leave now."

His bleak gaze met hers. "You've been throwing me out
of here ever since I arrived. I've told you more than once
that I'll go when I'm damned good and ready. Tell me
about this shadow book you were looking for in my garden."

"Book of Shadows," she corrected as she took her seat
again—not because he refused to leave but because Sybilla
whispered an order into her mind to do just that. Sighing,
she picked up the speculum, but it mocked her with its
nonresponsiveness. She laid it back down and looked at
him.

"My mother's Books of Shadows were a chronicle of
her life, as well as a list of her magic spells. All true witches
keep one—more than one, if their life has merited it." He
sneered at that, but she let it pass. "They're both a book
of spells that work for us and a way to record our lives for
continuity down through the years."

"I don't believe in this magic shit."

"That's extremely clear, by your actions. However, for
some reason you're still here listening to me. So why don't
you suspend your disbelief for a few minutes and pay attention."

With a scornful twist to his lips, he gave a curt nod,
indicating for her to proceed.

"I'm not exactly sure why, but I feel you need to know
something about us in order to understand what's brought
you here. You see, witchcraft is not an evil practice with
us. It's a oneness with the earth and part of what we are.
It's the religion we honor."

"So is voodoo," he sneered.

"No. No, voodoo is different, but I'm not going to get into that with you. Our witchcraft is white magic, and we don't use it for harm. In fact, we believe if we harm someone, the harm will come back on us threefold."

Her words seemed to spark some memory in him, but he maintained the thread of their current conversation.

"That's not what the common consensus is."

"And the common consensus is always right, monsieur?"

Her question lit the pain in his eyes again, and she caught a sense of longing in him. A deep longing to come home from a faraway land, but a knowing he would be unwelcome. For a flickering second, she thought he might make an attempt to understand, but he stayed quiet, his fingers whitening on his walking cane the only other sign of his emotions.

"Do you believe in life after death, Monsieur Bardou?" she asked.

"No," he snapped. "Hell's right here on earth, and it's enough to make me look forward to the void of death."

She blew out a breath, chasing a stray curl from her forehead and noticing his gaze follow it. "Well, whether you personally believe or not, you need to understand that we do. And I'm getting to what this means as to the Books of Shadows," she said to the impatient look on his face. "My mother's Books of Shadows should be mine, but her violent death has done something to my karma—and perhaps to yours, since you've been brought back here from so far away, when you believed you never wanted to see New Orleans again."

He at least had the grace to acknowledge she'd voiced something she couldn't have known. Still, the skepticism on his face could have been written in words.

"My magic should be growing as I get older," she went

on. "But it seems to be stalling and, at times, even to be blocked for some reason. And Aunt Sybilla's magic is weakening. We need the second Book of Shadows to try to figure out what's going on."

"And you thought it was in my garden." He didn't question, but stated a fact.

"Aunt Sybilla had a vision. She saw a marble statue of Aphrodite, and she remembered my mother saying there was one in the Bardou gardens. Your father told her."

"Yes, my father," he snarled. "In bed or out?"

"Look," Wendi said in exasperation. "Your father and my mother were lovers. There's no getting around that, and we all know it. And the consensus is—you killed my mother, but there wasn't enough evidence to arrest and try you. The resulting scandal over your possibly killing your father's mistress devastated your mother and she died by her own hand."

Mentally she applauded his control. She didn't even know herself where those words came from, and had she flung them at any other man she knew, he'd probably have his hands around her throat right now. Nick only tightened his fingers on his walking cane instead of her throat, until she thought the knob on top would powder into dust, and stared steadily at her.

"You really are either foolishly brave or bravely foolish," he said in a musing voice. "I may have been gone ten years, but the Bardou name still has power in this town. And the *consensus* is, I got away with murder once."

Wendi pulled her courage around her, somehow knowing what had to be said even without Sybilla's mental agreement with her thoughts. "Did you? Or is that one of the wrongs that needs to be righted before the karma can be corrected?"

"Damn your karma." He said it mildly and, leaning

heavily on his cane, rose to his feet. "I came here to warn you to stay out of my life. I'll only be in town a few days, and that alone is making me miserable enough. If you cross my path again before I leave, I'll make you wish you'd never heard the name Bardou. And when I depart for good again, I'll leave behind word that if you're ever seen on Bardou property, you're to be arrested. When I'm notified of the arrest, I'll be back here to see that you're tried for witchcraft and, at the very least, banned from New Orleans."

His cold, deadly glare told Wendi he meant every carefully chosen, lethal word. Somehow she held his gaze, although her hands twisted in her lap to hide their trembling. Anything she said right now would only make matters worse, and at least he appeared to be leaving. That's what she wanted, wasn't it?

He limped toward the door, jerking it open.

"Monsieur." Oh, Great Goddess, what on earth had she done now? She bit down hard on her tongue to keep it from moving, but he looked back over his shoulder with a sneer of contempt and she let her tongue loose.

"I can help that pain in your leg."

His contempt crumbled into disbelief, matching the stunned amazement in her mind. Now what, or who, on earth had made her say that?

"I'd sooner die from the pain than let Sabine Chastain's daughter lay a hand on me," he spat.

The door crashed behind him, shaking the walls of the small house. After a moment a horse galloped away, and she wondered how he could stand that frantic pace with his injured leg. A second later the kitchen door opened behind her.

"I couldn't give him a reading, Aunt," she said without

looking at Sybilla. "The speculum stopped glowing after only a moment."

"I thought that might happen."

Wendi didn't question Sybilla's enigmatic words. Her aunt had no way of knowing whether the speculum's non-responsiveness meant Nick Bardou had no future.

She'd barely met him, so why did that thought bring her as much pain as when she'd seen the same thing for Cherie Bonheur?

Five

Wendi allowed two days to pass—two days when she and Sybilla had to turn away a half dozen clients each. The Fates appeared to be conspiring to force them in some direction, as yet unclear but not to be ignored. The speculum wouldn't glow. The cards, dealt as a last resort, foretold nonsense neither one of them wanted to interpret for their customers. Instead, they sent them away, explaining they would get word to them when their abilities appeared to have returned. If something didn't happen soon, they'd be out of food again.

The second evening of the troubling days, she and Sybilla shared a pot of tea before going to bed.

"You know you're going to have to go see Nick," Sybilla said.

"And ask him what?" Wendi demanded. "To search his garden again? To look in the house? 'Oh, by the way, Monsieur. By any chance do you think your father may have brought my mother here into the house—perhaps into one of the bedrooms—maybe while your mother was gone somewhere? Could I look and see if there's a statue anywhere that my mother might have hidden her Book of Shadows beneath?''

Wendi shook her head. ''You know as well as I do that being a witch doesn't make me immortal, Aunt. You better pick out which gown you want to bury me in before you send me on *that* mission.''

''You don't really think the man who was here killed Sabine, do you?''

Wendi set her teacup down and stood to pace the room. Twilight lingered these days, but they'd lit a couple of wall sconces in the parlor, anticipating each would read for a while before they went to bed. The threadbare rug on the floor only slightly muffled her footsteps as she gave the question careful consideration. Pausing in front of the window, she turned to look at Sybilla.

''Can you honestly say you're sure he didn't?'' she asked.

Sybilla's face creased with a frown of worry. ''No,'' she admitted. ''No, I can't. I believe that's what's nagging at me as much as anything—whether or not he did or didn't kill her. And I don't understand why ten years have gone by with nothing happening. Then all of a sudden . . .'' She shrugged and patted the hound at her feet.

Wendi crossed the room and sat in the horsehair settee beside Sybilla. ''If you'll think on it, Aunt, like I have been the last two days, you'll realize our problems began about a month ago, probably around the same time Nick Bardou started thinking of coming back to New Orleans.''

''He was on one of the ships that comes out of Galveston,'' Sybilla mused. ''So he probably came by rail across the country that far. Yes, a week to get his business ready so he could leave it for a while, and two or three weeks to get here.''

Wendi agreed with her. They both read anything they

could get their hands on, including the weekly papers when they could afford them—week-old ones tossed in the trash when they couldn't. They knew as much about politics and how the country was growing as any man in the city did. Rail travel was quickly growing throughout the country, but had not yet reached New Orleans. But they had both been paying careful attention to how fast one could travel across country.

"Think about it, Aunt, it makes perfect sense," Wendi said. "My mother died a violent death, an unavenged death, yet her soul hasn't made itself known. You can't contact her, and neither can I. And now something's happening, and none of our other guiding spirits appear to be willing to let us in on what the plans are. And it all seems to be happening since Nick Bardou entered our lives."

"We need Sabine's second Book of Shadows. Sabine's magic always was stronger than mine, even though I was so much older. There's got to be an effective spell in her book to contact a reluctant soul. We need to talk to your mother and see what's going on here."

"Either that, or the karma is playing out the way it should, and there's not a darned thing we can do about it. If that's the case—"

"If that's the case," Sybilla finished for her, "we need to confront Nick Bardou even more than ever."

"I don't understand."

"He's the key to everything, Wendi. These problems aren't just happening because he's entered our lives. His life is intertwined with ours—has been, ever since his father and your mother first talked in the park so many years ago."

"So we're missing the subtleties, and that's why we're being forced into action by not being able to earn enough even to buy food." Wendi smiled wryly. "Hunger can be a powerful motivator, I guess."

Sybilla stood and patted one plump hip. "Well, I can last a little longer than you can, but I'd rather not let Alphie here go hungry. He does such a good job keeping that nasty cat next door away from me." The dog lying at Sybilla's feet thumped its tail in response to her loving look.

"Some witches like cats, Aunt. In fact, they use them for familiars."

"Well, I'm not *some* witch," Sybilla said with a huff. "I don't understand how anyone can like one of those sneaky, hissing creatures!"

Wendi leaned back on the settee and laughed as Sybilla waved a ta-ta motion with her fingers, ordered her not to stay up too late, and headed for her bedroom. The hound— not a male as the name indicated, but Wendi didn't have the heart to tell her aunt—padded after. Alphie had been Sybilla's unswerving companion since the day it raced out of the bushes during one of Sybilla's ongoing confrontations with the neighbor's cat. Her aunt had even resorted to making a cross with her fingers to ward off the cat, but it hadn't fazed it. The hound managed to send it back across the fence, however, and earned Sybilla's unflagging gratitude.

Wendi thought the cat had figured out on its own that Sybilla was scared to death of it, and took advantage of the situation to torment her. The game continued with Alphie, although the cat would rub itself on Wendi's ankles should they both be in the yard without anyone else around.

She wished her aunt had stayed up a little longer, but then she glanced at the mantel clock and realized how late it was. After nine, and they always rose before dawn, a good time to spend a peaceful period meditating and preparing for the new day. Dark had fallen outside now, but

Wendi was afraid she would toss and turn again if she went to bed at her normal time.

She hadn't told Sybilla, but she'd been restless for a month or more—the beginning of the period when Nick had decided to return to New Orleans. A couple of times she'd even risen from her bed and taken a long, vigorous walk in the dead of the night. And she definitely wouldn't tell her aunt where those walks took her.

Getting up from the settee, she strolled over to the window and peered at her face in the reflective pane. Yes, she was well aware her restlessness had started about the time Nick Bardou—a continent away—decided to come home to the city of his birth. But by the Goddess, she would not admit a man could have anything to do with her feelings!

Madame Burneau might need a man, even at her advanced age and after having buried one husband, but Wendi Chastain would never again have anything to do with letting a man into her life—human or not.

She'd tried one of each. Colin O'Grady had been a warlock her own age, with whom she'd practically grown up. They'd married more in friendship and loneliness than love, ending their marriage shortly after Cassandra arrived in town.

Madame Burneau's nephew, Charles, was a different story. She gritted her teeth. If she saw Charles lying in a ditch on fire, she'd have to think long and hard before she decided whether it was worth the effort to conjure up a rain shower to put out the flames. Maybe then he would think there was a reason for her magic other than to make her a freak—a freak he wasn't above using to try to make his own fortune without having to overcome his inbred laziness.

Charles didn't invade her dreams, though. He was blond, as was Colin. A dark man lived in the shadows her mind couldn't penetrate during the deep, quiet nights. A tall man. She'd thought for many years it was just the normal yearnings of a young woman for a tall, dark, and handsome stranger. Now she knew the dreams were unclear visions, a result of her psychic powers foretelling things to come. Foretelling, yet not telling, as they sometimes did.

That dream figure had climbed down the ship's gangplank the other day. Had sat across from her at the parlor reading table. Had kept her awake the last two nights, with the reality of his presence in the city instead of his former shadowiness in her dreams. He had made her attempts to delve into his mind rebound on her own senses, scrambling them until she could barely think.

Nick. His name was Nick, and the sharp bite of the name curled through her stomach. Filtered into the nether regions of her mind—and body. The regions where she'd buried the longing for a life partner—someone to hold her as much as kiss her. Someone to laugh with—someone to share life's sorrows. And joys. The regions she thought had died into hard coals instead of tantalizing flames when Charles Burneau tried to rape her, then laughed at her and called her a freak of nature.

Why, then, did both her mind and body reach out to Nick Bardou? He would obviously never accept her witchcraft, thinking her as much a freak as Charles had. Why did it bother her even to think of the two men in the same breath of thought?

Charles didn't truly believe, but he assumed others did and he could profit from it. Nick didn't believe at all—or so he said. It was very possible that, given his disgust over the relationship between his father and her mother, he thought Sabine had snared Dominic with magic rather than love. It was far from the truth, but it wouldn't be the first time a human had misinterpreted magic.

She should be worried about the failure of her magic instead of how a ten-year-old scandal was still affecting her world today—and she was. But as hard as she tried to concentrate on pondering the reason the magic was failing to develop as it should, as the magic of every witch in her genealogical line before her had developed, her thoughts kept wandering to other things.

Her nighttime thoughts veered down different paths until she was caught in the remembrance of every nuance she'd studied on Nick's face since she first saw him. The way he looked when he tried to pretend the brandy she could smell on his breath protected him from the pain in his leg. The way his blue eyes darkened when his memories crowded his consciousness, threatening to break through the protective barriers he'd erected. The way the pain caused him to howl in an anguish no one could hear except her.

Could this indeed be why her abilities had stalled? Could his presence now be part of a star-crossed path hindering her future? A path filled with pitfalls and obstacles to overcome? A path with Nick Bardou blocking her footsteps from reaching the distances where she'd find true happiness? Blocking the development of her magic until she put the present right—or more probably the past?

Tomorrow night would be Bealtane Eve. She should wait until after then and hope the May Eve celebration would make the spirits more receptive to her questions. More receptive to answering them.

But she already knew she couldn't wait.

She didn't bother with a wrap, since the evenings this near full summertime were already muggy. She'd walked the path between the small house Dominic Bardou had built for her mother and the Bardou mansion on St. Charles Avenue many times before. She wasn't exactly sure why it fascinated her. She'd been twelve when her mother died—was murdered—barely entering into the formative years of her magic, a time when she needed her mother dearly.

Wendi closed the door of the little house behind her. Aunt Sybilla had filled in as best she could, but Wendi admitted a simmering anger at her mother's lack of contact after her death. Any other self-respecting witch would have let her daughter know she hadn't completely abandoned her.

Sybilla believed her sister had never been inside the Bardou mansion, but since Wendi hadn't found the courage to visit Belle Chene, the Bardou plantation outside New Orleans, she'd settled for the mansion. At least there she could stay in the dark recesses beneath the live oaks and imagine how different her life could have been. Imagine what would have been, had her father not died. Imagine what would have been, had Nick's father not loved his wife.

She made the trip between the two worlds of Canal Street and St. Charles Avenue in half an hour. Stopping beneath the live oak across the street, she gazed at the Bardou mansion.

Silence reigned here at night, unlike the nightly carousing in her end of the city, where brothels and bars teemed with activity until dawn. Here the carousers' mothers, wives, and daughters lived, and heaven forbid their delicate sensibilities be offended by a man's baser actions, sending them into a swoon.

Pleasant scents reigned here, too, unlike the smells of nearby wharves and warehouses, dead fish and muggy salt air, which were very much a part of her own neighborhood's atmosphere. Night-blooming jasmine, one of her favorites, filtered on the breeze. And roses. She did love roses.

"The other side of the street is my property."

Wendi stiffened, but for some reason Nick's voice coming out of the darkness didn't totally surprise her.

"I don't imagine I could make a charge of trespassing stick, with you on this side of the street," he continued, his voice low but clear. "But if I ever find even one toeprint from your slipper on my property, I'm calling the police."

"No, you won't." Wendi turned, smiling wryly, her night vision able to see him in the hanging tendrils of Spanish moss. "You wouldn't want the entire town of New Orleans hearing about another confrontation between the Chastains and Bardous, monsieur. Or might I call you Nick, since it seems our paths are destined to cross?"

Instead of a blast of anger at her audacity, she received a droll chuckle. Had she been able to see his face, she sensed she might find a spark of admiration for her conclusion. It hadn't taken much to make her well-founded defense and deduction, however. After all, she'd also lived through the ashes of the lives left after the scandal. Being on the fringes of scandal was nearly as bad as being one of the central, controversial characters.

He limped past her and started across the street. "Southern hospitality demands I offer you refreshment," he said over his shoulder. "But I'm sure you wouldn't wish to partake of Bardou refreshments."

"There you'd be wrong." She went after him. "As wrong as you are about some other things. I'd love to have something to quench my thirst. It's a long walk from Canal Street. From one world to another."

"Look." He stopped at the foot of the mansion's steps and gazed down at her, a troubled look on his face. "I know damned well how far it is—both in physical distance and in lifestyles. I'll call the carriage driver and have him take you home. You shouldn't be out this time of night alone."

Did she dare ask what had been on her mind for the past two days? Nothing ventured, nothing gained.

"Since I'm here, could I please look at my mother's portrait? I've never seen it."

He flinched. Hard and fast. "You can have the damned thing! I'll have it crated up and delivered to you tomorrow."

His stance told her she wasn't going to get any farther than the walkway, no matter how much she wanted a chance to see inside. She had absolutely no recall of her birth place, and she'd always wanted to see what she'd lost—the way she might have lived. Although, granted, Bardou mansion wasn't where she was born, it was a home such as she might have had, had Fate picked a different path for her.

But Nick obviously didn't want her to soil the memory of his mother's house.

She started back down the walkway. "Never mind the driver. I made it here alone, and I can get home the same way."

"Wait—"

The door behind him opened, cutting Nick off and causing him to groan under his breath.

"Monsieur, what on earth has come over you?" a sprightly voice said. "Entertaining here on the porch. Why, the neighbors will think California destroyed all your manners."

Miz Thibedeau. Wendi lifted a hand to wave at the cheerful, unassuming woman, who peered through the darkness where the light spilling from the doorway ended.

"Why, stars above, if it's not Wendi Chastain!" Miz Thibedeau said with a gasp. "Come in, my dear. Come in. I just finished some pralines. My sister's recipe, you know.

Remember the pralines I used to bring you when I came to see Sybilla?''

Wendi glanced at Nick, lifting an eyebrow and waiting for permission to enter. He glowered at her, but then looked at Miz Thibedeau and shrugged his shoulders. Wendi bit back a laugh at his definite change of attitude toward someone who had to be his servant. She'd venture there was a story behind that somewhere, and maybe some day she would find out what it was.

She started back up the steps, and Miz Thibedeau shooed her inside. Nick came in after them, shutting the door with a sigh of resignation.

''Now, you take her into the parlor, monsieur,'' Miz Thibedeau said to Nick. ''And I'll be right there with refreshments.''

She scurried down the hallway, and Nick turned abruptly into the first room on their left. When she followed, she found him standing just inside the doorway, and he nodded at her, then stepped back into the hallway.

''I'd prefer you limit your visit to this room, then leave. Feel free to have Miz Thibedeau call our carriage driver to take you home when you and she are done talking. I hope you have a pleasant visit with her. Good night.''

When he turned away and limped off, Wendi's mouth dropped open. Without even thinking, she chased after him.

Six

"Uh—" was all Wendi could think of to say when she grabbed Nick's arm and he glared down at her fingers on his white shirt sleeve. Leaning on his walking cane, he reached for her hand, hesitating as though reluctant to touch her before pushing it from him.

Disappointment filled her, lessening and bending toward a sly satisfaction when he rubbed his index finger over the spot where her hand had rested. Something told her it was an unconscious movement, an awareness on his part of the same tingles she'd felt herself when they touched.

Despite her unalterable decision to never let a man manipulate her life again, there was something fascinating about Nick Bardou. Could it be because they shared a past, which now appeared to be on a convergent path into the future? That had to be the only reason she felt drawn to him. Didn't it?

"I was wondering if you minded Miz Thibedeau showing me the portrait," she said when the length of the silence threatened to turn into embarrassment. "Since I'm here."

He glanced on down the hallway to the next doorway,

then shrugged and flicked his head in that direction. "It's in there."

"Thank you."

Taking his manner as an indication she didn't have to wait for Miz Thibedeau, she passed him and headed for the other door. Eagerly she opened it, then halted, stunned.

The portrait hung over the fireplace, and the realism and beauty of it took her breath away. The room was a library—dark, masculine, and lined with full bookshelves—and somehow the portrait wouldn't have looked as striking in a more feminine room.

Wendi marveled at it. The artist had captured her mother so authentically and with such a palette of distinctive colors that she appeared alive, eyes sparkling, lips quirked in a hint of a smile. A person could race across the room and fling herself into the long-lost, long-dead arms.

"Oh, lord," she murmured. "She's so beautiful."

Behind her, Nick grunted a sound of disgust, and once again she wasn't surprised at his presence. His not tossing her out on her fanny gave her pause and made her wary, ready to confront whatever threat he had in mind when he decided to use it. But it seemed right for him to be there in the library with her just then. Of course, his attitude could stand a major shift, but at least he'd allowed her this far.

She turned to look into his eyes. They were fixed on the portrait with an angry intensity that would have melted the oils into messy, indistinct pools had he been a warlock focusing his magical power of destruction.

"Why do you let it hang there if you hate it so much?" she asked logically.

He didn't answer, and the danger she faced if she forced conversation along those lines lingered palpably in the air.

Shrugging, she walked closer to the portrait and gazed up. "It's too beautiful to be hung in our little house."

Nick spoke in a reluctant tone, as though the words were forcing themselves past his throat. "The damage disappeared, but you'll never make me believe there was anything unexplainable about it."

"What damage?" Wendi asked. "It looks absolutely perfect to me."

He slowly lowered himself into one of the chairs in front of the desk, evidently familiar enough with the room to know it was there for him, since his eyes never left the portrait.

"I threw a crystal decanter of brandy at it," he said in a reluctant tone. "I didn't stay around to see what I'd done, but I heard the bottle shatter as I left the room. Yet when I came back from your house that day, there wasn't a sign of anything different about the damned thing. Not one tear. Not one ounce of brandy splattered on it."

He clenched his fingers on the cane between his legs. "Miz Thibedeau said she swept up a pile of glass in the corner, beneath the sideboard over there. She assumed one of the decanters had fallen off the shelf because I hadn't replaced it properly. But it didn't. I threw it *at* that damned thing, not at the side of the room. I have no doubt of that."

His eyes slid to her, then back to the portrait. "You could be her twin, you know, instead of her daughter."

"I've been told that more than once."

He continued, "I don't even know why I told you what I tried to do to the portrait. But I will tell you this." He tilted his head, indicating the chair beside him. "Sit down, damn it. It's bad enough to look at one of you, let alone two."

"Since you ask so nicely," Wendi gibed, nevertheless moving over to the chair.

She'd give anything for a private moment or two right now. The shock of seeing her mother looking so lovely in the portrait reeled her senses, although she'd lie down and die before she let Nick Bardou see how it bothered her. More important, she wanted some privacy to get her jumbled thoughts in order and try to figure out what was going on—why Nick didn't just throw her out of the house and be done with her. He must have some underlying purpose she should be wary of.

But she couldn't think. It was just the portrait, she assured herself while she studied it once more and waited for him to speak. It wasn't being in the room with a man who drew her, yet angered her. More than once while she matured, Sybilla had warned her about her easily lost temper. She warned Wendi to control and contain her anger if she wanted to maintain dominance over her magic. After her failed reading for Nick in their parlor, Sybilla had explained that the vibrations between her and Nick had caused the sparks to fly and wind to blow at their little house. She warned Wendi not to lose control again, lest she further disrupt the karma.

"What did you mean the other day when you said I *thought* I'd killed your mother?" Nick asked at last.

At that moment Miz Thibedeau scurried in, almost as though she'd been waiting for that exact moment. Wendi certainly hadn't heard the tea cart coming down the hallway.

"Here the two of you are. I thought maybe you'd come to the library, when you weren't in the parlor." She pushed the tea cart, which was loaded with dishes and platters of different foods, over beside the desk. Nick's stomach growled loudly.

"Now, here, here, Monsieur Bardou," Miz Thibedeau admonished. "You'll make Wendi think I don't feed you."

She gave Wendi a wink and said, "We had jambalaya and corn and potatoes and tomatoes for dinner. And sweet potato pie and banana pudding for dessert. My, my, can this man eat. The woman who marries him better make sure her cook plans huge meals. Land sakes, I don't understand how he can stay so slim, while I smell food when I'm cooking and put on five pounds."

"Miz Thibedeau!" Nick said. "If you're done chattering away, we can serve ourselves."

Wendi started to remind him that he'd more or less told her to visit with Miz Thibedeau, not him, but she quickly found that Miz Thibedeau handled herself perfectly well with Nick.

"I have no intentions of letting you break one of these delicate dishes, like you did the brandy decanter the other day," Miz Thibedeau said with a haughty sniff. "I'll take care of handling these myself."

"You said the decanter fell from the shelf," he muttered.

"Huhmph." She filled two china plates and then stirred two tall glasses of lemonade on the cart. Pushing the cart closer, she settled it equa-distant between them, gave a curt nod when it all suited her, and brushed her hands together.

"Don't try to bring that cart back into the kitchen," she said as she headed for the door. "I'll get it myself." At the doorway she paused and turned back, making her own comparison of Wendi and the portrait. "I never understood," she mused.

"Understood what?" Wendi asked immediately.

Miz Thibedeau shook her head. Without answering, she disappeared out the doorway before Wendi could question her further.

"Do you know what she meant?" she asked Nick.

"Hell, I didn't even know she was aware of who I was until the day we arrived back in New Orleans."

He lifted his shoulders in a shrug, then rose with an effort at masking the pain on his face. At the bar he picked up a decanter and carried it back to the tea cart, then poured the liquor into the lemonade glass nearest his chair. Moving the decanter over the other glass, he glanced at Wendi in inquiry.

"Just a tiny dab," she said.

He complied, then set the decanter on the cart and picked up his glass. Rather than sitting back down, he leaned against the desk behind him and drank a good portion of the lemonade. Wendi only sipped hers, then picked up a praline and nibbled.

"I'm still waiting for you to answer me," Nick reminded her. "I *thought* I killed your mother?"

"Is that the only reason you haven't thrown me out of here?" she asked.

"Yes. I'm sure you understand what your being in this house would do to my mother, if she were alive."

"The sins of the fathers and all that, I guess." Wendi dropped the praline back onto the cart and stood. "I think I'll leave now. You needn't bother showing me out."

Before she could take a step, he said, "I can make you a deal."

She studied him, and his eyes met hers, keeping contact while he lifted the glass and finished the lemonade. Ice tinkled as he lowered the glass and continued to stare at her. Blue. Yes, his eyes were blue, but not an ordinary color. Just now they were deep azure, filled with his thoughts and the pain in his leg. Filled with laughter, they could probably knock a woman to her knees, Wendi mused, wondering just how long it had been since he even smiled.

"You want to know what's in the Book of Shadows when we find it," she said.

"Reading my mind?"

"I don't have to read your mind to come to a logical conclusion. What you're not taking into consideration is that, even if we do find the Book of Shadows, no one's going to believe the words of a witch. Even the written words of a witch long-dead for ten years."

"Maybe I don't care about everyone else," Nick growled. "Maybe I just care about having all the available facts so I can make my own decision—draw my own conclusions—and live with them. And you're not going to be able to search this house without my permission. Belle Chene, either."

"Belle Chene?" Wendi took a step toward him. "Would you really let us search Belle Chene?"

"She was out there plenty of times over the years, so it seems that should be a part of any search I allow," he snapped. Then he broke contact with her gaze and grabbed the decanter to splash his glass half full of liquor.

Wendi sighed in commiseration. "I can help that pain," she made the mistake of saying.

"You keep your damned hands to yourself!" Nick snarled. "I've already suffered through one bout of needing laudanum so badly I couldn't sleep nights. It took me weeks to get over that dependency." He saluted her with the glass. "From now on, this will do perfectly fine."

"It can be just as addictive as laudanum."

"The hell you say. Look, you keep this in mind, if we're going to work together. I don't believe in witches or magic or any of your supposed *healing* arts! You keep your distance, and I'll keep mine."

"I haven't agreed that we should join our search efforts," Wendi reminded him.

"Fine. Then get out. And don't think you'll be able to search this house after I return to California. I've got plenty of money to hire a permanent guard here, to keep you out."

So, this confirmed her suspicions of the reason for his tolerance of her, Wendi mused, refusing to yield to his order to leave and staring at the portrait instead. He had been contemplating this since she told him that he might have erroneously assumed that he killed her mother, no matter what the wild rumors said. He wanted her to find the Book of Shadows for his own selfish reasons.

On reflection, taking into consideration what he had probably gone through the past ten years, she couldn't blame him. After what she said to him in their parlor, he must desperately want to know the truth about her mother's death, for his own peace of mind.

Her own need for her mother's Book of Shadows was different. Wasn't it? Wasn't it more of a need for survival of her magical powers than anything else? But the Fates were obviously forestalling her and Sybilla's efforts to correct their waning magic. Could it be they would have no luck at all until they allowed Nick to share their search?

She didn't know. She needed to talk to Sybilla before she made any commitment to allow Nick to infiltrate their lives any more than he already had.

"Tomorrow is Bealtane Eve," she told him. "We'll be celebrating the marriage of the Goddess and God in the evening and into the next day. We can't make any decisions until after that."

"I'm going out to check on Belle Chene tomorrow, then leaving for California the day after that."

"Then you'll have to go," Wendi said, refusing to allow him to dominate her. After a last brief look at the portrait, she left the room and walked down the hallway. At the door she glanced back as she opened it, but he wasn't standing in the library doorway.

She wasn't truly surprised that he refused even to discuss a compromise with her. She went out and down the steps.

She would have thought less of him if he had—and yes, been less satisfied with her own refusal to allow him control of their future relationship.

She hadn't seen the last of Nick Bardou by far. She didn't need her magic or scrying speculum to recognize that fact.

The darkness never bothered her. Should anyone approach her, they usually left as soon as they realized who she was. If not, a quick chant for protection could penetrate even a fog of drunkenness in an accoster.

Thrice around the circle's bound

got their attention. By the time she finished,

Evil sink into the ground

the assailant would be hightailing it to a safer area. She felt completely safe walking back to her house.

The encounter with Nick was troubling, but she couldn't allow him to ignore the ramifications of what could happen—things beyond their control. He had no idea the wrong he could do if he interfered with the powers that provided her with her magic. Not that she had any intentions of allowing him to do that.

Bealtane was one of the four major celebrations of the year, as important to her as Christmas and Easter to the Christians. In fact, she could argue whether the placing of Easter on the Sunday following the first full moon after the spring equinox wasn't derived from a pagan influence. Bealtane celebrated the marriage and joining of the Goddess and God, honoring the return of fertility to the earth and the resulting vitality, passion, and hopes. She would not dishonor her beliefs by failing to take part in this festivity, no matter Nick's threat to leave for California.

It was well-known that contact could be made with the departed during Bealtane, as on any of the other various holidays during the year. Her mother had failed to show her presence for the past nine years at Bealtane or any other celebration, though, but maybe this was the right time for her to make contact at last.

As she got closer to home, Wendi became aware of the sound of hoofbeats behind her. She tried a tentative probe and, not surprisingly, encountered the barriers she couldn't seem to breach around Nick's mind. For an instant she was tempted to let him know mentally that she was aware of him following her, seeing her safely home. Then she hardened her heart. He'd been using her at his mansion, trying to manipulate her into wielding powers he purported not to believe in to ease his own mind. He would have to come to her and apologize before she would even consider joining forces with him.

Ah, no. She'd been concentrating on her awareness of Nick behind her instead of paying attention to the path she'd taken. She should have turned left at the previous block, in order to miss Katzey's Bontemps. As she watched, two men staggered through the arched gateway on the bar's courtyard, stumbling over bricks fallen from the decaying structure.

Sure enough, they headed in her direction. She straightened her shoulders and mentally called the triple layer of purple light around herself for protection. She kept walking, since they'd already spotted her in return. Fleeing would probably urge them in their befuddled minds to follow her.

They approached, meeting her beneath a dim circle of light from a barely lit street post. She recognized one of them and smiled. Perhaps everything would be all right.

" 'Evenin', Mish Wendi,'' Doc Meneur slurred. He actually tipped his hat to her, swaying and nearly losing his balance at the movement.

"Doc," she acknowledged.

The other man, unknown to her, nodded a greeting, also, and they both passed on by. Sighing in relief, she hastened her steps in order to pass the tavern entrance before anyone else came out.

But the horse behind her snorted, and its iron-clad hooves danced on the cobbled street. Then she heard a frustrated shout of anger.

Seven

"Damn you, don't even think of trying it!" Nick shouted at the two men when one of them reached for his stallion's reins. Grabbing his riding whip, he slapped it across the man's hand. The man yelped and backed off, but his partner egged him on.

"Shit, there's two of us, Harry. Come on, go back after 'im. That fancy gentleman's probably got a pouch that'll keep us for a whole year! I'm tired a' Mary Jo havin' to work so hard."

Goddamn it, why had he left the house without his pistol? But he'd been anxious to make sure that little package of fake witchcraft made it home safely. Damn his southern upbringing, including the mistaken training that said women needed a man's nurturing and protection. The two men hadn't more than glanced at Wendi. She'd been perfectly safe.

Harry lunged for the horse again, and Nick slashed him across the face. But while he had his attention on Harry, the other one crept up behind him, grabbed his frock coat, and pulled on it to unseat him. His weight hit the left stirrup, and his injured leg screamed with pain while agony filled his mind.

"Stop it, right now! Or by the Goddess, you'll wish you had!"

A bright flash of light crackled through the air, accompanied by a crash of thunder and landing with a hiss of smoke in the cobbled street. Nick's stallion reared, whinnying in terror. Nick barely managed to stay in the saddle as the second man dropped to the ground, freeing Nick and lessening the pain.

When his vision cleared, Nick subdued the wildly dancing stallion and brought it to a standstill. Wendi stood a few feet away, her hair blowing as though in the wind, notwithstanding the night being still. Harry got to his feet, stared at her, and raised his hands in a warding-off motion. The other man was still on his feet, staring at Wendi.

"Mish Wendi," he pleaded. "We din' know this one was with you. Truly we din'."

"Doc," she told him, "if you ever want to use that manhood to make Mary Jo happy again, you better leave here right now. Otherwise, it's going to shrivel and drop off!"

"Oh, me god, no. Please," Doc whimpered.

"Leave! Both of you. Now!" Wendi ordered.

She pointed her finger at them, and Doc clutched between his legs and did as she commanded. Harry galloped right behind him.

Gripping his leg, Nick crumpled over the saddlehorn. He needed to get home.

Wendi's concerned voice cut through his suffering. "Let me help. Can you ride as far as our house?"

"No," he muttered, unsure if he was warning her away or refusing her offer of help. But she ignored him anyway. Gently she pushed his foot from the stirrup and mounted behind him. Reaching around, she took the reins from his unresisting hands and set the stallion in motion.

"This horse doesn't let anyone else ride him," he muttered nonsensically. The groom who delivered the stallion from Belle Chene had assured Justin that no one had been able to handle the beast since Nick left New Orleans. And hell, here she was on the horse, controlling it.

Wendi continued to disregard him, and he laid his cheek on the stallion's neck. All at once he felt a caress on his leg, and he gritted his teeth, trying to dredge up the energy to push her hand away. But she clenched her fingers, then rubbed his leg with her palm in a massaging motion. The relief was slight, but instantaneous. He groaned in reaction.

"If I had my herbs with me," Wendi said, "I could take the pain away faster. You'll have to wait until we get to the house."

"I can't go to your house."

"Shut up, Nick, or I'll shrivel your manhood."

His choke of laughter caught him by surprise. He jerked in reaction, startling the stallion, and Wendi's voice soothed the animal. Closing his eyes and stilling the laughter, Nick concentrated on the pain in his leg—now more the lack of it—as she continued to massage the scarred area.

"What happened?" she asked him, and he knew she meant the long-ago wound.

"The war," he answered curtly.

Finally the pain lessened enough that he could sit up straight, and he removed the reins from her hands. She made no protest, settling back on the horse's rump and disengaging contact with him. The sense of loss was immediate, but he told himself it was because, without the massaging motion, the nerves in his leg tightened again and the pain gave a warning throb. Then it subsided, at least for now.

He glanced around to get his bearings. Her house was

only half a block away, and he kept the stallion on the same path, pulling it up at the gate a few seconds later.

"I'll wait until you get safely inside."

Giving a resigned sigh, she slid from the horse, landing lightly in the cobbled street. But instead of going on into the house, she stared up at him. The nearly full moon gave enough light for him to make out the concern etched on her face.

"I can help, you know," she said. "There's herbs to use with the massage to ease the pain." When his lips lifted in a sneer, she hastened to add, "There's nothing magical about healing or pain-fighting herbs and massage. Eucalyptus and wintergreen have been used for muscle and nerve pain for hundreds of years, and even a lot of doctors use them in various forms. In addition, the massage soothes the nerve and muscle damage."

"Sure, just like you didn't use any magic to get rid of the disfigurement on that young woman's face."

Her pretty mouth moued into a tease, her eyes dancing with reflected starlight. Other than Miz Thibedeau, he'd never encountered a woman who didn't cower and slink abjectively away when he snarled.

"I thought you didn't believe in my magic," she said with a secretive smile. "But yes, that's what it was that got rid of the disfigurement. Sometimes it works and sometimes it doesn't, though. It depends on what the Goddess feels the Fates have in mind for the person who asks for our help. If it's what's supposed to be, then the Goddess assists our magic."

"Some would say your honoring a goddess is blasphemy."

"And what do you say?" she questioned.

"I quit believing ten years ago."

She nodded in a nonjudgmental way, then asked, "Are

you sure you won't come in and let me see what I can do for that leg?''

The pain throbbed again, a dagger stabbing him then subsiding. His leg dangled beside the stirrup, and he gritted his teeth, waiting for the next thrust. He didn't protest when Wendi stepped closer and laid her palm on his thigh, extremely close to what she'd threatened to shrivel on both him and the attacker. But it would take a lot more than a Chastain woman's touch to waken that part of him and make it stand to attention through the pain.

Or so he'd thought. Hell, he hadn't felt this much need since before his injury. He glared down at her, but she didn't seem to notice, which pissed him off even more. His condition reminded him there was one thing that always alleviated the pain for a while—

"Let's go inside," he gritted.

She looked up at him. "Of course. Do you need some help dismounting? There's a mounting block over there that some of the ladies use."

Pride-stung as usual at any mention of his disability, he disregarded her offer, dismounting on the other side of the horse to avoid any more strain on the leg than necessary. Cautiously he balanced his weight on his right leg, then grabbed his walking cane from where he carried it in what was usually the rifle scabbard. Looping the reins around a hitching post, he limped to the small iron fence and opened the gate.

"After you."

She walked past him and on up the porch steps, waiting at the door until he made his slower way to her.

"My aunt is probably sleeping," she said. He mentally hoped so. "But she sleeps soundly, so we won't disturb her if we're halfway quiet."

He could do that. Be quiet, that is.

She led him into the parlor and walked over to a wall sconce. After lighting it, she motioned to a horsehair settee. "I'll need to get some things. And you'll need to remove your trousers."

He stepped close to her, reaching out a finger and running it down her cheek, realizing as soon as he touched her that he'd wanted to do this since the day he saw her from the ship's gangplank. He assumed she'd jerk back, perhaps in fright, but instead she stood silently, returning his gaze with an unfathomable look.

"You want me to take off my shirt, too?" he murmured.

"You know something?" she asked in a musing voice. "Maybe we *should* get this over with. Once and for all." Stretching on tiptoes, she wrapped an arm around his neck and touched her lips to his.

Nick only thought he'd felt need when her hand massaged his thigh. It slammed him now with a force that almost brought him to his knees—would have, had he not pulled her to him and used her body to steady himself. Not that he was more than slightly aware of that part of it.

The majority of the hot, explosive sensations centered in his lips and his groin. Erupted with the growl of both need and want in his throat, into swirls of insensibility in his mind, seething heat in his blood.

He could have swallowed her, he wanted to be a part of her so badly. Wanted to be inside her thrusting until he lost his mind, his seed, his being. Wanted her out of that dress so fervently, the only thing that kept him from ripping it from her was the fact he'd have to let go of her long enough to do it.

That wasn't an option. Gripping her hips and rubbing the mind-threatening throb between his legs against her taut, yet soft, stomach was. The action nearly sent him over the edge without entering her, something that hadn't happened since his teen years when he'd wake in the middle of the night with soiled bed sheets.

Even then he could never bring himself to resent the lingering sensations of fulfillment, the same as he had no power now to forego the fast-rushing culmination he was on the verge of right now.

Suddenly she yanked his hair, struggling in his arms like a wild thing. For a moment he let her fight, drinking in her anger and fear, filling her mouth with his tongue and a feral chuckle of satisfaction that he was causing this wild response in her—this twisting and turning that shoved her soft, feminine curves against the hard planes of the body yearning for them.

She bit his tongue.

That got his attention.

He jerked back, throwing up his head and losing his balance. He had to let her go to keep from falling, and the cane didn't begin to take the jar of his imbalance well enough to keep the pain at bay. She backed away from him, her eyes finally reflecting the fear he'd been hoping to see in them before he kissed her.

Now he wanted to see—what? Now, instead of being satisfied to see her dread, he felt like a cad for causing that terrorized look on her face.

"I'm—sorry," he said, surprised to find it was the truth.

The fear cleared from her eyes, and she shook her head. "I started it. I don't know what on earth I was thinking of—what made me behave so foolishly."

Lifting his hand, he touched his tongue. There was a drop of blood on his finger when he drew it back. She saw it, too.

"I'm not going to apologize for that," she said. "I had to do something before both of us ended up in a situation we'd have been very sorry about tomorrow morning."

He nodded agreement, even while he stifled the twinge of masculine satisfaction at her admitting the embrace had bothered her as much as him. Unable to stop himself, he examined her flushed cheeks, lips pouted from his kiss. The fullness was caused from only one kiss, because he'd refused to relinquish her lips once he claimed them.

Her hair had come loose, tumbling around her shoulders in riotous waves of strawberry silkiness, hiding the breasts he hadn't had time to explore. They, at least, weren't shrinking from him. They perked to attention and burrowed through her curls, nipples beckoning as though they had a mind of their own, much like his own part acted at times.

She heaved a sigh, which filled her breasts with more yearning, and Nick licked his lips.

"I should get out of here," he growled.

"No. No, we can handle this. You're just a customer. And you're in pain, and I can help you."

"The kind of pain I have right now is only getting worse with you around."

Her blue gaze flickered right to the pain, increasing the pleasure of it until he thought he'd finally disgrace himself for sure. She drew in another breath, then whooshed it out, scattering curls from her cheeks and forehead but not cooling the heated flush on her cheeks one bit—nor the heat clamoring in his groin.

"I'm not a virgin," she said, her words exploding on his barely curbed senses.

"Jesus Christ, do you want me to rape you?" he yelled. "And damn it, why should you bother telling me that? I suppose the next thing you're going to reveal is that you're married."

"No. Divorced," she said, a tiny smile hovering around her mouth and her eyes lighting with mischief.

He groaned and staggered over to the settee. As surely

as he knew the world would keep right on spinning into tomorrow, as it had the past ten years, he understood he should have gone the other way. Out of that parlor. Down the hallway. Gotten on his horse and galloped the hell back to his own part of town.

"There's no way in hell I'm going to let you touch me again tonight," he said. "But go get whatever you have to treat this pain, and I'll take it home with me."

"He was a warlock," Wendi said as though he'd asked. As though he gave a good goddamn about another man who'd been between the beautiful legs. "We thought we could make a go of it because we were such good friends, and both of us really wanted to have a family. There's not a lot of us around, so we decided to give it a try. But about a month after we were married, Cassandra moved here from England, and when I saw the way they looked at each other, I realized she was his soulmate. We waited until we were sure I wasn't with child, then we dissolved the marriage, and he went with her."

"You make it sound awfully damned simple."

"It is. For us. We believe that each of our lives should be as fulfilling as we can make it. Had I thwarted Colin's love for Cassandra, it might have taken several lives to correct the disrupted karma."

"I keep telling you, I don't believe in that bullshit. Go get the stuff for my leg so I can go home."

She hesitated only another second, then left the room. Without her tormenting presence so near, the magnitude of what he'd done hit home with Nick. He'd kissed the daughter of the woman who gave his mother so much pain. The daughter of his father's mistress. Mauled her, even, and been damned delighted to be doing it.

Was that what had happened to his father once he touched Sabine Chastain? Was that why he'd abandoned his wife's bed—ended up causing a scandal that destroyed the Bardou name in New Orleans? At least, the respected part of their name?

Left behind a legacy of dishonor, which Nick himself had made worse?

He staggered to his feet. He had to get the hell out of here.

By the time Wendi caught up to him, he was out on the porch. The only reason he didn't totally escape was because his leg had stiffened and ached so badly, he could hardly walk. He knew he'd be forced to use the mounting block, another blow to his battered pride.

"Nick, please," Wendi said, laying a hand on his arm.

He shook her off and limped down the steps. She followed him—he could smell her presence, even while the pain roared too loudly in his mind to hear her soft footsteps. He went through the gate, untied the stallion and led him over to the mounting block.

She didn't say a word while he painfully got into the saddle—nor did she wound his pride by offering her help again. Damn her! He wished she would, so he could have someone to shout at!

When he sat astride the horse, she handed him a small cloth bag. "There's wintergreen salve in here, and some witch hazel liniment. Use them alternately, to see which one will help. And there's dried willow leaves and bark for tea. Use only a small pinch for an entire pot of tea. Let it seep for at least fifteen minutes, then drink only one cup every four hours or so. Don't overdrink that, because it can be dangerous if you do."

"How much do I owe you?" he asked grudgingly.

"See if anything works first," she said with a shrug.

"I'll be leaving soon, so I might not be around for you to collect your money from," he warned.

She studied him for a moment, and when she spoke, it wasn't about the money. "Aunt Sybilla and I are planning a ceremony with the rest of our coven for Bealtane, to see if we can contact my mother. You're welcome to join the ceremony, since you're involved in this, also."

"I'll be damned if I'll participate in a witch's ceremony!"

"You're already living as though you're damned, Nick," she murmured. "Why don't you make an effort to do something about that, instead of wallowing in your self-pity? Why don't you live your life like you have a life to live, instead of just passing time until it's your hour to die?"

"Goddamn you!" he snarled. "You don't have any idea what you're talking about or what I'm going through!"

"Oh, but I do." She took a step back from the stallion. "I suffered through the consequences of that same scandal, too. So I'm probably one of the few people on earth who truly does understand what you're going through."

She walked around his horse to the gate, then said, "If we find the book before you leave, I'll let you know. And if you change your mind, we'll be in the St. Louis Number One Cemetery at midnight tomorrow."

Eight

Stacks of white tombs gleamed in the moonlight as Wendi and Sybilla walked down the aisles toward the back of the cemetery. Three high in most rows, here and there the bottom tombs had already sunk into the ground part way. Separate family tombs rose into the air in their own private spaces, some square, with iron fences surrounding them and gates guarding the entrances. There were even two huge, round tombs, built to accommodate the nuns, priests, and poor at their deaths.

Aboveground burials were a requirement in New Orleans. Ground-water level made belowground burial impossible, and in the early days of settlement, coffins floated to the surface during hurricanes.

Strict edicts were necessary for the custom to work properly. The tombs were used over and over again by the families, but each body must be given at least a year and a day to decay inside the wooden coffins. Opening the tomb prior to that could spark an explosion of the body gases inside, causing the door to fly off and possibly injure someone. But if left the proper amount of time, the bones could be swept to the rear of the enclosure, the wooden coffin burned, and another coffin placed inside, holding another body to molder.

In the family tombs and the ones for the Catholic priests, nuns, and poor, an area was left open in the middle for the bones to be pushed into and left to turn to dust. And when a family died out, the rentals for those tombs not actually owned by a family would sometimes go unpaid to the church, necessitating the removal of a family's bones. They were then re-blessed by the priest and added to the area the church used for its own dead and for the bodies of the poor, the tomb then re-let.

Wendi shook her head. She loved graveyards and never understood why they frightened most of the rest of the world. It was only the body and then the bones left, the soul having entered the netherworld of the afterlife at the moment of death. Peace. Graveyards exuded peace and serenity. She couldn't fathom how people could purport to believe in the afterlife, yet not understand death being part of it. All of them would end up here or in a similar place some day, so why be fearful of it?

Truly, though, the unknown frightened most people, much as fear of her magic and witchcraft made them terrified of her and others like her. That worked to the witches' advantage on the days and nights of celebration, giving them privacy to honor their Goddess and God. Not even the priests at the nearby St. Louis Cathedral would confront them.

She and Sybilla rounded the end of one aisle and saw the gathering of their friends ahead. Wendi sensed the one person she expected hadn't broken down and joined them yet. But he would. She had no doubt he was already on his way.

Colin and Cassandra greeted her and Sybilla.

"You two are almost late," Cassandra said, giving Wendi a hug and kissing Sybilla on the cheek. "We've already gathered everyone's tokens for the tree."

"It's your turn to arrange the altar and light the candles and the incense in the censer," Colin said. "Cassandra's turn to cast the circle."

Wendi had prepared for her responsibilities this evening, and she carried her basket of sacred articles to the altar of stones someone had already propped back into shape. Unlike some covens, their group didn't have a singular leader or priestess. Their duties rotated, but always among the women, not the men. Their beliefs gave Mother Goddess stronger power than Father God.

"We're sorry we're late," she said. "Aunt Sybilla's hound wasn't home, and she refused to leave until he came back and she could put him in the house. She was afraid that animal might try to follow us and someone steal him."

"Alphie's a valuable animal," Sybilla said with a sniff. "I don't plan to chance anyone taking him from me."

Wendi patted her arm. "It's all right, Aunt. I was only teasing. You know I like Alphie, too."

She and Sybilla greeted the rest of the gathering, which consisted of nine other people besides Cassandra and Colin—thirteen in all, as was the custom rather than a necessity. Similar gatherings were going on in other areas of the city, but their coven had used this meeting place for more years than anyone could remember. It had been her mother's place of worship, also. The live oak beneath which they met grew just inside the back wall, in a spot near where the Jewish portion of the cemetery was set off. It seemed appropriate to Wendi, when she thought of it, to celebrate their religion at the spot where two other religions merged yet remained separate.

Ah, she sensed him coming. Better let the others know.

She walked back to the stone altar, but instead of beginning the ceremony when everyone quieted and gave her their attention, she turned.

"I invited someone to join us this evening. As you know, Aunt Sybilla and I really need to contact my mother as soon as possible. And the son of my mother's lover is back in town. Nick Bardou. He has his own reasons for needing to join us, and he'll be here in a minute."

There were few secrets in the coven, since the very survival of their worship depended upon one another, so no one was surprised at her referring to the old scandal. Agreeable murmurs responded, and the others returned to their own conversations until she was ready for them to participate in the ceremony. Wendi waited until she heard the hoofbeats plodding down the aisle, then walked to the edge of the gathering to greet Nick.

He appeared in the darkness like a satyr, the hat on his head shadowing his face. Still, she could see the outline of his lips and recall the thrill of his kiss. No one had brought her such pleasure before, and she'd spent more time than she should have recalling it—especially in the dark hours of the night.

Halting his horse, he stared down at her, his shoulders blocking the moonlight. The sight brought a tingle to her palms. On his horse he appeared perfect, exuding a masculine sexuality that would give any woman a weak-kneed response, and Wendi was a woman. Even his limp made him attractive, she mused, inducing a feminine desire to comfort him, to be a nurture to his maleness.

"I don't intend to join in whatever you're going to do," he said. "I'll watch from here."

"You can't. You'll disrupt the circle."

"Why did I know you were going to say that?" he asked. With a sigh of resignation, he climbed down from the stallion more agilely than the previous night.

"Have the herbs and tea helped your leg?" Wendi asked.

"Yes," he barked. "Where should I tie my horse, so it doesn't *disrupt* things?"

Wendi nodded at an iron fence surrounding a nearby tomb, and Nick limped over to it. After tying his horse to a spiked corner post, he returned to her side. She glanced at his face, not surprised to see uneasiness reflected on it. Their ceremonies could unnerve the uninitiated, but she had to give him credit for his fortitude.

"Am I supposed to do anything?" he asked after a moment.

"No. Just watch. We won't know ourselves what will happen until it actually does."

"You said this is a celebration of some sort."

"The marriage of the Goddess and God. It has to do with spring, new growth, and fruitfulness. A lot of our beliefs are based on the earth and its cycles, as well as their meanings in our lives. We never want to forget to show the proper respect for what we are given."

She led him over to the gathering of people and introduced him. "I know you won't remember everyone's names," she said when she was finished, "but you may remember a few of them."

He nodded. "So what will happen now?"

"We arrange the altar and light the candles and censer, then cast the circle. We've brought gifts that have a meaning to us, and we'll decorate the tree with them. After that, we'll see if anyone comes through to contact us. We ask that you remember not to break the circle once we form it, Nick. We'll release it when the ceremony is done."

"Since I came here at your invitation, I'll respect your purposes and directives," he assured her. "But that doesn't mean I believe for one damned minute I'm going to see you talk to dead people.''

"Souls, Nick," she said with a smile. "It's the souls we communicate with. Now, I believe we're ready to start."

Leaving Nick standing beside Sybilla, Wendi approached the altar again. The gathering grew silent, and she stood before the altar, preparing herself emotionally and forming the proper respect. She lifted her arms toward the moon, the symbol of their Goddess.

"Mother Goddess, our Queen, on this Bealtane we have come to honor you and your union with Father God." Picking up the ritual broom leaning against the altar, she turned and handed it to Cassandra.

"Mother Goddess, we cleanse our circle to honor you, showing our respect by giving you an orderly arena where you can show your presence," Cassandra said. She walked around the area, cleaning it with wide sweeps, while the others chanted "Mother Goddess, we honor you." Once the circle satisfied Cassandra, she began casting the circle of stones, which Wendi handed her one by one from beside the altar.

"Spirit of the North Stone," Cassandra said, taking the flat stone to the north side of the gathering and laying it reverently on the ground, "we call on you and all the energies of the north to aid us in our celebration this night."

She repeated the appropriate chant for each stone Wendi handed her, the South Stone, East Stone, and West Stone. Then she took the purple cord from Wendi and laid it around the circle, connecting the stones and enclosing them inside. Wendi added her mental strength to the minds of those of the other coven members, drawing a barrier around them, delineated by the purple cord. Like everyone else, except perhaps Nick, she could feel them being cut off from the rest of the world—their area become a sacred place to honor their Goddess and where they could petition their needs.

"Our circle is complete," Cassandra murmured. "We ask that no one break it until we release it."

Wendi turned back to the altar, lighting the candles and the incense in the censer as she spoke the age-old chants. Then she picked up the bowl of water and held it out, touching it with the point of the sacred knife in her other hand.

"I consecrate and cleanse this water, making it suitable to dwell in our sacred Circle of Stones. In the name of Mother Goddess and Father God, I consecrate it in their honor."

She repeated her actions with a stone bowl of salt. "I bless this salt and cleanse it to make it fittingly pure to dwell in our sacred circle, which we have prepared to welcome Mother Goddess and honor her union with Father God."

When the altar suited her, she turned. Everyone concentrated together during a long moment of silence. She could feel the energy in the air, the welcoming atmosphere waiting for the Goddess to honor them with her presence. One more step of the ceremony remained.

Wendi waved a hand at the tree. One by one each person walked up to the pile of wrapped offerings and picked up their own. In strong voices, unashamed to let the others know of their desires, they spoke of their respect and their needs at the moment. And also what they desired for their futures, which they hoped their gift would help the Goddess be more inclined to grant them. When it was Sybilla's turn, Wendi stepped away from the altar and joined her.

They picked up their separate cheesecloth bags, tied with bright red, white, and green ribbons. Wendi had no idea what was in Sybilla's, since they'd prepared them privately, but hers was a combination of things. The red and white ribbons were the colors of the Goddess and God, and she'd added green indicating money to assure them of having clients enough through the following season to keep their cupboards filled.

Inside, she'd placed one of the hairs from the curl Sybilla had clipped from Sabine's hair before her burial. She'd added some dried jasmine buds, her mother's favorite scent as well as hers, and a small segment of one of her mother's dresses. She'd written a plea on a piece of paper, using lemon juice so it would be invisible to anyone unless they knew how to manifest the writing. To honor the Goddess, she'd added dried red rosebuds and cinnamon, and some anise and yarrow to facilitate communication with the spirits and souls.

She hung her bag on the tree and tied the ribbons, then stepped back and said, "Mother Goddess, I come to you on this day of your union to honor you and Father God. I come also to beg your help and ask that you call upon my mother, who resides with you in your world. For all I do, it seems not enough to strengthen my powers and use them to help others as they are intended. More often than not, my speculum remains dark and the karma is unsettled."

She glanced at Nick, then back at the tree branch. "I believe something in the past is left disrupted, and that it's affecting me today. I believe it involves my mother, and I feel I need her final Book of Shadows to aid me in resolving the past, so my future can once again become what it should be."

She stepped back and Sybilla tied her bag onto the same branch. "I honor you, Mother Goddess, as I have all these years," she said. "My magic is weakening, and I believe it is for the same reason Wendi's magic is not developing. We ask your help, Mother."

Suddenly a wind grew, whipping the women's skirts and the men's shirtsleeves. Overhead, thunder growled and a cloud scuttled across the moon. The wind picked up a small cyclone of dust, which whirled toward the altar, rose into a vaguely human shape, then died along with the wind. Wendi heard Nick gasp, but the rest of the coven murmured a welcome, knowing their Goddess had blessed them with her presence.

In the resulting silence the candles burned brightly, their flames completely unaffected by the wind. Wendi chanced another glance at Nick and a probe into his mind, finding him suitably impressed by the candles' undiminished flames.

She moved over beside Nick and murmured, "Can you feel her presence?"

He stared down at her, a skeptical look on his face. "I don't feel a damned thing except a dampness from the humidity. By the way, when does everyone get naked?"

Clenching her hands, Wendi reminded herself he was a human, not a warlock. Still, a desire to turn him into a toad for only a brief instant, to see how he would react to *that*, filled her mind. And they had enough magic here tonight to do that, if she decided to carry through with it and her own magic fell short of the mark.

No, whispered in her mind. Sybilla's voice, with a tinge of laughter in it. She turned and caught her aunt's eye. A smile on her lips, Sybilla shook her head to confirm her command.

All right, Wendi thought back to her. *But he better watch his mouth!*

"Sorry to disappoint you," she said to Nick. "But this isn't a ceremony when we worship without the encumbrance of clothing."

"Too bad," he murmured, scanning her with his eyes.

Sick and tired of his effrontery, she returned his look boldly.

"Yes, isn't it?" she replied, satisfied to see him flick his eyes away from her for a brief second in discomfort.

Suddenly Cassandra called out, "She's becoming stronger!"

As soon as Cassandra spoke, Wendi felt the presence. Had she not been focused on Nick, she would have felt it immediately. Disgusted with her distraction and lack of honor for the important ceremony, she turned abruptly and joined the gathering, which had formed a circle around Cassandra.

"She's been honored tonight," Sybilla said in a soft voice. "The Goddess will speak through her."

"I'm only here for a brief moment," Cassandra said, but the melodious voice wasn't hers. "I deeply cherish the honor you bestow on me tonight, and you will all have my favorable wishes for your needs and desires to come true. I must go now."

"Wait!" Wendi leaped forward, but Sybilla grabbed the back of her dress and hissed for her to stop.

Cassandra looked at Wendi and said, still in the Goddess's voice, "I know what you want. It is time, but it is not time yet. You must have patience, but you must not wait. The courses of the stars have merged favorably, but you must be true to the pathway set out for you. This I say to you. This you must understand and do."

Cassandra closed her eyes, then wilted. Colin was beside her in a second, catching her before she hit the ground, picking her up in his arms and carrying her over to the altar to sit on one of the stones.

Cassandra woke quickly, sat up, and smiled at everyone. "Oh, I feel so wonderful. And I feel certain my child will be a girl now."

Nick harumphed behind Wendi, and she whirled on him. "You could at least have the courtesy to keep your skepticism to yourself," she whispered furiously, unsure whether her anger stemmed from his presence or the Goddess's enigmatic dictate. "I don't come into your church and mock your beliefs!"

"I don't go to church," he said in a bleak voice.

He started to leave, but Wendi grabbed his arm. "Don't! You can't leave until we release the circle."

His muscles bunched beneath her fingers and he glared down at her. "Then you better release the damned thing. I've wasted enough time here with this little farce."

She stepped back and studied him. "It was your own decision to come here. No one forced you. Evidently you had some hope that you'd find something here, or you wouldn't have wasted your valuable time on this *farce*."

"*Touché*," Nick admitted with a shrug. "But now I know I was right to begin with. Whatever powers you appear to have are some sort of trick with chemicals and mind-control attempts. All that happened here was that your chosen spokeswoman made some preselected remarks in a disguised voice. I didn't even have the pleasure of seeing a bunch of naked people dancing around a fire, as the rumors say happens at your witchcraft gatherings."

She gritted her teeth, refusing to continue the verbal sparring. "But you owe me in return now," she said. "Whatever you feel you did *not* get here tonight, you were given the opportunity. Now it's my turn."

"For what?" he snarled.

"To search your house for the Book of Shadows," she told him. "That was the understood agreement."

From the corner of her eye, she saw Cassandra pick up the sacred knife and walk over to the North Stone, ready to start the release of the circle. Afterward, they would go to her and Colin's small house near Wendi's for the feast of celebration, but Wendi wasn't going to offer that opportunity to Nick.

She needed to force him to admit their bargain quickly, then give her attention to the final portion of the ceremony. However, should he choose not to honor the unspoken agreement, she had nothing to use to compel him to do so.

"You seem to read a lot into things," Nick muttered. "I don't recall agreeing to let you return to my house and do any such thing."

"Forget it, then," Wendi said in defeat. She turned and gave Cassandra her attention.

Pointing the knife blade at the North Stone, Cassandra chanted, "Farewell, Spirit of the North Stone, O Ancient One of Earth. We give thanks for your presence here tonight, and for your aid in bringing Mother Goddess to us to hear our pleas. Go in power, Spirit of the North Stone."

A greenish mist rose from the stone, and Nick gave a start, but he controlled himself when Wendi glanced at him. Cassandra bent down and picked up the end of the purple cord. Winding it around her hand, she walked toward the East Stone.

"Farewell, Spirit of the East Stone, O Ancient One of Air," she said, pointing the knife blade at it. "We give thanks for your presence here tonight, and for your aid in bringing Mother Goddess to us to hear our pleas. Go in power, Spirit of the East Stone."

A yellow mist indicating air rose from the stone, and Cassandra repeated her chants at the South Stone of fire, where a crimson mist rose, and the West Stone of water, resulting in a blue mist. The mists filled the air, nearly obliterating everyone, as Cassandra stood again by the altar, holding the knife aloft.

Wendi added her mental powers to those of the others

and pulled the circle inward. The outside world slowly regained dominance over their combined magic, and after a
proper period of respect, the gathering broke into chattering
groups.

When she deigned to check on Nick again, she saw him
on his horse, riding away. Just before he would have disappeared down the aisle, he halted the stallion and looked
back. A cloud scuttled across the moon, making it impossible for her to determine the expression on his face, and
when Sybilla came up beside her, Nick turned his horse
and continued down the path between the tombs.

"So what do you think, Aunt?" Wendi asked.

"The same as you, Wendi," she replied. "That it's as
confusing now as it was before the ceremony. I have no
idea what we should do next."

"Nick said he was going back to California tomorrow,"
she reminded Sybilla.

"I doubt that," she murmured. "But if he does, it will
be what's supposed to happen."

Nine

Standing on the edge of back veranda, Nick stared up at the sky. Black clouds still blanketed it, but the rain had weakened to a listless drizzle.

Damn it, it ought to be about ready to quit. He'd been confined to the house, along with the rest of New Orleans, for the past two days, not even making it home after the ceremony in the graveyard without getting soaked. Behind the preliminary shower the winds strengthened into not exactly a hurricane, but damn close.

He couldn't remember another storm like this one. Wind blew in sheets, pounding continuously without abatement the entire two days. It was worth a person's life to venture out, since hazardous dead tree limbs gave way during the violence. He'd lost one live oak on the front lawn and would have to hire someone to clear the tree as soon as the storm died.

There was no use even thinking about leaving for California, since ships wouldn't sail until after the Gulf waves died. And he refused to believe any sort of magical power had caused the storm and kept him from seeking passage home. What he couldn't deny, however, was that for the first time since his injury, his leg hadn't completely disabled him in rainy weather. The ache was there, but not to the point where he had to take to his bed and wait out the end of the storm. It couldn't be anything else other than the preparations from Wendi, he realized resentfully.

"Would you like me to fix you some lunch now, monsieur?"

"I suppose," Nick told Miz Thibedeau, who joined him in his perusal of the weather. "Something light, if you don't mind. For some reason, I haven't been able to work up much of an appetite in this weather."

"It's strange, isn't it? I've never seen such a spat of steady wind and rain. Usually we either have a full-blown hurricane or periods of light rain, then heavy again. But it looks like it's going to quit now."

Even as she spoke, the clouds drifted off, leaving a gray sky behind. Nick heard one of the horses whinny, and the man Miz Thibedeau had found to care for the stable came in the back gate. She'd said he was a cousin or a nephew— something like that. He couldn't keep track of all the relatives she appeared to have, and it still amazed him that she hadn't once let slip that she knew who he was while they were out in California.

The relative waved at them, and Miz Thibedeau called back a greeting before she turned and went inside. Nick plucked at his shirt, grimacing at the quickly building humidity now that the rain had quit. The entire town would be a steam bath while the ground dried, and without the shade of the downed live oak, the front parlor would be barely usable in the summer. He longed for his home in California, where the ocean breeze kept him comfortable year-round.

He wasn't going to worry about how the small house on Canal Street had weathered the storm. Or if the weather had kept her clients at bay. There hadn't been that much room to store food in the kitchen the one time he'd been in it. They probably had to go out daily to restock their larder, while he ate heartily from the mansion's well-maintained pantry. . . .

"There's someone here to see you, monsieur," Miz Thibedeau said from the back door. "He says he's from Belle Chene."

"Belle Chene?" Nick asked as he turned. "Did he give his name?"

"From the way he's dressed, I assume he's just one of the hirelings. I put him in your study."

A stab of pain hit him when he took a step, and Nick cursed under his breath. It had been several hours since he'd rubbed his leg with the salve and drank a cup of willow bark tea with his breakfast. It could be the effects of the medication wearing off, or it could be a result of the stress building in his consciousness at the mere mention of the plantation. Or maybe the unwavering knowledge that Uncle Jacques wouldn't send anyone in through the nasty weather unless something was seriously wrong.

He'd had a long discussion with Jacques soon after he arrived. Jacques swore he had no idea what had happened to the tax money, because he'd paid the taxes on time. Though far from making anyone wealthy since the war, Belle Chene at least paid its own way, he assured Nick. And it also made enough to pay the taxes on the mansion in town, despite the heavy fees levied by the damned Yankee carpetbaggers flooding the southern states. Jacques had sent Nick periodic reports, and if Nick wished, he could come out to Belle Chene and confirm what Jacques told him.

Nick shuddered at the very thought as he limped toward the study. Though necessary, visiting Belle Chene would be worse than returning to the secrets and memories of the family mansion he was forced to live in for the present.

The boy waiting in the study didn't notice Nick's entrance. He stood enraptured with the portrait Nick still hadn't sent over to Wendi. Something about the tilt of his head tugged at Nick's subconscious, but a vicious pain stabbed his leg, making him gasp and grab a chair back for support. The boy turned at the sound, but clearly preferred the portrait to facing Nick.

Wet and soggy, his clothing bespoke the class of workers at the plantation, as Miz Thibedeau had indicated. Homespun cotton, it was the same uniform most of the Belle Chene workers wore. They'd used the identical form of clothing even when slaves worked the fields, and Jacques had evidently found no reason to change the dress style now.

Yet the boy's bearing opposed the outward evidence of his attire. Blue eyes met Nick's gaze without deference, although he nodded in a respectful manner. Shaggy, unkept dark hair escaped a leather thong, but more in the manner of a harried ride on horseback than the ill-cut lanks of those who couldn't afford trips to the town barbers. Or those with personal valets to keep their hair cut fashionably.

"She's beautiful," the boy breathed in a husky voice unsuited for his age.

"You have a message for me from Belle Chene?" Nick reminded him shortly.

The boy's eyes clouded in worry. "Yes, sir. Yes, sir, I do. It's your uncle, sir. There's been an accident, and he's hurt badly. Monsieur Julian sent me to tell you that maybe you better come."

"Why the hell did Julian send a boy out in the weather we've been having? It must have taken you two hours to get here."

"I rode one of the better horses, sir. But if you'll be needing to come in a carriage"—his eyes flicked to Nick's leg, then back to his face—"you might better use a sturdy type instead of your Sunday church buggy. There's a couple pretty bad spots of bog on the road."

"Who are you, boy?" Nick asked.

"Lucian, sir. My mother keeps house at Belle Chene. Cecile, she is."

"I remember her."

The front door chimes pealed, and Nick glared over his shoulder. Now what the hell? Miz Thibedeau's footsteps sounded in the hallway, so he turned his attention back to Lucian.

"What happened at Belle Chene? How badly is Uncle Jacques hurt?"

"He fell from the hayloft. No one knows how it happened, sir. He's unconscious. Fact is, Monsieur Julian thought him dead, and it was my ma who saw a flicker of life in him, sir."

"Damn it, call me Nick," Nick spat. Something about the boy's deference ate at him.

"Yes, sir." When Nick frowned at him, he hurried to say, "Uh . . . Monsieur Nick."

"Monsieur," Miz Thibedeau said from the doorway.

With a huge sigh, Nick turned and faced her. Instead of speaking, Miz Thibedeau crooked a finger at him, indicating for him to join her in the hallway. Catching the concern on her face, he reluctantly limped out of the room.

"Miss Wendi's here," she said quietly. "She insists on seeing you, although I told her you were tied up right now. I put her in the front parlor."

"Well, she didn't stay there," Nick growled as he glanced over the woman's shoulder and saw Wendi watching him from outside the parlor door. "Look, you'd better try to catch that relative of yours who's taking care of the stable before he leaves. He—''

''Fred,'' Miz Thibedeau put in.

''What?'' Nick asked in confusion.

''Fred,'' she repeated. ''He has a name, you know. It's Fred.''

Gritting his teeth, Nick continued, ''You'd better have *Fred* hitch up the carriage, because I need to go out to Belle Chene. Ask him if he can drive me, also.''

''He can,'' Miz Thibedeau assured him. She looked briefly at Wendi, shook her head, then started down the hallway toward the back veranda.

Wendi approached him without hesitation. ''I want to go with you. I can be packed by the time you come pick me up.''

''Packed? What the hell for? I'm only going out to Belle Chene to check on Uncle Jacques and see if I need to find another manager for the plantation for a while. Then I'll come back here and book passage.''

''Monsieur Julian said to tell you he could take care of things if you didn't want to bother with it,'' Lucian said.

Nick had almost forgotten the boy. And it damned sure wasn't because the strawberry-blond beauty who haunted his dreams night after night stood within touching distance. Her troubled gaze touched on his leg, and immediately the pain abated a bit.

''I think you'll be there for more than just a check-in visit,'' Wendi murmured before turning her full attention on the boy. ''Who are you?''

''Lucian, Mademoiselle,'' he replied. ''Cecile's son.''

Wendi drew her bottom lip between her teeth in a worried gesture, but nodded at the boy. ''I'll go get ready,'' she said in a distracted voice. ''Your uncle might need some care.''

Nick stared after her in stupefaction as she hurried down the hallway and out the front door without waiting for either an acknowledgement or denial from him. She hadn't even told him why she'd come, and within the blink of an eye, she was gone. Gone, but she'd be waiting for him at that damned house on Canal Street, the sight of which curled his stomach every time he went there.

And what made her think Uncle Jacques might need some care? Lucian hadn't explained the injuries where she could hear. Nick glared at Lucian, and almost as though sensing the deadly gaze, the boy gave a guilty start and jerked his eyes away from the portrait.

Nick diverted his gaze to the one-dimensional layers of brush strokes some artist had fashioned into a portrait that curled the dread in his stomach even more than the sight of the Canal Street house. Ignoring the growing pain in his leg, he limped over to the fireplace and grabbed the bottom of the frame, yanking the portrait from the wall. Splinters of plaster scattered on the mantel as the nail gave way, dusting the dark marble in a layer of white.

He jammed the portrait face-side-in against the wall, then snarled at Lucian, "Go ask Miz Thibedeau for a towel to dry off and something to eat before we start out. I'm not going to have you grumbling that you're hungry all the way out to Belle Chene."

"Is the lady in the portrait going with us?" Lucian asked.

"She's not the lady in the portrait," Nick growled.

"But is she go—"

"Get out of here!"

Lucian ducked his head into his shoulders and scurried from the room, his bare feet silent on the shining floor. Miz Thibedeau could clean up the mud he left behind, Nick thought, along with the plaster dust on the mantel. Incongruously, or perhaps to keep his mind off the trip he'd been dreading even more than arriving in New Orleans, he hoped Lucian's bare feet indicated his preference to go barefoot. Surely Uncle Jacques wouldn't begrudge money for shoes for his hirelings.

Then he wondered why the hell that fact even bothered him? As soon as he got things under control at Belle Chene, he'd book his passage for California, even if he had to buy a damned ship!

Far too many encumbrances were encroaching on him back here in the city from hell. In California the responsibilities of his businesses were a welcome distraction from the haunted memories that sometimes strained the lid of entrapment in his subconscious. Here, the responsibilities didn't even notice the fetters of restraint.

Ten

The damned coach had never seemed this small. But hell, it hadn't been designed for this many people. Lucian rode on top with Fred—*he has a name, Fred*, Miz Thibedeau's voice singsonged in Nick's mind. The boy—*he has a name, Lucian*—rode up there not so much by choice as necessity. The three women inside with Nick took up every inch of space except that which he occupied, with their full skirts and baggage that didn't fit on top of the coach. Sybilla had even attempted to cram that stupid ragged hound in here, ignoring Nick's order to leave it behind and sending the animal scrambling to the top of the coach in defiance.

"He won't be any trouble at all," she had assured him. Harumph. Periodically he could hear Lucian thumping around on top with the animal. They'd be lucky if one of them didn't fall off before they reached Belle Chene, preferably the dog!

How the hell the women had all managed to cram so much into so many portmanteaus so quickly was beyond him. Not one of them appeared to have heeded his caution that they'd only be at Belle Chene long enough to get a new manager in charge. One portmanteau even sat between

Sybilla and Miz Thibedeau, who chatted away like long-lost friends, as he supposed they were in a way. On his side of the seat Wendi swayed against him now and then when the coach hit a rut or rounded a bend. At odds with the chatter across from them, Wendi kept her gaze fixed on the passing scenery, a troubled expression on her face.

"I still don't know why I allowed you to accompany me," Nick grumbled when he could abide the tense silence of her presence no longer. "If Uncle Jacques needs nursing care, I'm sure there are plenty of people at Belle Chene to take over that duty."

The coach tilted on the road, and she slid a couple inches across the leather seat. A delicious thigh made contact with his before she grabbed the window strap and pulled herself away.

"I assumed you knew why I wanted to go with you, in addition to offering to help with your uncle," she murmured. "My mother died at Belle Chene, and I've never been to where it happened. Plus her Book of Shadows might possibly be hidden there."

"You'll never find it, if it is. The plantation manor house alone has eighteen rooms. And the barn, where she died, connects to the carriage house and stables, where they kept over two dozen riding horses before the war. Belle Chene threw week-long extravaganzas in my grandmother's day, and she would have been mortified at her lack of hospitality had one of her guests wished to ride and a horse not been available."

"How did Belle Chene escape destruction during the occupation of New Orleans?"

"I don't know," he admitted. "Maybe because it's far enough outside of town that it was inconvenient for the Yankees to worry about it. But it didn't escape notice when the carpetbaggers descended. Thankfully, my father ordered

Uncle Jacques to bury most of Belle Chene's gold and silver when it became clear the Yankees were going to be in control of the city. After the war my uncle shipped everything to me in California, where I sold it and got the plantation back on its feet. As well as giving myself a start on capital for my businesses.''

"I see."

He frowned at her, the thought flickering through his mind that he had no idea why he explained things to her. No one, not even Miz Thibedeau, had bothered to ask him so many questions. He'd made a lot of lonely decisions without anyone to discuss the pros and cons with.

But the daughter of his father's mistress damned sure didn't have any right to have input into Bardou affairs.

"I'll bet Belle Chene is beautiful," the daughter said in a wistful voice.

Instead of telling her it was none of her business—as he should rightfully do—Nick grumbled an agreement. "I always preferred it to the mansion in town," he admitted. "Aside from the two balls my mother grudgingly hosted each year to follow the tradition set by my grandmother— one at Christmas and one in the springtime—Belle Chene always held for me the freedom from all social obligations."

Wendi nodded, and he scanned her profile, allowing his gaze to travel over the rest of her while she looked out the window. She wore a cotton gown, white but sprinkled with tiny pink rosebuds. As usual, her strawberry curls escaped the confines of her hairpins, tumbling over a slender shoulder, with tendrils twirling across her forehead.

She'd be even more beautiful in a silk ball gown, he thought, then contradicted himself. No, the cotton suited her perfectly, the capped sleeves and semi-low neckline cool in the humidity. The skirt draped her thighs, and when she bent to peer out the window further, the material snugged against a shapely hip.

"I see a stone fence and a gate up ahead," she said in controlled excitement. "Is it Belle Chene?"

"Probably. There's a quarter-mile line of live oaks planted on either side of the drive leading up to the manor house. They were planted by my great-grandfather, at my great-grandmother's direction, shortly after he received his land grant. Belle Chene means beautiful oaks."

"I know," Wendi said, no touch of resentment in her voice for his explanation.

Her fingers clenched in her skirt, and Nick realized he'd misjudged the tone of her voice. It wasn't excitement, but trepidation, if the whiteness of her knuckles was an indication of her feelings. For some crazy reason, he reached out and took her hand in his own.

"I don't want you going out to the barn alone," he said when she glanced at him, then down at their clasped hands. "The emotional shock will be too hard for you."

"Will you go with me, then?"

He tightened his grip, and she flinched. Quickly releasing her hand, he rubbed his palm on his trouser leg, not answering. He had no intention of going out to that barn. There were plenty of servants to bring either the carriage or a riding horse to the front veranda for him.

He closed his eyes, but still he saw the body on the dirt floor—the face that was almost a twin to the one beside his shoulder. Saw the horrible damage—

The pain in his leg throbbed, and he clutched the head of the walking cane propped between his legs.

The coach pulled into the circular drive in front of Belle Chene and halted. A second later Lucian appeared at the side door and opened it, then pulled down the steps and held out a hand to Wendi.

"Mademoiselle," he whispered in an awestruck voice. "Might I have the honor of helping you descend?"

Nick frowned as Wendi smiled at Lucian and gave him her hand. The boy was an incongruous piece of work, with his field-hand clothing and cultured voice and manners. He couldn't blame the lad for wanting to better himself from his position as the housekeeper's son, although others might disagree with his getting ideas unconventional for his class.

He decided right then to get to know the boy better, and perhaps offer him the chance to improve himself even further. He obviously had the ability to learn, given what he'd seen so far of him.

And if he wanted to fawn over Wendi, he supposed the boy was young enough to be excused for his lack of experience with women. Nick's hand tingled again from the touch of the soft, feminine one, and he rubbed it against his trouser leg again.

He waited for the ladies to descend, then climbed out himself. Lucian offered a sturdy arm for him, in an unabashed way that somehow didn't demean Nick's disability. Then he stepped back respectfully as Nick stood by the coach to examine the Belle Chene manor house for a moment.

"Monsieur Jacques has done the best he could," Lucian murmured as though understanding Nick's perusal.

Incredibly, Nick felt a stab of discontent as he studied the manor house. He'd thought himself beyond caring what happened to anything he owned back in New Orleans, but the needed repairs tugged at some distant part of him.

He'd spent a lot of happy hours at the plantation, and it had always seemed perfect to him. Now paint peeled in places, the bright white dulled to a sickly gray. Here and there a shutter dangled beside a window, black paint faded. He watched the women climb the steps, and a groan of weakness sounded when Miz Thibedeau and Sybilla both stepped on the same one at once. Wendi's gown snagged on a splinter, and she bent to loosen it before it tore.

The house reminded him of a shabby lady, down on her luck but still desperately clinging to her former glory. Someone kept the bright red, pink, and yellow begonias in baskets hanging along the veranda roof well-cared for, and the curtains he could see on the windows had the whiteness the paint lacked. The windowpanes sparkled with cleanliness, even though he saw a rotten sill beneath one. It must have recently given way, because a flowerpot that had graced it lay broken on the floor.

He couldn't see any of the outbuildings from here. They were all scattered in the far rear of the manor house, well away from the back gardens. He could see, however, weeds that would never have been tolerated before growing in the expanse of the lawn, where the grass had always before been clipped closely so it wouldn't stain the ladies' dress hems when their hoops swayed with delicate hip movements or infrequent breezes.

With a sigh, he walked toward the veranda steps and the women waiting for him before they knocked on the door. Only a thin layer of crushed oyster shells crunched beneath his feet, rather than the full two inches his father had always demanded be raked and evened out on the walkway. He instinctively climbed the steps on the edges, knowing they would be more supportive of his weight there.

The door opened before he could knock, and a beautiful older woman with dark-gray hair stood there. Cecile's brown eyes were rimmed with red, indicating that she'd been crying fiercely. She gulped back a sob and greeted them.

"Monsieur Nick," she said in a ravaged voice. "I am very sorry, but your uncle died about half an hour ago."

Nick fought the urge to take her in his arms and comfort her. Cecile had been part of his childhood, also, and word had been whispered that she was his uncle's mistress, although he didn't recall ever hearing why they hadn't married. Cecile had always treated him with respect and teasing chastisement, like a member of the family.

"Oh, Mama," Lucian cried in a heartbroken voice, shoving past Nick. The boy was nearly as tall as his mother, and she buried her face on his shoulder. Both of them wept, and Wendi moved forward and put an arm around them.

"Let's go on inside," she said. "Find you somewhere to sit down."

"The parlor's on the right," Nick told her when she glanced at him with a questioning look. He held the door open and allowed Sybilla and Miz Thibedeau to enter before him.

Instead of following the others into the parlor, Nick moved toward the staircase leading to the upper floors, grimacing at the long climb ahead of him. The stairwell wound completely around once before the landing for the second floor, and a duplicate of it connected to the third floor. Constructed from teak imported from the East Indies, it shone in its polished glory as it always had. Steps wide enough for both a man and woman to descend side-by-side and make a proper entrance during a fashionable evening stretched upward. He assumed Uncle Jacques would occupy the master suite on the second floor, cutting the necessary climb in half for him.

Feminine skirts whispered behind him, and he recognized Wendi's scent without turning.

"Cecile is in good hands with my aunt and Miz Thibedeau," she said. "Would you like me to go with you to view your uncle? Cecile said he's in the master suite, with his valet and son preparing him for the lying in."

Funny, he really did want her with him. And it didn't even bother him to admit it. He indicated for her to join him, and they climbed the staircase together.

At the head of the stairwell he turned right, toward the master suite, and a man emerged from the doorway almost as though he'd heard them coming up the stairs. Which he probably had, given Nick's distinctive gait.

"Cousin Nick," the man greeted.

"Julian," he replied. "I'm very sorry for your loss." Although Nick hand't seen him in years, Julian looked much the same.

Julian shook his head and wiped at his eyes. "It was so very sudden. I still can't believe he's not going to sit up in there and ask me what the hell Zed and I are doing, trying to put him to bed this time of day."

Suddenly he centered his gaze on Wendi, then gave Nick a startled look. To his credit, he kept his mouth shut, but Nick knew a hundred questions were rushing through his mind. And another expression flickered briefly, a narrowing of his eyes at Nick's audacity, even as the owner of Belle Chene.

"I'll see you in the study in a few minutes, Julian," Nick said without introducing Wendi.

But Julian evidently couldn't overcome the same set of drilled-in manners as Nick had been raised with. "Miss Chastain," he said with a nod. Wendi murmured an acknowledgment, and Julian left them, his booted feet clattering down the stairwell in a cadence Nick had long been denied.

"You'll need to wait out here," Nick told Wendi. "Zed's been my uncle's valet for forty years or more, and he'd be shocked if you came in while he was preparing him. I imagine he'll leave to go live with his son in New Orleans now that Uncle Jacques is dead."

She stepped back agreeably, and Nick went through the door. Zed glanced up from washing Jacques's face, his eyes streaming tears.

"Monsieur Nick," he choked. "He's gone. I don't know what I'll do without havin' him to take care of."

"You've devoted your life to my uncle, and I'll see you have a stipend when you go to stay with your son," Nick assured him in a distracted voice. His attention focused on his uncle, stretched out naked on the bed except for a sheet Zed had placed protectively over the man's privates—the servant doing what he could to foster his uncle's dignity even in death.

One more of his family gone—but Nick couldn't allow any grief inside his emotions. He'd used up his quota of grief years ago.

Jacques had always been fit, working in the fields or the tobacco curing sheds along with the field hands when necessary. His barrel chest had not an ounce of fat even at his age, and his legs were muscled and firm. On the ride to Belle Chene, Nick had tried to understand how a man born and raised on a plantation—a man who had done every chore without a hint of clumsiness—could have slipped and fallen from a hayloft. He hadn't seen a single sign of weakness in the man who came to the St. Charles Street mansion to report on the plantation. Yet he recalled one of the plantation's neighbors dying from being kicked in the head by a factious horse, and the neighbor had been renowned as the top horseman in the state.

No matter what people who consulted fortune-tellers like Wendi and her aunt believed, no one could ever predict what the next minute would bring into their lives. Death was all the more startling and disconcerting when it occurred so suddenly. He could still recall the horrible emptiness those who had survived the battles in the war felt, sitting around campfires later and missing the voices that had been there only hours earlier.

On further examination, Nick saw the only mar on what could have been a much younger man's body was on the side of Jacques's head. A concave spot, still uncleaned of clotted blood, mishapened the face. A huge bruise, which had formed beneath the tanned skin despite death, marred the side of the face.

Zed followed Nick's gaze and said, "He hit his head on the iron wheel of the hay rake when he fell. Otherwise, he probably would've just gotten a broken bone or two out of it. I don't even know what he was doin' up there. He'd been headed out to check the cane fields, and his horse was tied outside the kitchen house, still saddled and waitin' on him."

Zed sniffed and rubbed the back of his hand beneath his nose, an action he never would have stooped to beneath Jacques's stern gaze. Nick pulled a handkerchief from his pocket and handed it to the man.

"Do you need any further help with him?"

"No, sir. I sent Monsieur Julian on because he was carrying on somethin' fierce and not bein' of much help. Guess he felt some guilty."

"Guilty?"

"He and Monsieur Jacques hadn't been gettin' along lately again for some reason. They'd had their fights and made up plenty of times over the years, though. But you know how it is. Death be a great gap no one can bridge, and now there ain't no chance for them to make amends, like they done in the past."

Nick knew. No time for one final *I love you* for his mother before they found her dressed as though attending one last ball and laid out in the same repose as though in her coffin already.

No time for one final "Why?"—even if I had given Father the chance to explain, he thought, then quickly grimaced in disgust at the idea. There was no possible explanation his father could have given for driving a wonderful woman like his mother to suicide by taking a mistress. For setting the scene for the scandal that had ruined her life and driven her to the final desperate act. For setting the scene that Nick himself had kindled into the flame that destroyed the Bardou family.

He could never forgive his father for that, although he admitted his own part in the events that played out. While Nick received his punishment for his part in it every day, his father had initiated the chaos.

Hearing a stir in the doorway, Nick turned to see Wendi. Wendi, the daughter of the woman who had played the major role in ruining the Bardou family reputation and driving his mother to an early grave. Much as she hadn't liked Belle Chene, his mother was probably still turning over in her grave at Wendi being present in the manor house.

"I told you to stay the hell out in the hallway," he snarled.

Her face whitened when she looked at him, but she gave him a nod and disappeared. By the time he limped to the doorway, he saw her head disappear down the stairwell—heard her skirts whisper on the steps, a much less audible sound than the acres of crinoline his mother wore the times he escorted her down.

Remorse filled him, but he shoved it away. He hadn't asked her to accompany him, and there was no need of her services now that Jacques was dead. He'd send her back to New Orleans as soon as they could reload the coach.

First he had to talk to Julian. Despite the loss of its manager, the plantation work would continue to need attention. It was the season of cultivation for the cotton plants, with the first picking of the year perhaps already overdue. And the cane would need to be flooded, if it were to produce suitably.

He hadn't even realized he knew that much about the seasonal harvests at the plantation, but the conceptions sprang into his mind easily. He hadn't thought to ask Uncle Jacques if his son was capable of taking over control of the plantation during their last discussion. He recalled Lucian telling him that Julian would be willing to assume the management, but he'd make that decision after he renewed his acquaintance with his cousin.

Eleven

Miz Thibedeau met Wendi in the hallway outside the parlor. "I've been waiting for you, dear. Sybilla took Cecile to her living quarters over the kitchen house. The poor woman's in no shape to handle what's necessary for the funeral, so I'll take over. Cecile was able to give me a quick rundown of the layout of the manor house and which rooms we can use. There aren't any regular servants, since Cecile took care of the house and cooking for both Jacques and Julian, but I'll find someone to bring your things in immediately."

"I doubt Nick's going to let us stay here," Wendi cautioned.

"Pooh." Miz Thibedeau waved away the concern. "There's lots of things need done if Belle Chene is to provide proper hospitality to the people who'll be coming to pay their respects. And Monsieur Nick does remember how important hospitality is in this area of the world."

She gave Wendi a wink. "Besides, if Monsieur Nick wants his belly filled with the food he likes—and that man does like to eat—he better let me keep you and your aunt here as companions and to help me. I won't be able to concentrate on my cooking in a houseful of strangers."

Miz Thibedeau hurried away, and Wendi found herself at a loss as to what to do next. Catching a movement out of the corner of her eye, she saw someone disappear into a room on the other side of the hallway. The door slammed shut with a positive thud.

Julian, she supposed. She understood his agitation very clearly. He resented the hell out of her presence at Belle Chene.

She couldn't blame him, she guessed. Or Nick, either, for recalling her connection to the scandal and snarling at her, although it had hurt her deeply. She turned and detected her reflection in the corner of a mirror, which someone had carelessly covered with a black mourning scarf. As usual, a younger version of her mother's face stared back at her. It reminded her that Nick had never sent the portrait over to her Canal Street house, and she hadn't found the courage yet to ask him why.

Despite Miz Thibedeau's assurance, she wasn't going to depend on being able to stay at Belle Chene once Nick got around to finding time to order her gone. The very least she could do was make her pilgrimage to the site of her mother's death before he chased her off.

Knowing the probable layout of the plantation, she went down the hallway and out to the rear veranda. The back gardens were badly in need of care, nevertheless with a wild and scattered beauty. She hurried through them without pause. On the left Miz Thibedeau was talking to Aunt Sybilla on the kitchen house porch. No doubt Cecile was resting in the upper living area provided for servants. Wendi walked on down the garden pathway without acknowledging the two women, opening the back gate to examine the new surroundings and allowing it to swing shut behind her. The gate squealed, desperately needing oil.

There, through the trees, stood the barn. A path led directly there from the gate, with another wider driveway intersecting on the right. The horses and carriages were routed to the front of the manor house to pick up their riders and passengers, and the driveway showed recent hoof and wheel prints leading toward the barn from the coach that had brought them to Belle Chene.

The gate squealed again behind her, and Wendi turned to see Aunt Sybilla come through it.

"I'll go with you," Sybilla said. "We might need each other's support."

"All right."

They walked toward the barn, and Wendi tried desperately to tune into the other-world sensations she should have felt. Beside her, she could sense Aunt Sybilla doing the same. When they emerged from the trees, both of them stopped of one accord and waited for the feelings to take shape.

The barn rose majestically above them, a faded, weathered gray but in better shape than the manor house. Only peace greeted them, however, instead of vibrations of discontent or disruption. Perfectly in tune with each other's thoughts, they looked at each other, then walked on.

An iron bar propped the barn door open. Inside, they paused again to get their bearings. Far back in the recesses, they heard movement and sound—footsteps and the pleasant nicker of a horse. Light entering from a similar door on the other end of the structure gave plenty of illumination to see, although the interior was shaded.

Comfortable smells lingered—the scent of newly cut hay, harness leather, and horses. Dust motes danced on the streams of sunlight. Sybilla tensed and gave the several cats and half-grown kittens lying here and there a wary glare, but they remained perfectly at ease with the human intrusion of their space.

All in all, Wendi could sense no lingering trace of the two deaths that had occurred here, the one so recently. Jacques Bardou had died in his bed, not in the fall, so perhaps that answered the question of why she didn't feel his spirit here. She hadn't really sensed it in the bedroom, either, though.

Make no mistake, however, her mother had definitely died here. On that floor. Her throat cut, bleeding into the dirt.

" 'It is not time, yet it is time,' " Sybilla quoted from the words of the Goddess. "If She's playing games with us, I'm ready for recess to be over."

"Me, too," Wendi agreed. "Let's move around and see if we can feel anything."

"We'd feel it already if there was anything here," Sybilla griped, but she walked with Wendi deeper into the interior.

Wendi headed for a piece of machinery against one wall. Above it, the hayloft shadowed the machine even further, but there was a window on the wall. Wendi opened it, allowing more light to stream in.

"Is that a hay rake?" she asked Sybilla.

Her aunt shrugged. "I suppose so. See those wicked-looking iron hooks across the back? Looks like they probably harness a horse or mule into the traces and someone rides on that seat on top while those hooks drag the hay into rows. But I'm not a farm girl, so I could be wrong."

Given it was the only piece of machinery sitting below the loft, that's what it had to be, Wendi decided. She examined both the huge iron wheels on the machine, her forehead creasing in a deep frown at what she didn't find. She looked above her, and determined that a person falling from the loft would probably indeed encounter the hay rake.

"There's no sign of him hitting his head," she mused.

"What are you talking about?"

"Nick's uncle. I was in the hallway, but I heard his valet say that Jacques had hit his head on one of the hay rake's iron wheels. That he might have lived through the fall, if that hadn't happened. And look how unused and rusty the wheels are. Don't you think if something as hard as a man's head had hit them, there would be signs of it?"

"Probably at least some hair caught on that rough surface," Sybilla agreed. "But—"

Suddenly a frightened whinny split the air, followed by a man's loud curses. The cats leaped to their feet, the pair closest to Sybilla arching their backs and hissing at her. She shrieked and lifted her skirts, heading for the barn door.

But someone had carelessly left a pitchfork on the ground, and Sybilla's right foot encountered the handle. Full skirts and petticoats flying, she tumbled end over end, landing with a thump against the barn wall.

"Aunt!" Wendi gasped, racing over to her. "Oh, Aunt, tell me you're not hurt."

A man stomped down the middle aisle of the barn, dragging an animal with him and cursing, obviously unaware the two women were there. Sybilla opened her eyes and scrambled to her feet as though unhurt.

"Alphie!" she said. "What are you doing to my dog, you brute?"

The man stopped as though he'd run into a wall. His hold on the dog loosened, and Alphie bounded over to Sybilla, jumping up to lick her face. A nearby cat, a tom from its size and manner, took offense at the dog and arched its back, hissing and growling a weird "meowrrr" of warning, which got Alphie's attention immediately. The dog decided the cat needed to be put in its place.

Before either Wendi or her aunt could act, the cat swiped a vicious claw across Alphie's muzzle, and the dog jumped back "ki-yie-ing" in pain. Wendi remembered the man watching them at the same time she saw Sybilla lift her hand and heard her begin the chant that would change the cat into a mouse.

"Don't!" she hissed, sounding almost like the cat and reaching for her aunt's arm. She managed to swat the arm down before much damage was done, and only a small hole in Sybilla's skirt verified her magical attempt. A tiny stream of smoke rose from the hole, a result of the lance of magic Wendi had interrupted. Wendi quickly used a silent chant to repair it and dissipate the smoke.

Sybilla glared at her, and Wendi whispered, "Darn it, that man who had hold of Alphie is watching us! Do you want him to spread the word that he saw you working magic in here? Want this entire plantation in an uproar and a lynch mob after us because they're afraid of witches? Knowing how Nick feels about us, I doubt he'd offer much resistance to them!"

Sybilla glanced guiltily at the man watching them, then straightened and faced him. "Sir, I'll thank you not to man-handle my dog in the future!"

The man stared from her to Alphie, who was cringing against the wall and fearfully eyeing the tom. As far as Wendi knew, the dog had never run across a cat that stood to fight—at least, not since it took up residence with them. The neighbor's animal had always fled to a high tree branch before it faced the dog below with false bravado, giving Alphie the impression it was afraid. And the cats they met around town fled at the first soft growl of confrontation on Alphie's part.

The tom hissed again, and poor Alphie turned tail, racing out of the barn. Sybilla drew in an indignant breath.

"Now see what you've done," she told the cat. "He'll never be of any use to me again with your sort of animal! I ought to—"

The cat stood from its crouch and laid its ears back, baring its fangs and taking a step toward the end of the hay bale. With a shriek, Sybilla lifted her skirts and followed Alphie.

When Wendi turned to look for the hired man, she saw him disappearing out the rear barn door. She looked back at the cat, and it sat down, giving her a placid gaze before bending its head to bathe itself with a pink tongue. Wendi started to shake her head, but the cat froze, then leaped up once more and arched its back. A second later it raced toward the rear of the barn, the rest of the pack appearing from their hiding places and following.

Wendi felt the changed atmosphere at once. The hair on the back of her neck lifted in a scattering of pebbled goose bumps, and the cascade of chills spread over her shoulders, down her arms, and across her stomach. Even her legs chilled, and she frantically searched the dim recesses of the barn to find the cause.

Something was there. Someone. But no one responded to her mental attempts at contact.

"Mother?" she whispered at last. She thought she heard a sigh—felt a faint caress on her cheek—but as suddenly as the chill had descended, it left. Had she been a plain mortal rather than a witch, she would have passed off the experience as her imagination.

But she was a witch. She knew beyond doubt someone had made brief contact with her, and the cats had verified it. Animals were as in tune with the other world as witches. She would have to provide a more welcoming atmosphere for the entity before she could sustain the contact.

But how on earth could she do that? During the day, the

hired hands were probably in and out of the barn with frequency, caring for the horses and equipment. A plantation the size of Belle Chene would also have dozens of field workers besides the stable hands, as well as their families. They would live near the barn on plantation grounds, close enough to investigate any unusual sounds or disturbance in the night. Nick would never grant her permission to perform a ceremony where his workers might discover them, even if he did allow her to stay past the time it took him to order the carriage prepared to deliver her and her aunt back to New Orleans.

Whatever or whoever had tried to contact her was completely gone now. The peaceful, serene atmosphere in the barn had returned. Except for one thing. She smelled jasmine, her mother's favorite scent. Hers, too, but she hadn't taken time that morning to use the bottle of perfume on her own dresser.

"Mother," she whispered again.

The scent faded, replaced by the odors of horse and harness. Still she smiled. Somehow, some way, she'd perform the ceremony before Nick banished her from Belle Chene. The next magical holiday was White Lotus Day, with the following three days the celebration of Lemuria. One of those nights she needed to try to contact her mother.

Miz Thibedeau had settled Wendi and Sybilla in two of the second-floor bedrooms, the ones farthest down the hall from the master suite. When Wendi asked where Nick was staying, Miz Thibedeau told her he'd ordered them to clean the *garçonniere* for him. A separate, semiround building used as the more private bachelor quarters for the plantation's sons after they entered their teens, the *garçonniere* set off from the main manor house.

Wendi could see the small, two-story structure from her

bedroom window. Lucian came out the door as she watched, carrying a pail of water, which he tossed into the grass by the doorway. Crossing to a nearby cistern, he attached the pail to a rope and lowered it for a refill. He must have been pressed into service to prepare the rooms for the guests, but she wondered why he wasn't with his mother.

Turning away from the window, Wendi was once again struck by the shabby elegance of her room. At least four inches on the bottom of the curtains on the windows dragged the floor, an earlier-times indication of wealth of the owners, evidencing the prosperous owner's disregard for the cost of the expensive material. The bureau and dresser were cherrywood, as were the corner posts, headboard, and footboard of the bed. A cherrywood armoire stood in the corner, and when she'd checked, she found her meager wardrobe already hung inside.

She could barely recall the room she'd lived in the first four years of her life, but this one vaguely reminded her of it. A carpet that had once been plush but was now threadbare in places covered most of the floor. The room had been cleaned sometime recently, as she could smell lemon and beeswax, intermingled with the mustiness fast receding with the windows open.

She needed to make the room her own, if she were to stay here for a while—

The knock on the door came a brief instant before the door opened, and Wendi turned, expecting Sybilla to enter. Nick stood there instead, and her temper flared.

"Most people have manners enough to wait until they are invited past a closed door before barging in."

"My overseer said you and your aunt were out in the barn." His lips were in a flat line, his words coming through gritted teeth. "I thought I told you to wait until I could go out there with you."

"Excuse me, but I recall you offering to go *with* me, not ordering me not to go alone. Your negative vibrations would only make it harder to see if there was anyone still lingering there anyway."

"I am the owner of Belle Chene. You'll do as I say, or else—"

"Or else what?" she prodded when he fell silent. "Or else you'll pack us up and send us back to New Orleans? Why do I have the feeling that you want us here? That you're interested in what we can find out?"

When he didn't respond, she continued, "Have you been out to the barn, where your uncle supposedly fell to his death?"

"Supposedly? What the hell do you mean by that?"

"I'd prefer you go out there and look and make your own determination." Wendi turned away and tugged on the chain around her neck, pulling out a small key from her bodice and unhooking it. She headed for the armoire.

"I need to make this room my own—give it a welcoming atmosphere, if I'm going to stay here. If I'm not, you need to tell me now."

She took her portmanteau from the armoire and drew out the smaller satchel inside, sticking the key in the lock to open it. Nick stood unmoving in the doorway. She quirked a questioning eyebrow at him, and when he remained silent, she shrugged and set the satchel on the bed.

Removing three small, round candleholders and an incense burner from the satchel, she carried them over to the mantel to set up her altar. Pausing to determine the location of her bedroom in relation to the four directions, she set the holders in the appropriate spots: the one to hold salt instead of a candle to the north, the one she filled with water from the bedside pitcher to the west. The last candleholder she set to the south, where the flame, once lit, would be the symbol for fire. The incense holder went to the east, where burning it would indicate the last basic element of air.

She took two more candleholders and four candles from the satchel, then a bottle of jasmine oil. When she detached the stopper, the scent filled the room. She slipped a surreptitious look at Nick. Good Goddess, he actually looked like he was interested in what she was doing.

Closing her eyes, Wendi murmured her welcoming phrases, then prepared each candle by dipping a finger into the jasmine scent and slowly rubbing it up and down the sides and around the tips of her candles. She could feel the bubble of magic enclose her, and she continued the process until her altar satisfied her. Then she propped a small tintype of her mother near the incense, where the scented smoke filtered across it. Last she added the light-blue crystal she carried in her pocket at times, a stone that symbolized her desire for peace and harmony.

She turned to look at Nick. His aura in the magical atmosphere shimmered and rippled a deep red, indicating tension, his hooded gaze impenetrable. After a second, he turned and limped away.

Twelve

It rained again the day of the funeral. The very next day, in fact, since there was no way they could keep a body very long in the southern climate. Wendi watched the drops slide down the window pane, finally tiring of the trapped heat in her bedroom and raising the lower portion of the window.

There. The open window afforded little relief, but at least it gave the illusion it would.

She hadn't let the idea of attending the funeral service grow to a full thought in her mind. She and Sybilla had spent most of yesterday and all of this morning with Miz Thibedeau in the kitchen house, helping prepare food and drinks for the visitors at Belle Chene.

Visitors. Yes, she couldn't truly call them mourners. The vibrations she sensed were more curiosity than sorrow, and she'd bet the fictitious broom people thought witches rode upon that the curiosity stemmed from their desire to see Nick after all these years, rather than pay their respects to Jacques or the Bardou family. Cecile and Lucian appeared to be the only true mourners for Jacques Bardou. Even his son, Julian, didn't act overly heartbroken.

Catching a vague reflection of herself in the window,

Wendi reached up and pulled off the frilly cap Sybilla had
found for her to wear when her aunt realized Wendi meant
to mingle with the Belle Chene visitors. In a plain gray
gown and with her well-known strawberry hair hidden beneath the cap, no one noticed her. Indeed it rather irked her
to see how nondescript she became in her role as a servant,
even though the near-invisibility, unless someone wanted a
drink, served her purpose well.

She didn't catch anything interesting in the furtive murmurs when she paused unnoticed here and there to listen
to conversations. The mourners knew no more than she
about the scandal and death, their whisperings fueled by
speculation and innuendo. And it didn't look like she'd
learn anything more today, if there was anything to learn.
The rain had most people heading for their carriages to
return home, rather than stay for visitation after the service.

Miz Thibedeau had anticipated the rain would result in
people leaving instead of staying over, if only to remove
their damp clothing as soon as possible. Some would linger,
though, and Wendi wanted one last chance at uncovering
any clues about her mother's death. She left the room and
headed down the rear stairwell—the one the servants used.
It opened onto the back veranda, and she could go to the
kitchen house unobserved that way.

She sighed as she crossed the veranda. She'd come to
Belle Chene hoping to find a ghost lingering here; to contact it and ask it for some answers not available in her
present world. Now it looked as though she'd have to learn
how to investigate in the human way—with human senses
and her brain instead of her magical abilities.

Not that her magical abilities had shown themselves as
anything but average and mundane so far. At her age she
ought to be able to demand her mother appear to her, or
use her skills to breach the barriers of the two worlds if

necessary. She pursed her lips wryly and shook her head. In this disrupted karmic condition, even her aunt, with years and years more experience with magic, couldn't do that.

A small figure sat coiled up, head on knees, on the far edge of the kitchen house porch. Something flickered in the recesses, and a light danced on the wall. A wind chime tinkled, but above that sound, Wendi heard a muffled sniff.

Lucian. The boy's place at Belle Chene and relationship to the rest of the occupants was a mystery to her. However, his sorrow at the loss of Jacques was undeniable. The idea of him being Jacques Bardou's son had probably crossed more than just Wendi's mind, but right now the boy needed comfort instead of questions about his ancestry.

Wendi started for him, but the porch squeaked behind her. Before she could turn, Nick caught her arm.

"I'll take care of him," he said. "Go on about whatever you had planned to do."

"I had planned to offer Lucian some comfort," she said in a soft voice, not wanting to upset the boy further by having him overhear her and Nick arguing about him. "I'm sure you have guests to take care of."

"Curiosity seekers, you mean," Nick said. "I long ago quit giving a damn about appearances and the false decorum demanded by some outdated code of conduct in Louisiana. The few people who stayed behind will get tired of waiting for me to make an appearance and leave soon enough. Why weren't you at the service?"

She stared at him in amazement. "I didn't expect you'd want my aunt and me there. We've been trying to keep ourselves inconspicuous."

"Maybe your aunt has accomplished that." Nick chuckled drolly. "But you've been in evidence everywhere I look lately. Did you learn anything we didn't already know about what happened here when your mother died?"

"How—?" Wendi shook her head. "It shouldn't surprise me that you were aware of what I was doing. There's been a connection between us ever since you walked off that ship. Even before."

"What do you mean, even before?"

He frowned, his eyes darkening in that pattern she was coming to know meant he wasn't impressed by any reference to her magical abilities. And his body tensed in the manner she knew meant he wouldn't take evasion for an answer.

"Our lives have been entwined since my mother met your father," she said, attempting evasion anyway. It didn't work; she knew it immediately.

"I think you're referring to something more recent." He took a step closer to her, bending his head. "Maybe even something very recent. Entwined, you say? I can remember being entwined with you."

She forced herself not to retreat. She'd been wanting him to kiss her again since the first time, but not here. Not in the open and not like this. Not with his attitude.

What on earth was it about him? She wanted him, even allowed him to invade her space. Was drawn to him more than she'd ever thought it possible to crave a man's touch. Even now a warmth settled in her stomach, crawled down a little further to the area between her thighs. By the Goddess, her knees even trembled and her toes curled!

He didn't kiss her, though. He stopped with his lips still several inches from hers, the pull of them an almost physical sensation. Different emotions sparked and died, one after the other, in his eyes. Desire was the most prominent one, hot, wicked, and undeniable. Yet it intermingled with hesitation, uneasiness, and indetermination.

The counter sensations to his desire flooded Wendi with humiliation. He wanted her, but he only wanted to satisfy his lust, not take her as woman to his man. Not as a partner to share something more than his body with. Nothing could be clearer to her than that, and she sensed it with her femaleness, rather than her magic. It made an even greater impact on her that way.

She stepped back, feeling as though she were swimming to the top of a deep pond after having touched the sandy bottom and the movement taking every bit of her concentration.

"You'd better see to Lucian," she murmured, escaping into the kitchen house.

Escaping, yes, she admitted as she leaned against the wall inside the doorway, surprised to find the house empty. Not escaping the desperately desired kiss, though. Instead, escaping the blow to her pride and undermining of her yearnings. She almost felt as if she needed a bath, to wash away the feeling of Nick's lewd craving rather than the meaningful caresses she wanted him to give her.

"He's the son of my mother's lover," she reminded herself in a whisper. "He tolerates me for his own purposes. And if he ever did get me into bed, it would probably only be an act of revenge, not an act of love."

She compelled herself to move over to the side window and make certain Nick had indeed gone to comfort Lucian. She didn't need the guilt of knowing the boy was out there alone in his sorrow added to the already heaping pile on her shoulders. Relief filled her when she saw Nick sitting beside Lucian, and she started to turn away before the scene registered on her.

Nick probably didn't notice, but then, he didn't have magical abilities. He probably thought the pile of magnolia leaves between Lucian and the porch wall was just a pile of leaves. Wendi saw the layout, however, and hastily turned to shush her aunt when she came down the stairs from the upper story of the house.

Motioning with her finger, she drew Sybilla over to the window and pointed at the porch floor. After glancing outside, Sybilla looked at Wendi in stunned amazement. Almost at once her brow furrowed in alarm.

"This only complicates things, if it's not just coincidence," she whispered.

The next morning Wendi paused outside the *garçonniere* door. Surely nothing could happen in broad daylight. But it had been daylight yesterday afternoon when Nick had almost kissed her.

Not that she enjoyed labeling what he'd been prepared to offer her a kiss. The word was too special, meant too much to her as a woman, to degrade his actions by calling it that.

Colin had kissed her. Warm and tender, though unfulfilling, his kisses had at least meant something—meant he cared and considered her a partner in his life, someone special and important to him. Charles had mashed her lips with his own, dug his hand between her legs demanding she open for him, rather than coax her to respond.

Nick. She had no earthly idea what the pull between her and him meant. As surely as there was magic, there was a pull there.

And it deepened the moment he opened the door.

"You need something, or are you here to clean?" he asked.

"Clean?" she gasped, then gleaned his meaning. He was putting her in her place.

"I wasn't, but I can be," she said, struggling to keep her voice neutral. "I don't mean to be staying here without paying my way. Far be it from me to expect your charity."

"Get inside, Wendi," he snarled. "We've got things to talk about."

Yes, they did, but all of a sudden it didn't seem like a good idea to discuss them right now. Discuss them in the privacy of his quarters. She shook her head and moved back a step.

"I—"

By the Goddess, she'd be darned if she offered him any more medications! He moved as though his leg didn't bother him at all today, grabbing her arm in a firm grasp. But as soon as she looked into his eyes, she saw he'd only managed to cover up the pain for a brief instant. His grip tightened, and she winced, knowing he didn't mean her discomfort; he was fighting the weakness brought on by the pain his abrupt movement had caused him, using her to steady himself.

She instinctively moved closer, offering herself for him to lean on. His grimace told her he'd rather die than admit he needed her support, and she preceded him inside, hoping he'd follow and sit down.

He followed, and she went into the first room she found, on her right. Inside the door, she realized her mistake. His bed was in the corner of the room, rumpled bed clothing strewn on the mattress and dragging on the floor.

Nick staggered past her and sat down on the bed with a groan. Pity stirred in her when she noticed his white, strained face, and she took advantage of his closed eyes to move closer.

"You seemed to be getting better with the medication," she murmured.

His eyes flew open, and he studied her guardedly. "I was, but I was forced to be on my feet most of the day yesterday. And I didn't feel as if I should be walking around the guests smelling of that medication."

"Lie back. Let me see."

The fact that he obeyed her without argument indicated to her how bad the pain must be. He laid with his head toward the foot of the bed, and she quickly retrieved one of the pillows from the floor and placed it beneath his head.

"It looks like you spent a pretty restless night," she murmured, reaching for the sheet and draping it over his lower body.

"What are you doing?" He grabbed her hand when her fingers neared his belt buckle.

"You'll need to remove your trousers so I can see the wound," she said reasonably. "A massage will probably help the pain a great deal."

"Just get me the liniment over on the bureau and go tell Miz Thibedeau to brew me some of that damned willow bark tea," he ordered. "I don't need you *massaging* anything on me."

He shifted his leg, his face going stark white as he grabbed his hip and groaned in agony.

"Please, Nick. Let me help."

"Maybe you'd better," he gasped.

Wendi reached for the belt again, ignoring the trembling in her fingers as she undid it. She'd nursed others before—even helped Sybilla tend wounds festered by neglect and putrefication. Her stomach had never curled with dread as deep as she felt seeing Nick in such misery, though.

She tugged at his trousers, and Nick used his other leg to lift his hips and give her room to pull them down. His indrawn hiss of breath accompanied the movement, and she could feel the bellow of pain he repressed. When she saw the scarred flesh on his hip and thigh, bile rose in her stomach, but compassion and concern chased it away.

She'd felt the wound that night on his stallion, but that hadn't prepared her for the actual sight of it. The muscles bunched and twitched from the nerve damage, and the skin was hardened and rigid with scars. A deep indentation showed where the flesh had healed over after a musketball blew away a large chunk of it. But the destruction was even more widespread than could be accounted for by a small musket ball.

"I got hit with grapeshot," Nick said, and she sensed he was talking to try to take his mind off the pain. "I'd only read about such stuff in books, and no one could believe the Yankees were using it against us. They had plenty of cannonballs and rifle bullets without resorting to that. But I guess they just wanted to do as much damage as they could in every possible way."

"Like Sherman did when he marched to Atlanta," Wendi murmured, standing to go to the dresser and retrieve the witch hazel liniment she'd given him. "I read afterward that he wanted to show the South what their resistance was doing to their own families. That's why he destroyed everything in his path, including the fine old mansions that weren't doing anything to benefit the South's cause. He wanted the families homeless and needing their men to take care of them. He wanted them to realize what holding out and refusing to surrender was doing to the families they left behind."

Nick slit his eyes, watching her return to the bed. "I must have read some of the same stories you did." She caught a measure of respect, and perhaps a tad of surprise, in his tone. "It worked, but it sure was a hell of a loss."

"You went out to California," Wendi reminded him. "The South's downfall didn't effect you."

"You're wrong," he murmured, then fell silent.

She poured some liniment in her palm and allowed it to warm for a few seconds before she spread it on his hip and thigh. Setting the bottle on the floor, she kneaded the scarred area, firmly and to the point where Nick clenched his fists in response to the pressure of her fingers. To his credit, he didn't protest the increased pain, and after a few moments, his fists relaxed.

He opened his eyes. "Whatever you're doing is working," he admitted grudgingly.

"I told you it would."

She stood to get a different grip on him, now working her fingers around his thigh, toward the inside.

"Don't get that damned medication any closer to my co—my privates," he snarled. "That stuff will burn."

She blushed violently, not only at his language but at his reminder of the area of his body where she was working. Her tongue fought to utter the comeback flashing through her mind, but she clamped her teeth shut around it. She concentrated on the sturdy thigh, covered with a sprinkling of black hair and muscled and firm despite the damage to it. She leaned forward, remembering that she'd unbuttoned the top of her bodice in the morning heat at the same time she felt her dress gape open.

A bulge she'd been trying to ignore beneath the sheet elongated and jumped far enough to distinctly mound the material. Immediate heat and moisture flooded between her legs, and Wendi straightened, moving back from the bed and licking her dry lips.

"I—I believe that's about all I can do."

"That's not even close to what you could do if you wanted to," Nick growled in a voice laden with unmistakable want and need. "And you better get the hell out of here before I decide to make you admit it."

Wendi rushed toward the door, stopping as though she'd run into a barrier when Nick almost silently murmured her name.

"What?" she asked, refusing to turn around.

"Thank you," he said.

The simple acknowledgment did what his carnal comments couldn't. She turned to face him again, losing herself in his eyes for a yearlong moment. She glanced at his mouth, finding his lips pursed in a pout. Full and tempting, they called to her as though he'd spoken again.

What would happen if she actually walked back to that bed? Touched his lips with her fingertip? Bent down and kissed him?

Colin's lovemaking had been tender and sweet. She had a feeling Nick's would be violent and wild, filled with all the contradictions in his soul. Gentle yet fierce. Confused yet determined. Frantic yet all-consuming.

Nick's lovemaking could fulfill her as a woman in a way Colin's never had, basically because Nick was more of a match for her than the more passive Colin had been.

She couldn't imagine Nick agreeing to marry a woman just to dispel the loneliness facing him from a life without a partner. When he married—a pang of hurt went through her at the thought of him with another woman—it would be forever. It would be a total commitment to the two of them as the whole they would then be.

She finally realized how long she'd been standing there, caught in the flowing vibrations stretching between the two of them. Nick's hooded eyes and slightly parted lips spoke of his responsiveness and acknowledgment of the sensations, too. His naked leg lay outside the sheet, his body more tempting partially clad than if it had been totally nude.

"You need to get the hell out of here." Nick's voice almost begged her, spurring her more than if he'd ordered her, as was his usual bent.

"You're welcome," she said belatedly, then turned and made it through the doorway, not stopping this time until she exited the *garçonniere*.

The world was still turning. The sun still shown. Birds still sang and flowers still bloomed, their dew-soaked heads nodding in the misty morning light. So why did she feel as though she'd left part of her appreciation for life inside the bachelor quarters? Why did she feel as though she'd never get it back until after she joined her body with the man inside, where the other part of her, lost now, waited for her to find it?

She got a grip on her emotions and walked toward the kitchen house. She needed to concentrate on trying to contact her mother before Nick ordered her off Belle Chene. Now that the funeral was over, he'd have more time to realize her presence was an intrusion here.

Thirteen

God, she was beautiful. Nick wanted her with a desperation he'd never before felt, even in his teens when it seemed like all he could think of was how soon he'd be able to sweet-talk his way beneath some girl's skirt.

He stared down at his bare leg, imagining a smooth, feminine thigh wrapped around it. Wendi's thigh. Her skin was the pearl-pink of a redhead, unmarred by the freckles those with hair darker than her strawberry blond usually sported. It gleamed with that pearlescent glow, beckoning a man's fingers to its warmth and silkiness. Her blue eyes danced with merriment when she teased him, sparkled with desire when she was as tempted as him.

And make no doubt, he mused, she wanted him, too. But did the same thing keep her from lying beneath him as kept him from kissing her senseless and eating those beautiful breasts until she opened for him to plunge into? Did the thought of who they both were—he the son of her mother's lover, she the daughter of his father's—keep her from surrendering to what he was sure would be a mind-blowing passion?

Or did she succeed in holding him at arm's length because she thought he might have killed her mother? Was she able to resist the pull because she shuddered at the thought of making love with her mother's killer?

Damn it all, those people are dead now. Wendi and I are very much alive.

Nick drew in a sharp breath. What part of his subconscious had opened and allowed that thought to see the light of day? Had he been standing, he might have fallen to his knees, the emotional impact was so strong. Turning over, he buried his face in the pillow, his mother's shocked voice ringing audibly in his ears.

Why hadn't he let his mother know he was there for her that night? That he would stand by her and face the consequences of their reputation being maligned, a direct result of both his and his father's actions?

No one, not even the servants, knew he'd slipped back to the St. Charles Street mansion the night his mother killed herself. Word of Sabine's death and whisperings of her being his father's mistress had proceeded him, since Nick had taken a piroque and gone into the swamps for the night, not returning until the next day. And he didn't go to her when he overheard her soliloquy in her dark bedroom. He was too ashamed of his own part in the outcome.

Why have they done this to me? he remembered her saying in a voice breaking with agony, while he stood in the hallway, unable to force himself to face her. *My punishment is too harsh. I can't go on any longer.*

Had he known her words meant she was preparing for suicide, would he have found the courage to comfort her? Remind her how much he and Pierre loved her? Remind her he needed her, especially now that his heart had hardened against his father?

Nick shook his head and sat up on the side of the bed. He'd gone over and over that night in his mind. Then over it some more. He couldn't change what had happened—what he had done and what he had failed to do.

He needed to concentrate on Belle Chene now. After his interview with Julian the day he arrived, he still wasn't sure his cousin was the right one to take over management of the plantation. Something didn't sit right, much as he wanted to get the hell out of here. Hell, not only get the hell out of the city, but the entire state of Louisiana. Get back to California, where his demons faded into near oblivion—dim enough to be locked into the box in his mind and ignored.

Locked away for the most part, anyway. Every once in a while—just often enough to remind him they hadn't died off completely—one or two of them managed to force a gap in the lid of the box. Managed to sneak a claw out and dig it into his belly. Into his heart.

He washed in the common room used by all the young men who had occupied the *garçonniere* over the years, dressed himself and headed for the house. His leg bothered him more with the lack of pain than it did when the ache would distract him from his responsibilities.

No, he admitted honestly. It wasn't the lack of pain bothering and distracting him. It was the reason for it. The slender fingers that had massaged the pain away. The woman those fingers belonged to.

The way she ignored his rude demands for her to leave him alone and tended him anyway. The caring he felt in her touch. For that matter, she seemed to want to take care of him, too.

He stopped on the back veranda, stunned. Could he possibly be overcoming his aversion to her being Sabine Chastain's daughter? Be beginning to care for the total woman she was, rather than just wanting to get beneath her skirts? Get to know her in other ways instead of scheming to plunge his hardness into that delectable body and eliminate this want for her?

Hell, he needed to get out of here fast. Get back to California, a continent away from this hell.

"Julian!" he bellowed as he strode down the hallway. "Someone tell Julian to get his ass into the study so I can talk to him!"

Miz Thibedeau stepped out of the front parlor into his path. "You don't have to bellow like a bull this early in the day, monsieur! And you know there's no servants left in the house since the funeral."

"Why aren't you out in the kitchen house fixing breakfast?" he demanded.

Her eyes narrowed, and his stomach tightened in warning. Damn it, his belly seemed to have a mind of its own whenever Miz Thibedeau got that look in her eyes, like he better treat her right or his belly would go empty. Blackmail, that's what it was. Absolute blackmail.

Nevertheless, he softened his voice.

"I mean—look, I just got up on the wrong side of the bed a while ago. And I'm hungry for one of your delicious breakfasts. By the way, have you seen Julian this morning?"

"No, I haven't. And Wendi already asked me to make you a cup of willow bark tea. It's steeping on the counter in the kitchen house. I'll bring it to you in the study."

"Thank you. Is there anyone else around who might go find Julian for me?"

The front door opened, and both of them looked up. Julian came in, wiping his face with a handkerchief, his clothing rumpled as though he'd slept in it.

"Whew," he said. "It's already steaming out there."

Miz Thibedeau hurried down the hallway without greeting Julian, and Nick felt a twinge of annoyance. Miz Thibedeau wasn't normally that rude. Julian probably deserved it, though. He'd already noticed his cousin didn't deign to greet the servants, and should they have the audacity to speak to him for no important reason, he disregarded them.

Nine years younger than himself, Julian hadn't been one of Nick's playmates when he visited Belle Chene. He didn't remember Julian's mother, either, vaguely recalling that she'd died in childbirth.

"You look as if you've been up all night," Nick said.

Julian gave him a wicked grin. "Part of me was," he said with a wink. "But I got some sleep—enough to function on today."

"Let's go into the study."

Julian followed him, and Nick took the seat behind the desk, catching Julian's frown of irritation when he did so. Julian evidently thought the manager's chair should be his now, given his father's death, but Nick wasn't ready to fully relinquish control of Belle Chene to his cousin just yet.

"Is the woman you spent the night with someone who means something?" he asked as Julian settled into one of the chairs in front of the desk. "Or just a passing stand?"

"We're betrothed," Julian said, a satisfied smirk on his face as he leaned back. "Unofficially, for now. We would have announced it, had my father not died. And I still don't intend to wait an entire year to make her my wife, despite what the mourning period dictates. Rest assured, however, the wedding won't interfere with my duties regarding Belle Chene. In fact, she'll be perfect for Belle Chene's mistress, and the plantation does need one."

"I have to agree with you there. Who is she?"

Julian hesitated for a moment, then shrugged. "Felicite Debeau," he said. "There's no stain on her lineage, cousin."

Nick whistled under his breath. No stain, for sure. In fact, he wondered how the hell Julian had pulled that off. The Debeaus were one of the original families of the parish, and he recalled that Felicite had been their only daughter. At least, when he'd left New Orleans.

"Quite a catch. For a Bardou," Nick murmured.

Julian bristled. "I suppose you'll dig into everything until you figure out how the hell I managed to get her to agree to marry me," he growled. "So I might as well tell you that her family isn't as rich as it used to be. Even being gone as long as you have been, you've still got contacts enough to find that out. And her only brother died in the war, so there's no male hair to inherit their plantation, Candlemas."

"In other words," Nick said, "she wouldn't have looked at you before her family fell on dire straits, given the scandal of the Bardou family."

"True," Julian said without remorse. "But have no doubt about it, Nick. I intend to have Felicite for my wife. And Candlemas borders Belle Chene, so that will give me my own plantation, yet allow me to keep supervising Belle Chene."

"Then I suppose that gives you another reason to take your responsibilities at Belle Chene seriously. Good points in your favor."

Julian rose to his feet, a scowl on his face. "Do you have a list of bad points?"

"Not really. I'm not one to make hasty decisions, but let's just say that I don't see any reason not to get on out of here and leave Belle Chene in your hands. Except—"

Anger darkened Julian's face, and Nick continued in a warning voice. "Except for the way you treat the servants and workers at times. Like they are only good for you to wipe your feet on."

"I expect them to handle their jobs and not bother me with the details," Julian said. "I've got more important things to do than follow house servants around to see if there's any dust left behind after they perform their duties. Or walk up and down the fields to check for weeds. When Felicite moves in, she'll want to entertain her friends, as she does at Candlemas, and she can handle an expanded household staff here herself. She's had the necessary training."

"I agree. For the present, Cecile can continue as she's doing. At least, when she gets her grief under control. For now, what do you have in mind for the plantation's fields and crops?"

They discussed Julian's work plans, and Nick found himself in agreement with them. When Julian left to wash and change clothes before he went out to check with the overseer, Nick folded his hands and propped his chin on his fingers in contemplation.

He couldn't fault Julian at all. His plans were adequate, even sensible, and would assure the most profit for Belle Chene's crops this season. He even had some ambitious future intentions, which should benefit the plantation.

Nick made his decision. He'd stay here for another couple days, just to study the books and make sure he had a firm handle on the workings of the plantation after all this time away. Then he'd get the hell out of here and go back to California.

Blue eyes, strawberry curls, and delectable body be damned.

The delectable body walked into the study just then, carrying a china cup in her hand.

"Miz Thibedeau said you were in here. How does your leg feel?"

His leg felt fine, but another part of him sprang into an

ache immediately. Thank God for the heavy desk between them.

"The leg is better than it has been in a long while," he admitted. "Thank you."

She sat the cup on the desk, where steam rose from it.

"Willow tea," she said. "Miz Thibedeau said to tell you she warmed it up again."

He grimaced. "That damned stuff works, but it sure tastes like sh—crap."

Wendi giggled. "The only thing I know tree bark tastes good to is some animals. I imagine, had man not discovered fire and meat, we might be extinct right now."

He glanced at her in surprise, then shook his head. "You amaze me at times, especially when you mention stuff like that."

"Why? Because I've read books and educated myself?"

"Well, yes. I've met very few women who know the things you do. Few men, either, for that matter."

She ran a finger across the desk surface, the motion drawing his eyes and making him recall how those same, slender fingers had soothed him with massage. How those same, slender fingers had shot fire the night the two men had attacked him. How those same, slender fingers could probably make another sort of fire shoot through him.

Suddenly her words penetrated his jumbled thoughts.

"You want to do what?" he asked.

"Have a séance in the barn," she repeated. "We'll do it late at night, after all your workers are gone and in bed. I—"

"We? Who is this 'we' you intend to have with you?"

A tiny smile curved her delectable lips, and she shot him a mischievous glance from deep blue eyes beneath silky lashes.

"My aunt, of course. And maybe a couple others, who would have a stake in the outcome."

"Like me, I suppose."

"Like you," she agreed.

"It's impossible." He hardened his heart at the disappointment in her eyes. "All it would take would be one restless person walking around the plantation at night. If they stumbled onto that ceremony, every worker on Belle Chene would leave as soon as they could find another job, fearing that voodoo was being practiced here. Julian would be left without fieldhands. I can't allow it."

"*Allow* it?" she murmured, her eyes narrowing. "All right."

Before he could rise from his chair and detain her, she swept out of the room. Halfway to his feet, Nick reversed direction and sat back in the chair. Dropping his head onto his chest, he shook it back and forth. He had no doubt she would go through with her ceremony, with or without his permission. He could post a guard in the barn, but how would he explain that to Julian? Or the guard, for that matter? And he'd be damned if he'd spend his remaining nights at Belle Chene sleeping out in that barn.

That left talking Wendi into moving her ceremony somewhere she wouldn't get caught, and taking part in it himself, to keep an eye on her. But this damned sure didn't mean he believed for one bit that her blasted ceremony would work!

Fourteen

~

"Do you get naked at *this* ceremony?" Nick asked.

Wendi whirled on him, certain she caught a quickly masked teasing glint in his eye. Glancing around to make sure no one could overhear them, she saw Sybilla and Miz Thibedeau across the small clearing, although her aunt could tune in to their conversation psychically, should she desire.

"No, we don't get naked!" she said in a harsh whisper. "And for future reference, *you* will never see me naked at any of the ceremonies you participate in."

"Does that mean other men have seen you naked at other ceremonies?"

By the Goddess, if she were younger and less mature, she'd stamp her foot at him!

"None of your business!" His face darkened into a scowl as she continued, "However, we don't consider the body something ugly, which should be kept covered up with clothing."

"Oh, I don't believe for one minute your body is ugly, Wendi." He barely breathed the words, bending close to her and snaking one hand around her waist. "And if you hadn't run out of the *garçonniere* this morning, I'd have shown you just how beautiful I believe your body is.''

He bent his head closer, moonlight gleaming in his eyes mesmerizing her as though he were a demon appearing from its lair. A demon ready to match its magic with hers. Not that she'd ever seen a demon, but she'd heard tales. And each and every story reiterated that the antithesis to her magic had the ability to make itself stunningly handsome in an effort to sneak beneath a witch's defenses.

Somehow, some way, she managed a step back from this potential demon. Her retreat only fueled his blasted conceit, and his full lips curled into a satisfied smirk. In a fit of pique, she lifted her hand, pointed her finger—then dropped her arm as Sybilla's voice whispered in her mind.

Been me, I'd have let him kiss me.

A giggle bubbled in her chest, and she turned toward her aunt, meeting her gaze across the distance as clearly as though it were daylight. *Want me to ask him if he'll kiss you?*

Sybilla laughed and walked toward her with Miz Thibedeau following. Nick had only shaken his head in defeat when he saw his housekeeper arrive with Aunt Sybilla and climb into the buggy carrying them to this isolated portion of Belle Chene.

"I think we're wasting our time here tonight," Sybilla said. "I don't feel any receptive atmosphere for our magic at all. It's bad enough that White Lotus Day is only a minor holiday, so there won't be any push on the other side to make contact with us like on more important days. If there aren't any vibrations here, we can do a ceremony, but it won't do us a bit of good."

"We've got to at least try, Aunt."

"Let me remind you," Nick put in bluntly, "that I won't

have the two of you trying your so-called magic anywhere Belle Chene's workers might see you.''

"For your information," Sybilla said, the warning note plain in her voice, "we don't need your permission. I can turn you into some innocuous little pest and continue on with what I need to do.''

Wendi gasped and took Sybilla's arm. "Aunt! Let's go over here and talk.''

"No." Sybilla shook off her hold. "I believe it's time Nick realized the seriousness of this situation on our side of the coin. It's our lives as witches at stake, but the only reason he's even abiding us being on Belle Chene is because he thinks he might convince you to lift your skirts for him at some point.''

"Aunt!''

"Hush, Wendi." Sybilla's stare challenged Nick. "Isn't that right?''

Nick actually sputtered, and Wendi felt sorry for him. Her aunt didn't pull her stern act very often, but when she did, there was no doubt she'd once been a powerful witch. The last time Wendi recalled seeing this side of Aunt Sybilla was when they'd run across a man beating his poor old horse in one of the New Orleans alleyways a couple years ago. Sybilla had let the man run around in his state as a sewer rat until his squeals convinced her that he'd never raise a whip to the horse again.

"Well?" Sybilla prodded when Nick didn't reply.

"I'm going back to Belle Chene.''

Wendi's heart fell even further. He hadn't denied it, and until that moment, she hadn't even realized it mattered to her. Yes, he'd kissed her. Yes, she'd enjoyed it. And yes, she'd told herself the only attraction she felt toward him was a bodily one. He was too dark—too injured—for her to ever consider anything more than maybe a night in his bed.

Besides, he might be her mother's killer. At the very least, he was a bad seed from her past, part of what kept both hers and Sybilla's magic from working. Part of the disrupted karma, his disbelief in their magic a further complication.

Still, she'd lied to herself without realizing it. More than anything else at the moment, she wanted to be able to join forces with Nick and find the answers to the karmic disruption. Perhaps work out the problems between them, too. And perhaps—a big perhaps, but still it lingered irrepressibly in her mind—perhaps see if there was something between them over and above this fiery desire to make love together.

Nick didn't even reach his stallion before Wendi knew what was going to happen. Horrified, she glanced at Sybilla, who had her arm lifted. The warning glare in her aunt's eyes told Wendi to keep her bloody magic to herself, even if the whisper in her mind hadn't confirmed it. She obeyed.

The stallion disappeared in a huge poof of smoke. Nick stumbled but caught himself, and Wendi felt the pain in his leg as though it were her own. She knew better than to interfere, however, but perhaps Sybilla had a touch of compassion left within her anger. Nick's cane, which had been in the saddle scabbard, danced out of the smoke and into his hand.

He leaned on it, staring back and forth from the smoke to the trio of women. Miz Thibedeau had joined Wendi and Sybilla, but she didn't appear a bit surprised at the horse disappearing. Nor did she appear shocked when the smoke cleared and a brown, fluffy puppy sat on the ground, a red ribbon on its neck and a pink tongue peeking out in a pant.

Nick's shock and anger thundered around them, though, an almost discernible force in the air. His aura darkened to scarlet as the deep rage filled him. Had he been a warlock, Wendi knew without doubt all three of them would have been in trouble enough to threaten their very existence.

Nick faced Sybilla. "Turn that goddamned dog back into my horse!"

"Oh," Sybilla said coolly, "so you admit it was my magic that turned your horse into a puppy?"

"I'm not admitting one damned thing! Do what I said, or get your ass off Belle Chene. Along with your niece."

Sybilla propped her hands on her hips. "And just how do you think you'll enforce that dictate, should I decide to disregard your orders, monsieur?"

"That's enough, both of you!" Wendi stepped between the two of them, although they weren't close enough to actually have a physical confrontation. "Aunt, turn the horse back. Nick, we'll leave here in the morning."

"Wendi—" Sybilla began.

"You might be older than me, Aunt," Wendi interrupted her, "but I can tell this is useless. All that's happening here at Belle Chene is we're stirring up more disruption to the karma with this fighting between us."

"You're wrong, Wendi," Sybilla replied. "Back in New Orleans, my magic had weakened to the point where it would never have done what I just did. It's been strengthening ever since I got here. Yours has, too, but you haven't used it enough to realize it."

She overrode Wendi when she began to speak. "And the reason you're not using it is standing beside that puppy. You're thinking that if you weren't a witch—if you didn't have magical powers—you might have a chance with Nick. A chance to have a relationship with him."

A flush of embarrassment heated Wendi's cheeks and she

hissed at her aunt, "Hush! You've no right to say things like that to me!"

"I've every right, my girl. Both as a fill-in for your mother all these years, and as someone who loves you and doesn't want to see you hurt again."

"Your love doesn't give you the right to make my decisions for me. Or hurt me like this yourself."

Nick moved, limping around her and facing Sybilla. "You can do what you want to me, you . . . you witch! But you keep your nose out of whatever happens between Wendi and me. And your vicious tongue off her."

He turned and took Wendi's arm. "Come on. We'll talk at Belle Chene. We'll take the buggy, and these two can walk back." He tossed a sneer at Sybilla. "Or your aunt can fly on her broom."

Wendi sniffed and wiped a hand against her cheek. The wetness there indicated a tear had escaped the confines of her lashes, and her aunt's image blurred before her. Perhaps that was why she thought she saw a brief, satisfied twist to Sybilla's lips.

She followed Nick's urging and walked to the buggy, which the three women had used to get out to the site Nick had suggested they use for their ceremony. It had been a tight fit for them in the one seat, but when Nick climbed in after her, there was adequate room for only the two of them. He picked up the reins and turned the horse. As soon as they were out of sight of the other two, he reached over and pulled her closer to him.

"I'm sorry," he said.

"I don't know what came over Aunt Sybilla," she said with a repressed sob. "She's never treated me like that before—said those sorts of things to me."

Nick tightened his hold, and she laid her head on his shoulder, the sobs breaking free.

• • •

Sybilla's stance wilted, and Thalia Thibedeau put a comforting arm around her friend's shoulders. "You had to do it," Thalia said. "Much as it hurts, you had to drive her closer into his arms. Otherwise, he'd have run us off and we couldn't continue our search."

"I know." Sybilla straightened and faced her. "This has been a long time in coming about, Thalia. All those times you hid your witchcraft from Wendi, and especially Nick."

"Well, I was afraid Nick would figure it out when I repaired Sabine's portrait, but he didn't. And I'll tell you one thing. I'm sure glad to be back in New Orleans. I thought those years out in California would never pass!" She patted one less-than-slender hip. "The only good thing about them was that the way to keep Nick Bardou under control was through his stomach, so I got to use my cooking skills to make food I enjoyed, also. His businesses prospered, although I'll admit I didn't have all that much to do with that part of it. And I kept him away from here until it was time for him to return. Until the planets were in the right configuration."

"We aren't even positive we *have* chosen the right time, Thalia. Darn that Sabine! She hasn't contacted me even once! You'd think she'd check on Wendi at least. Let her know she loves her and is watching over her."

"There may be some reason. In fact, I'm sure there is. Now let's get started. Unless you want to fly and play swoop-the-loop in front of our Nickie boy, just to see his face."

"It's a lovely night for a stroll," Sybilla said with a laugh as the pain she felt at hurting Wendi subsided a little. Thalia always could make her see the sense of things. "And I have this feeling Nick and Wendi are supposed to be alone for a while. Besides, maybe we'll both lose an inch or so walking back to the plantation.''

"Why don't you just turn the puppy back into a stallion and we'll ride?" Thalia asked logically.

"I thought I'd keep him around as a companion for Alphie." She gave Thalia a wink. "And also as a reminder to Nick Bardou of just how strong my magic is.''

"Good idea," Thalia said.

Fifteen

After they dropped the buggy off at the stable, Nick steered Wendi toward the *garçonniere*. She balked as soon as she realized the direction he was taking.

"I better go on in the house. I need to wash my face."

"There's a washroom in the *garçonniere*," Nick said. "And I don't want you to be alone right now. You're still upset."

Reluctantly Wendi responded to his hand in the small of her back, urging her toward his bachelor's quarters. She knew she must look a mess. She wasn't a pretty crier, ending up with a swollen, red nose, streaky eyes and clumpy lashes. The knowledge of what she must look like and knowing he would light the wall sconces in his quarters were as much a part of her reluctance as anything else.

Had she looked her best, she would have no compunction about being alone with him. After all, she wasn't some simpering virgin, both curious and apprehensive about what happened between a man and woman. And she could handle Nick Bardou. She'd done it before.

Of course, that was before she'd started to get to know the more sensitive man beneath that angry aura. Started to think maybe she was beginning to fall for him. Knew as soon as she felt his solicitude a while ago that she was already well into the plummet.

She couldn't believe how he'd stepped in to comfort her and protect her from Aunt Sybilla's unfounded wrath. For that matter, she couldn't believe her aunt had acted as she had. Perhaps this entire situation was getting to them both, and Sybilla's fear of losing her magic was affecting her emotions.

She frowned in concentration. But Sybilla had said her magic was actually strengthening at Belle Chene, plus told Wendi hers was, also, if she'd just try to use it.

Before she could pursue that thought, Nick opened the door on the *garçonniere* and led her into the hallway. Someone had already lit the hallway sconces, but when Nick opened the door to his bedroom, it was dark. She preceded him into the room, and he shut the door.

"I'll have a light on in a second."

"Don't," she urged, taking his arm. "I—"

"I'm warning you, Wendi," he growled in a low voice, obviously mistaking the reason she wanted darkness. "If we don't get some light on the subject very quickly, I might have to concede that your aunt had a point."

"About you only letting me stay here at Belle Chene because you're trying to get under my skirts?" she asked in exasperation. "Don't you think the two of us are a little too mature to be playing those sort of games?"

"Oh, no," he denied. "Being more mature—having played those games before—only means we both know how much pleasure is in store for us." He took the hand on his arm in his own, slowly pulling her closer to him. With his other hand, he traced an index finger back and forth beneath her chin. "It means whenever we anticipate searching out that pleasure with someone new, there's the possibility of this time culminating in that trip to nirvana we've always heard about but never experienced ourselves. The place we've been temptingly near now and then, but never exactly experienced.''

His low, throbbing voice went through her like a lazy day, stealing into her senses and winding down her body to settle in her belly—and a little lower. When it made its way to her knees, she clutched his waist to steady herself and keep from wilting on the hard floor. Pulling him down after her.

He was right. Knowing what could happen filled her with anticipation. While lovemaking with Colin had been satisfying, she'd never attained the nirvana Nick evidently also searched for.

He bent his head and nuzzled her neck. ''Don't you agree?''

''Yes. Uh—agree about what?'' she gasped, realizing she didn't recall what he'd said previously.

His lips nibbled a path toward her ear. ''Hmmmmm? What?'' he asked, the quaver of the sound mingling with his nibbles and sending a delicious surge through her. The wave chased away every vestige of lazy lassitude, bringing each receptive pinpoint to full alert, as well as others she hadn't even known she had.

''I forget,'' she said.

When he murmured a ''me, too,'' she wound an arm around his neck, the action lifting her breasts to settle against his chest. The contact sent a new stab of pleasure flashing between her sensitive nipples to arch to the place below her belly.

Nick slowly turned her around and pushed her against the wall, his lips and hands finding new territories to explore—additional areas she wasn't aware of until he touched them. The sensations dizzied her and made her almost completely unaware of her movement. But when he lifted her onto a sturdy little table beside the door, she instinctively wrapped her legs around his waist.

With a groan that went straight into her belly, he pushed against her, rocking his hard readiness on her and flooding her with both moisture and warmth. She exploded immediately, the reaction taking her by complete surprise.

It caught Nick unaware, also, if the words he murmured, which barely penetrated her senses, were true. But the few words she could understand kept her release undulating far longer than it ever had before. Left her entire body relaxed and fulfilled, wrapped around Nick but barely clinging. As soon as awareness crept back into her consciousness, it left her yearning for more, this time a joining with the man who had given her such pleasure.

But that man stepped back from her, shaking his head in bewilderment, his expression barely readable in the dim light from one of the windows.

"I—God, Wendi," he murmured. "I'm actually afraid of what I'll do to you if this goes any further."

"I'm not," she whispered. "As wonderful as that was, it's not enough. I want you with me the next time I find nirvana."

She slid from the table and took his hand. Unresisting, he followed her over beside the bed, where she stopped and turned to face him.

"Listen, Wendi," he said before she could speak. "You're upset because of what happened between you and your aunt tonight."

"Yes, I am," she admitted, reaching for one of the buttons on his shirt. "But what's that got to do with this?"

"It's got—I—" She unbuttoned the top button on the front of her dress next. "I—I don't want you to regret this in the morning," he finally stuttered as she unbuttoned the next shirt button and reached for the next one on her dress.

"Like I said," she murmured, "we're both mature. We're surely mature enough to make our own decisions and live with them. Live with the regrets, if that's what happens." She finished unbuttoning her own dress, allowing it to gape open but not pulling it from her shoulders.

When she reached for him again, Nick cupped his hands around her face and pulled her toward him. His mouth was soft, all the more softer because she sensed the restraint in him. He feathered across her lips, nibbling and tasting, then parting them with the very tip of his tongue and curling it back and forth. She tugged his shirt from his belt to reach the very last button, and undid it while she opened her mouth to him.

He deepened the kiss and she ran the back of her hand across his hardness, feeling it flinch against her touch. Way too fast for a man with a less-than-sound leg, Nick swung around and sat on the bed, swooping her with him and pushing her back on the mattress.

Looming over her, he said in a warning voice, "I've never wanted a woman as badly as I want you, Wendi. I've told myself it's for a lot of reasons, and I've told myself that if I could only have you once, I could get you out of my system. But what happened back there at the doorway proved me wrong. Do you want to know why?"

Suddenly she felt small and helpless, a maiden again, unsure of what lay in store. All her feminine wiles deserted her, including the sense of power she'd experienced while she tempted him to continue. He was so huge measured against her smallness. And he was completely in control now, leaving her no doubt it would be up to him whether or not he stopped. Or continued.

She licked her lips. "W-why?"

Very gently he touched her cheek. "Because I was jealous of you going over the edge without me," he murmured, and she felt herself climbing toward fulfillment again with only his words. "I wanted to be with you so badly, I could taste it."

That scared the hell out of her. It also brought every sense alive again, filling her with femininity and assurance that this was right. That she could handle it—needed it. That she'd never be able to overcome the loss if he didn't continue.

"And I'm going to taste it before the night is over," Nick said, slipping her dress off her shoulder with one finger and leaning toward her nipple. He flicked it with his tongue. "And taste more than your breast." He cupped her between the legs. "I might even taste you there."

She throbbed against his hand, grabbing his head and pulling him down to suckle her breast while she writhed in pleasure and completion once more. When she quieted, Nick actually chuckled against her breast, his hand bunching her skirt and working it up her legs. Overcoming her languor, she sat up, stood for a second and jerked the garment off, then stripped her petticoat and chemise in one motion. He lay there watching her, eyes hooded and features indistinct in the moonlight.

"Now you," she insisted. Clad only in her panties, she faced him and propped her hands on her hips. "Get naked, Nick. We'll have our own ceremony." She couldn't actually believe she was teasing him so easily, but then, she and Colin had been easy and free with each other—had sparred in a jokingly sexual manner.

Nick lifted one leg. "You get me naked if you want me. I think you owe me that. I want to prolong this as long as I can, and believe me, it's getting harder and harder." He flicked his eyes between his own legs in a double entendre, and she giggled along with his chuckle.

"All right," she said, bending down and reaching for his boot. Her breasts swung free, and she heard him groan. Tugging his boot off, she slipped him a look beneath her lashes. "And harder?"

She pulled that boot off, but in the meantime, Nick had his trousers open and was sliding them down his hips. By the time he got them as far as his knees, her hands were free and Wendi met him there, taking over the removal. Negligently, she tossed the trousers over her shoulder, then stared at what was now revealed.

"It's hard," she said with a satisfied smirk.

"Wench," Nick muttered, reaching for her.

"You're not completely naked," she said, backing up so he couldn't touch her.

"Neither are you."

She quirked an eyebrow. "Both together?"

"Both together," he agreed.

He sat up and removed his shirt, while she untied the ribbon holding her panties in place. Teasingly, she held the ends together for a long moment, enjoying the way Nick's gaze centered on her fingers and the pink ribbon, the way his eyes narrowed to bare slits. Suddenly she released the ribbon and gave a jaunty swing to her hips to hasten the drop of her panties.

Nick surged up and grabbed her, tossing her on the bed and covering her with his body before she knew what was happening. He nuzzled her neck again, a semisensuous and semitickling action, gripping her tighter when she giggled and wiggled against him. Her giggles died the instant he moved his lips to her breast.

He licked her nipple, then blew on it. She moaned as the hardening tip sent a flash of sensation through her and the other nipple puckered in fellowship with its mate.

"Beautiful," Nick said, his breath continuing to cause the reaction in her nipples.

"Love me, Nick," she pleaded. "Now. Please."

"In a minute." He licked the other nipple, then around the lower mound of her breast, tracing a path over to the opposite one and back to the same nipple again. "I want to enjoy your body entirely. Every delectable inch of it."

She wanted her own part of his delectable body, especially the hard inches pulsing against her thigh. And she recalled one way she used to get Colin to hurry when he seemed bent on prolonging their play. She moved her thigh against that pulsation, then managed to turn herself and push her ache against him.

Nick groaned a half-gasp and pulled her closer. "Witch," he growled.

"That I am," she agreed, rubbing on him.

He moved over her and settled between her legs, which she wrapped greedily around his waist. "Open your eyes," he ordered. "I want to see your feelings when I fill you."

She opened her eyes, and the look on his face mirrored what she could feel in herself. Her lips parted and he slid into her, easily, smoothly. Fulfillingly.

"Oh, God," he said. "It feels so good it almost hurts."

How he managed she didn't know. Didn't care. But she crested two more times in quick secession before he rode with her into that nirvana he made her believe in. And she had absolutely no doubt that was the special place they found.

Or that he'd found it with her. His collapse over her, his shout of her name the only sound penetrating her swirling senses, assured her of that.

During the lingering flutters of aftermath, she realized he was still ready for more. Eyes opening wide, she said, "I'm not able. Any more will kill me."

"Then I'll die with you," he said with a smirk, moving within her again.

Nick was awake when Wendi stretched languorously into full consciousness the next morning. She opened her eyes to see him with elbow bent, head propped on one hand, hair adorably messed and blue eyes watching her appreciatively.

"I've never had so much fun with sex," he murmured, reaching out and running a fingertip down her cheek and around her lips.

She tucked her palm beneath the side of her face and smiled secretively at him.

"Well?" he prodded. "Don't you have anything to say?"

"I don't kiss and tell," she said.

He lifted one raven eyebrow. "But you do kiss. Right?"

"Do I?" she teased.

"I wish like hell I had time to investigate that comment further," he said, regret in his tone. "But I promised Julian I'd ride out and check the cane fields with him this morning. And I've noticed he rises pretty early—when he spends the night at Belle Chene, anyway. He'll probably be out here looking for me any minute."

Uneasy, Wendi started to slide out of bed, but Nick caught her.

"Whoa. He'll knock first He knows better than to barge in here without an invitation. Come here."

He pulled her close and bent his head, kissing her gently and lingeringly. "Good morning," he said when the kiss ended.

"Good morning," she whispered. "Last night was wonderful."

"Very," he agreed.

"At least, after we got back here."

She realized her mistake at once. Nick's eyes darkened, and the barriers between them slowly but inevitably rose. To give him credit, she watched him struggle, but the reminder of her witchcraft unfortunately brought with it the reminder of her mother. Of the scandal. Of all the reasons she and Nick Bardou were the last two people on earth who should be lying next to each other after a delicious night of lovemaking. Sabine's daughter and Dominic's son.

The reminder also carried with it the reasons she and Nick were the last two people on earth who should have experienced the total abandon and mind-bending pleasure they had last night. Given all that, the ending result crashed into Wendi's mind in the same manner as a bolt of intense pleasure, only causing the opposite reaction in her.

It had been pure sex between them—nothing else. Purely physical—nothing emotional. Heaven forbid what happened between them be anything leaning toward lovemaking. Toward love.

She sensed the same conclusion in Nick's mind—on his face—in his quickly shuttered eyes.

"There's still no reason to let Julian find you in here," he said. "Would you like to use the washroom first?"

Pain stabbed through her. Given the circumstances, he'd only reacted the way her rational thoughts indicated was the logical way to react, yet some tiny ray of hope had burned somewhere in her. But no longer. They'd shared their bodies and found nirvana together, but it was purely a physical release on his part. And he clearly expected her to judge it the same way.

After all, hadn't she been completely agreeable last night? Maybe even more of the initiator than he was?

She slid out of bed without opposition this time, heading toward the washroom. Shutting the door behind her, she leaned against it and closed her eyes against the tears. A few slipped through her lashes anyway, but she grabbed a linen towel and mopped them away.

Through the door, she heard someone knock on the hall door, then Nick's voice calling for them to wait. He padded across the floor, and she heard voices. Julian must have arrived. Hurrying over to the washbasin, she poured some water from the pitcher and picked up the cloth. A few minutes later, she wrapped the towel around her and peeked through the doorway.

She didn't see Nick anywhere. He must have already dressed and gone out with Julian. Sniffling in self-pity, she checked around for her clothing, seeing it piled on one of the chair seats, beneath the high arms. Nick had obviously picked it up, so Julian wouldn't chance seeing it when he opened the door.

Goddess forbid anyone in his family find out he'd spent the night with the daughter of his father's mistress!

She realized the contradiction of her thoughts immediately, but she didn't much give a full moon right now. As she dressed, she firmed her resolve as to the séance. One way or another, she was going to rectify the disturbed karma and get on with her life—a life without Nick Bardou.

Hungry, she headed for the kitchen house, where she and Sybilla took most of their meals with Miz Thibedeau. As she climbed the porch steps and reached for the door, she felt a furtive sensation tap on her mind. Could it be her aunt was discussing something secretive with someone and had forgotten to close off her thoughts? Feeling sneaky herself, Wendi stopped at the door without making her presence known and tuned into the vibration.

By the Goddess and God! That wasn't Aunt Sybilla. It was Miz Thibedeau. Thalia Thibedeau was a witch!

How dare Nick decry her witchcraft, yet have a witch for a cook and housekeeper?

Wendi pushed open the door and stomped into the kitchen. Both Sybilla and Thalia started in surprise, then identical guilty flushes stained their cheeks. Wendi propped her hands on her hips and glared at them without speaking.

She didn't have to speak. Her mind told them both exactly how she was feeling—reported back to her their confusion for a brief instant before both of them closed their own thoughts to her.

"Wendi—" Thalia put out a hand. "Don't jump to any conclusions until you hear the entire story. You were young when all this happened, and there are things you don't know."

"By the full moon, I have a right to know them," Wendi stormed. "I'm part of this, and I resent like hell the two of you keeping secrets from me!"

Suddenly something dawned on her, and a mixture of hurt and disbelief filled her.

"You manipulated me last night, didn't you, Aunt Sybilla? You wanted me to spend the night with Nick. Maybe make him fall in love with me so he wouldn't force us to leave Belle Chene."

"Wendi, it wasn't like that." Sybilla looked quickly at Thalia. "Not exactly, anyway."

"Not exactly! Aunt, I'm very close to hating you right now for using me like that. I thought you loved me. I thought we were friends, rather than just aunt and niece. Give me one reason why I should forgive you for what you did."

Sybilla either couldn't—or didn't want to. Wendi couldn't decide which. Sybilla avoided Wendi's gaze, looking down at the floor without answering. The glare Wendi then turned on Thalia was returned with a vacant, unreadable look.

Instantly Wendi realized the blank look on Thalia's face covered up her intentions. Darn her, while Sybilla distracted her, Thalia was working a spell in her mind! Thalia reached out to take Sybilla's arm, and Wendi stepped forward.

"Don't you dare!" she cried.

But the two witches disappeared in a poof of smoke.

Hurt beyond measure at Sybilla's defection, Wendi stared at the spot Sybilla and Thalia had stood. The kitchen was quiet, not even a trace of smoke lingering in the air. The clock on the wall ticked and tocked, and the metal coffeepot on the stove crackled as it cooled.

Ever so slowly, Wendi sank into a chair at the table. Now she was totally alone. Who knew when—or if—Sybilla and Thalia would return. Toenails clicked on the wooden floor as Alphie came out of the corner and trotted over to her, laying his head on her knee.

"I can't believe it," she murmured to the dog, stroking his head. "Thalia Thibedeau is the most powerful witch I've ever seen. Yet I never had any inkling at all of her magical abilities."

Alphie whined in sympathy, but didn't answer. The puppy peeked up over the woodbox beside the stove, trotted out into view, and sat down to scratch a flea. The little elbow on his back leg beat a tatoo on the floor, and the now-bedraggled red ribbon on his neck danced with his movements.

"I'll give you a bath today, darling," Wendi told him.

Then she sniffed back a sob and buried her face on Alphie's neck. But she didn't allow herself to cry. She was a Chastain, and she and her mother had borne plenty of sorrow in their lives. Her mother had always had the strength to get through adversity, giving Wendi the best life she could after they were kicked out of the mansion where they lived.

Wendi had had plenty of time to formulate the type of woman she was to become under Sabine Chastain's tutelage before her mother's death. She'd lived with her mother twelve years. One thing Sabine had taught Wendi to value above anything else was her witchcraft and resulting magic. It made her different, and at times unacceptable. But it made her special, Sabine had said. It was as much a part of her as her femaleness—to be valued for that very reason.

The Goddess was more powerful than the God in their beliefs, and only death could keep a witch from using her magic. Death had indeed stopped Sabine's magic, but Wendi was alive.

She'd been more gloriously alive than ever in her life last night. Nick's arms had held her tenderly yet firmly, with her exulting in her femaleness against his maleness.

Those memories made this morning's letdown even more difficult to bear.

But she'd get through it somehow. Some way.

Sixteen

Shortly before noon, Lucian appeared in the courtyard, heading for the kitchen house. Wendi stopped the rocking chair, realizing she'd been sitting there trying to work out a plan but failing to climb out of her misery ever since her aunt and Thalia Thibedeau had disappeared.

Lucian walked up the steps and paused to speak. "Is my mother in the kitchen?"

"No, Lucian. I haven't seen her this morning."

"Why don't I smell anything cooking?"

Wendi jumped from the chair. "Oh, no. I didn't think of that. My aunt and Thalia . . . uh . . . they had to go back to New Orleans. I guess I better see what I can throw together for the noon meal."

Lucian stared through the screen door, then straightened his shoulders. "I miss Monsieur Jacques, too, but it's time my mother got back to work," he said in a strangely adult voice. "I'm going up to tell her that."

"Lucian—"

But he was already gone. Oddly enough, if Wendi hadn't known he was human, she'd have thought he moved as quickly as a warlock at times. She'd seen them move in that graceful way, which anyone with magical powers of their own could discern as an ability they repressed in front of humans.

She shook her head. Her misery must be overworking her imagination. After realizing Thalia Thibedeau was a witch, she envisioned everyone around her with magical powers, even a child who was probably Nick's younger cousin. A child probably the result of a liaison between Cecile and Jacques—the strange form of the magnolia leaves she'd seen before notwithstanding.

Except for Nick. She had no doubt at all that he was completely human. All his sensuality and masculinity were total maleness, not magical.

She looked around in the kitchen, opening drawers and cupboards, peering into the spring-fed cooling room off the rear of the structure. By the time Lucian came down from talking to his mother, a forlorn look on his face, she had slices of ham frying in a skillet and potatoes boiling in a pot. While Lucian sat dejectedly at the table, she opened jars of canned green beans and corn, mixing them together for succotash and adding some seasonings.

"I assume your mother has decided she's not up to cooking again yet, Lucian," she said as she set the succotash on the stove, wiping her face in the heat from the fire.

He nodded, and she continued, "Grief takes time. It's different with different people. We have to let each person work it out on his or her own."

"Monsieur Nick says that hard work is the best way to overcome grief," he responded. "But Mama just lies there in bed. She talks to me when I come up, and she gets up sometimes and sits in the rocking chair by the window. But she stares out at the graveyard and rocks. I may be only a boy still, Mademoiselle Wendi—"

"Please," Wendi interrupted. "Just call me Wendi. For one thing, I'm not a mademoiselle."

"You're married?" he asked in a confused voice. "But where—"

"No, I'm not married. Not now. But we were talking about your mother." As a woman who had experienced grief of her own, Wendi knew she should have paid more attention to helping Cecile overcome hers. But she'd assumed her aunt and Thalia were handling it.

"Will you go talk to her, Ma—Wendi?" he pleaded. "I'm worried about her."

"I will. Right after we eat, I promise. Now, how about you going out to the pump in the garden and filling the water pans for Alphie and the puppy? I noticed they were almost empty when I passed them. Come back in about fifteen minutes, and the food should be ready."

Lucian pushed his chair back and headed for the door as Wendi hurried to the stove, rescuing the ham at just the right instant to turn it. One side was crispy brown, and the grease spattered gaily as she turned it to cook the other side. The potatoes were boiling, and the succotash was beginning to steam. She took some red, ripe tomatoes off the windowsill and carried them over to the table to slice. Luckily, she'd seen some pies in the cooling room for dessert.

Nick met Lucian in the courtyard, and the boy told him that Thalia and Sybilla were gone, and that Wendi was cooking. Hot, tired, and dusty, he stormed up the steps to the kitchen house. He didn't mind Sybilla's absence at all, but when he got his hands on Thalia Thibedeau, he'd fire her, despite her being the best damn cook in any state!

And he'd have a talk with his stable master right after lunch and chew his ass out for allowing the two women the use of a buggy without first asking Nick's permission. Stopping with his hand near the door, he shook his head. No, it wasn't possible. Surely Sybilla hadn't used her witchcraft to transport the two of them back to New Orleans as a punishment for Nick's attitude the previous night at the thwarted ceremony. Miz Thibedeau would probably have a heart attack if that happened.

Changing his mind, he headed for the stables. Not more than five minutes later, he walked back to the kitchen house, confused, after being assured by his stable master that no one had used any of the carriages or buggies that morning. Indeed, no horses were missing. He'd find out from Wendi what the hell was going on.

He made the mistake of glancing in the window before he plowed through the door. Wendi stood at the table, cheeks flushed from the heat, strawberry hair curling wildly and enticingly around her brow and cheeks. She'd piled her hair on top of her head, but curls and tresses tumbled around almost as though alive, bouncing with her movements as she arranged a plate of bright red tomato slices. His palms tingled as he recalled that her hair felt even more silky than it looked.

A drop of sweat fell from her nose, and she flicked her tongue out to catch it, wrinkling her face at the salty taste. She wore a capped-sleeve dress with a low neckline, cooler for her but one that made her even more sexy in the heat and humidity. It clung damply to her breasts, and a rivulet of sweat trickled down between them, making him yearn to follow it with his tongue.

Men sweat, ladies perspire. Damn, that was his father's voice. He well recalled that chastising, teasing manner Dominic used to teach his sons the better points of manners toward southern womanhood. The reminder of his father cooled his libido more effectively than if Wendi had grown a wart on her nose.

He pushed on through the door and into the kitchen. When Wendi glanced up and saw him, a brief smile of welcome flickered on her face before she evidently remembered how they'd parted this morning. Or perhaps she caught the thunderous look he could feel on his face.

Maybe she was even inside his mind again. That thought fired his anger higher.

"I want to know why the hell your aunt took my cook out of here," he demanded. "When I get hold of either one of them again, I'll—"

"My aunt?" Wendi cried.

The plate of tomatoes hit him in the face, then slid over his chest, leaving behind juice and seeds, which oozed down his chin. The china plate broke on the floor, drawing his amazed stare to the blotches on his white shirt. They almost looked like blood stains.

His eyes then settled on Wendi. She stood at the table, hands gripping the edge, a warning glare on her face and a sharp knife dangerously close to one hand.

"You can flip yourself around and take that ill attitude of yours right on out of here," she snarled, "and don't come back until you can be polite. I've been sweltering in this heat, cooking to fill your darned stomach, and by the Goddess, I won't be treated like some prewar slave!"

"You tossed those tomatoes at me," he said in a surprised voice.

"Understand this," she warned. "I threw them myself. I didn't need magic. I'm sick and tired of your changeling personality. One minute you're growling at me like a dragon disturbed in its lair, and the next you're stroking me and trying to kiss me! Then, when I give in and you get your satisfaction, you sneak off to *work* and turn back into the dragon!''

"All I wanted to know was where my cook was!''

"No." Wendi leaned on the table, thrusting her chin out at him, her blue eyes shooting warning sparks. "You wanted me to tell you that my aunt had used her witchcraft to steal your cook away. To get back at you for the way you acted last night when we tried to perform a ceremony.''

"Stay the hell out of my mind," he said, quickly realizing his comment had confirmed her words.

"I don't need inside your mind to follow my thoughts to a rational conclusion. Just because I'm a witch doesn't mean I need witchcraft to think with. I have a perfectly fine brain all my own! And your actions and comments are very easily read!''

"Well, we'll see how my actions are read when I go into New Orleans and find Miz Thibedeau—rescue her from your aunt's clutches." He started for the door, but at Wendi's gale of laughter, he stopped in his tracks and turned to face her again. "You think it's funny that I'm going to turn your aunt over to the authorities?''

"My aunt didn't take Thalia out of here," Wendi denied. "Thalia took my aunt with *her*.''

"Oh, sure," Nick snarled. "If that were true, that would mean that Miz Thibedeau is a—''

His face tightened in reaction as the blood drained from it. Shaking his head, he stumbled unsteadily to the table, easing himself into the chair opposite Wendi.

"That would mean Thalia Thibedeau is a witch," he said in disbelief. "That she's been living with me for over five years without me knowing that.''

Wendi shrugged. Instead of answering him, she rose to her feet and walked over to the windowsill, where she picked up two more tomatoes. After washing them in a bowl of water in the dry sink, she pointed her finger at the broken plate. It flew back together, then swooped over to the sink, into the pan of water. Retrieving a clean plate, Wendi came back to the table. While Nick sat silent, she cored the tomatoes and started slicing them onto the plate.

Something itched on his face, and Nick reached up a hand to scratch it, his movement drawing Wendi's gaze. A tiny smile—more of a smirk—curved her lips, and he drew his hand back to find a tomato seed on the end of his finger. Surging to his feet, he went to the dry sink and grabbed a dishtowel, dunking it in the water bowl and cleaning his face. He didn't bother with his shirt. It was probably only good for the ragbag now.

He caught Wendi staring at him when he turned around, but she quickly shuttered her eyes and reached for the second tomato.

"I notice you're not limping as badly this morning as when I first met you," she murmured. "Are you still using the liniment and tea?"

"The massages work better," he said without thinking.

Her eyes flew to his thigh as though to examine the wound through his trousers, and he groaned in discomfort, mixed with disbelief that he'd allowed her to sidetrack his thoughts. It took him several more seconds to gain control over the instant response her gaze caused in the part of his body adjacent to the wound. Well, not control, but at least enough composure to walk back to the table and sit down again.

Wendi concentrated on the tomato.

"Look," he said at last. "Maybe I owe you an apology for storming in here like a . . . a dragon," he admitted. "But you owe me an explanation about your comments."

"Why?" she asked, quirking an eyebrow and cutting off the last slice of tomato. "I didn't have a damned thing to do with Thalia Thibedeau moving in with you without your realizing she was a witch. In fact, I didn't even know it myself until she took Aunt Sybilla's arm this morning and the both of them disappeared in a poof of smoke. Right over there by the stove.''

She pointed the knife blade at the spot she meant, then said, ''Furthermore, *I* didn't have a damned thing to do with the scandal ten years ago.'' She dropped the knife and rose to her feet, leaning toward him across the plate of tomatoes. ''*I* was a child, twelve years old. *I* didn't choose my mother's lover, although knowing why it happened like it did, I didn't fault her. Or judge her.''

''What do you mean—''

But Wendi leaned even closer to him, ignoring his attempt at interruption. ''*I* lived through the results of that mess, too, however. Steeped in your self-pity, you seem to conveniently forget there were other people involved in that mess—hurt by it, and their reputations damaged. You seem to think you were the only one affected—or at least, the one affected the most severely. I stayed here and suffered, yet made a life for myself. A life where I helped others, instead of living in pitiful recluse. You ran off and didn't even try to bring the truth to light.''

Rounding the table, she stomped to the door, and Nick swiveled in his chair to follow her.

''Serve your own meal!'' Wendi yelled over her shoulder. ''And don't forget to clean up when you're done!''

''Get your ass back here—''

The plate of tomatoes flew up from the table and hit him in the side of the head, cutting off his angry shout. Nick had no doubts this time magic had done it. The plate hit the floor and broke, and his eyes widened in disbelief as he got to his feet. His movement sent more tomatoes slithering messily down his cheek and chin.

How dare she?

He took one step after Wendi, and his foot landed on a slippery piece of the china littering the floor. His boot slid out from under him, and he barely managed to land in the chair instead of on the floor amidst that mess. His wound throbbed and pain filled his vision with blackness strewn with pinpoint stars of agony.

Dropping his head into his hands, he gritted his teeth. Something tickled his nose, but when he swiped it, he didn't encounter a tomato seed. Opening his eyes, he saw a cup of tea on the table, steam swirling upward, carrying the scent of the willow bark he'd become used to. Wendi's magic again.

Grimacing in both pain and the knowledge that he'd acted like an ass and deserved every bit of agony, he picked up the teacup.

Seventeen

~

Wendi paced her room. She could go after them, she supposed. But it wouldn't do any good. From what she'd both seen and sensed when Thalia Thibedeau disappeared from the kitchen with Sybilla, even hers and her aunt's magic combined wouldn't touch Thalia's. And her aunt had made it clear who she had aligned herself with!

No, her best bet was to try to find a private time to perform the séance.

Or she could find Nick and wring his neck. Force him to listen to her.

Sure. And pigs could fly without a magical spell on them.

She climbed the step stool beside the high-mattress, four-poster bed and flung herself onto the comforter. She couldn't decide which hurt the most—the fact her aunt had obviously been working with Thalia Thibedeau all these years, or the fact that Nick had made torrid, devastating love to her and it didn't appear to have affected him. Hadn't made him care for her as a woman rather than only a bed partner. Hadn't made him love her, in spite of her being Sabine Chastain's daughter.

Their witchcraft doctrine acknowledged the superiority

of women to men—the control they had over them. But she was fully aware the culture Nick grew up in fostered the opposite presumption. In Nick's culture women were inferior both in their brain power and their physical abilities. Women were to be handled delicately and restricted to things within their capabilities.

Flipping onto her back, she propped her head on a pillow and forced her thoughts away from the man she'd like to have here beside her. Sybilla's words kept flooding her mind. Had her magic really begun to strengthen at Belle Chene?

She was almost afraid to try. But then, magic not used was magic lost. The tale making the rounds of her circle of friends last year had been about a powerful witch who'd given up her witchcraft to marry a mortal man four years previously—a man who couldn't bring himself to accept her magic. The man died in an accident a few years after they were wed, and when the witch attended a ceremony after his death, her magic wouldn't even light the candles on the altar.

Of course, the witch's magic would return with time and practice. But Wendi needed her magic to be as strong as possible now, in order to take advantage of every bit of time she had left before she was forced to leave Belle Chene. She held her hand up, holding her breath as she gazed around the room. Pointing a finger at a candle on the mantel, she barely whispered the incantation before a flame sprang up on the wick. Continuing to lie quietly on the bed, she lit the other three candles, then snuffed them out.

Scratching sounded in the corner of the room, and a tiny mouse scurried around a small hole in the baseboard, as though afraid to get too far from safety. It eyed the doorway into the hall, then sat up on its haunches and glanced at where Wendi lay, whiskers twitching in excitement and anticipation.

A second later a sleek panther paced the room, and Wendi gaped in astonishment. She changed mice into small cats before when she practiced her magic, but never a wonderful creation like this. Silky, shining, and black, the panther stalked back and forth beneath the window for a few seconds, tail coiling and whipping behind it. Then it sat down and threw back its head, opening its mouth and preparing to announce its newfound form to the world.

Wendi hurriedly reversed her spell to squelch the roar before the sound drew the entire Belle Chene population to investigate. The mouse scurried off, racing past the bed and into the hallway just as a crash by the armoire on the other side of the bed jerked Wendi's attention to it. She sat up in surprise as Lucian picked himself off the floor, cheeks flooded with embarrassment and eyes wide with fear. The child had been hiding in the armoire, probably with the door cracked to peer out at her.

"I—I—" was all Lucian could say. After quickly looking at Wendi, he stared around the foot of the bed, at the far corner where the mouse/panther had paced. Then he followed the path the mouse had taken out the door with his gaze.

"Where did it go?" he asked in an awestruck voice.

"What?" Wendi asked, feigning puzzlement and trying to maintain her poise. She hoped Lucian would think he'd fallen asleep and dreamed the scene. "And what were you doing in the armoire spying on me?"

Lucian faced her defiantly. "You practice magic. This isn't the first time I've watched."

"You're wrong, Lucian—"

"No! No, I'm not!" He clenched his fists at his side. "I'm not a liar!"

Wendi scooted to the edge of the bed.

"Lucian—"

But when she held her hand out, he screamed and raised his hands as though to ward her off. Then he raced from the room, his bare feet slapping across the floor and down the hall, down the rear stairwell.

Forgetting the height of the bed, Wendi jumped from it, twisting her ankle when she carelessly hit the floor. Pain stabbed her, and she fell in a crumbled heap. The rear veranda door slammed shut with a resounding thud, and she scrambled to her feet, limping over to the bedroom window facing the gardens in time to see Lucian disappear through the back gate. Instead of heading toward the barn, he ran toward a patch of woods on one of the few undeveloped areas of Belle Chene—the same area where she and Sybilla had tried to work their spell the previous night.

Testing her ankle, she found the pain bearable. It was only a slight sprain and would probably heal quickly. She chewed her bottom lip for a second, trying to decide whether to go after Lucian or wait until she saw him again. Knowing the damage the boy could cause if he spread the tale of what he'd just seen around the plantation, she realized she had no choice.

She couldn't fly after him in the daytime. While she had at times been able to perfect the flying spell, it didn't include the ability to make herself invisible at the same time. All she'd need would be for one of the workers to look up and see her in the sky! She wouldn't have to find her own way back to New Orleans. Nick would throw her all the way.

A couple minutes later she slipped into the woods after Lucian. She hoped the boy was too upset to do more than follow the path through the brush and trees. Suddenly she stopped beneath a huge oak and frowned, recalling the pattern of magnolia leaves she'd seen beside Lucian on the porch.

How could she have forgotten? She and Sybilla had considered that Lucian himself might have some magical powers, but neither of them had had time to follow up the possibility. If he did—

But he couldn't have. Surely Sybilla would have mentioned it if she thought his mother, Cecile, had magical powers. And it went beyond the realm of possibility for Nick's uncle, supposedly the boy's father, to be a warlock.

Shaking off the contemplations that could reach no logical conclusion without further investigation, Wendi closed her eyes and concentrated. It took only a second before she tuned into the confused thoughts of the boy. He didn't appear to be still moving. Instead, his thoughts were centered on one certain area. Almost as though she were looking through his eyes, she saw a shaded spot beside a pond, smelled a pleasant dampness in the air unconnected to the ever-present humidity.

Opening her eyes, she walked on into the woods. There had been a pond close to where they'd attempted the thwarted ceremony. She followed the path, pausing at a fork in the trail. It looked different in the daytime. She closed her eyes again, attempting to connect with Lucian's mind and see which way to go.

The world exploded into brilliant stars, then blackness.

Nick swept up the last tiny piece of china plate, threw the broom in the corner, then limped over and tossed the dregs on the dustpan into a waste tin. Grabbing a wet dishtowel out of the sink to wipe up the tomatoes from the floor, he went back over to the spill.

The scorched smell lingered in the air even now, after he'd scrounged enough food to at least curb a portion of his hunger. While he'd stared furiously and futilely after Wendi, the ham had burned, the potatoes had boiled dry and charred, and the succotash had overcooked into hard kernels of corn and stringy green beans. Fortunately for his stomach, unused to missing a meal, he'd found a loaf of bread on the windowsill and one lonely slice of edible ham.

When he straightened after wiping the floor, two brown, soulful eyes gazed at him from the other side of the screen door.

"Horses eat hay," he told the puppy, which had been his stallion the day before. "But I suppose it's not your fault you're a dog now."

He got the skillet from the stove and carried it out onto the porch. He'd put both the hound and the pup out when the pup kept jumping up onto one of the chairs, then the table, reaching for his food. The darned animal had behaved and obeyed better when it was a horse!

He didn't see the hound anywhere, and he set the skillet down and let the pup have at it. Someone else could worry about washing it later, perhaps Cecile.

He couldn't believe the woman hadn't come down when she smelled the food burning. Even Lucian hadn't been able to get his mother to leave her room, and according to the boy, he'd been trying ever since the day after the funeral. Nick had left the business of comforting Cecile and also caring for the household chores to the women, but it didn't appear there were any women left now to handle either of them. He supposed he should go see what sort of shape Cecile was in.

The hound bounded onto the porch, barking wildly. Mistaking the dog's fury for an attack, Nick threw up an arm, but the hound raced back off the porch, then turned around. It bounded onto the porch again, gripped one of Nick's trouser legs in its teeth and pulled, toenails scrabbling on the wooden floor. The material ripped, and the dog sat down with a thump, a piece of cloth dangling between its teeth.

The cloth fell to the floor when the dog opened its mouth, threw back its head, and howled wildly. The sound tore through Nick with a wrench, and Wendi's name filled his mind.

Something had happened to her. He knew it with an ir- refutable certainty he could not ignore. He hadn't paid any attention to where she'd gone after they fought, but she was in danger now.

"Go!" he ordered the hound, flinging out an arm.

The hound obeyed, heading for the patch of woods be- hind the kitchen house. Nick followed as fast as he could, never more disgusted with his disability than at that mo- ment. When he tried to run, his toe caught on a stone in the trail. Stumbling, he crashed forward into a tree trunk, his shoulder hitting so hard it split the bark. Cursing his clumsiness, he gritted his teeth and staggered on down the trail, one hand on his injured shoulder, the other massaging his leg.

The hound raced ahead, and each time Nick thought he'd lost sight of it, it appeared again to lead him onward. Nick knew the area, as he knew every square inch of Belle Chene's four thousand acres. He hoped the hound would wait at the fork up ahead until he caught him again. Other- wise, he doubted he'd be able to follow its footprints in the spongy dead leaves littering the trail.

He didn't need to. Around the bend, where he could see the fork in the trail, he also saw Wendi. She lay on her back, but with her head turned away from him. Incongru- ously she looked as though she were asleep on the trail, beneath a dancing pattern of sunlight filtering through the leaves. The serene scene heightened Nick's dread.

The hound bounded forward and stood over her, washing the side of her face with its tongue. When it looked back at Nick, it whined deep in its throat and wagged its bushy tail.

As soon as he reached Wendi's side, Nick went to his knees. He reached out a hand, then drew it back. Afraid. He was so damned afraid he'd turn her over and her sightless, dead face would stare back at him. He was too distraught to try to see if she were still breathing.

One other time he'd seen a woman lying like this. Only he'd been lying beside her, not kneeling over her. When he'd opened his eyes, for a brief instant all he'd seen had been a strange, bloody grin staring back at him before he realized he was looking at Sabine Chastain's gaping, slit throat.

He gagged, pushing himself backward on the dirt floor— away from the horrible sight. Vomit spewed between his fingers, leaving a smelly path in the wake of his body. He came up against the barn wall with a thud, managing to gain his knees with its support, but knowing if he tried to stand, he'd lose the battle.

Turning his head, he emptied the rest of his stomach, the vileness of the gall giving him dry heaves for long, tortured minutes, which seemed like hours. When he finally gained control, he couldn't bring himself to turn his head back toward the body.

And it had to be a body. She couldn't conceivably still be alive with a wound like that. Yet could it be possible?

Reaching deep down inside him to a place where he didn't ever realize he had stored strength, Nick slowly turned his head.

Blood. There was blood everywhere. It covered the front of her, her breasts, her stomach, even her skirt. It had soaked into the ground, leaving a spongy and slick wide circle in the dirt. Turning the dust a sickening rusty color.

The smell. Oh, God, the smell. He'd cleaned animals he'd killed before, and helped butcher hogs on the plantation. But their blood had never smelled like this. Maybe it was because there was so much of it, but then, even the deer he helped butcher weren't any smaller than Sabine. And they didn't give off this metallic odor, this nauseating, almost sweet sourness.

He forced his gaze to her face. Her head lay back at a sharp angle from the rest of her body, and a glance showed him her spinal cord had been severed. More than likely, she hadn't suffered then. At least he had that much.

But . . . had he killed her? Or had—he shook his head. He couldn't remember. He couldn't even follow the thought to a conclusion. Had there been anyone else in the barn? Or was he falsely recalling another voice—hoping there had been? Otherwise, there was no doubt who had done the deed.

Nick threw back his head, covering his face and howling in pain. Emotional pain, a much deeper, slashing pain than physical pain. Finally realizing he had to look at Wendi, he took a deep, hollow breath and dropped his hands.

The hound growled viciously. It sprang, right at Nick, and he jerked in reaction, tumbling to the ground when the hound's body hit him. The animal leaped on past him, though, heading into the woods. Brush crackled, but it could have been the hound instead of whatever it was chasing. Or whoever.

Wendi moaned, catching his attention and filling him with relief.

He rose to his knees again and gently touched her shoulder, cupping her chin and turning her head toward him. He couldn't stop himself from examining her throat, releasing a sob when he saw it smooth and clear. Her head lolled, but her eyes flickered open, then closed. She was alive.

But how badly was she hurt?

"Wendi?" he said anxiously.

She didn't respond. God, he needed help. His damaged body wouldn't permit him to carry her all the way back to Belle Chene by himself. Cursing his weakness once again, he brushed a silky strawberry tress from her cheek, seeing the discoloration the curl had helped hide.

He bent forward and examined her more closely. The opposite side of her head was stained with blood, encrusted with dirt and leaves. Someone had hit her with something heavy, which had injured but not killed her.

Which had the attacker meant to happen?

But now wasn't the time for questions. Now he had to get Wendi back to Belle Chene and send for a doctor.

From the opposite fork from the direction the hound had taken, Nick heard a sound. His head sprang up alertly, and he staggered to his feet, prepared to protect Wendi if necessary. He hadn't brought a weapon, except for the pocketknife he carried for small chores now and then. Taking it from his trouser pocket, he snicked the blade open.

Lucian came into sight, his face wet with sweat and etched with concern. He hurried over to Nick while Nick closed the knife blade.

"I knew she was hurt," Lucian said with a frown. "I don't know how, but I knew it."

"Thank God you're here," Nick said. They could discuss anything else later. "Get back to Belle Chene and fetch a wagon from the stables. Bring some blankets, too, and tell your mother she has to come with you. If she doesn't, tell her I'll wring her neck when I get back, because Wendi needs her right now. She's been injured badly."

Lucian started off, but Nick grabbed his arm. "And tell

one of the stable hands to find Julian and have him send someone into New Orleans for a physician. Someone who's able to handle the fastest horse we have.''

"Yes, sir," Lucian replied.

A second later he disappeared down the trail, and the hound emerged from the woods. Nick ignored him, kneeling beside Wendi again and taking off his shirt. He gently lifted her head and cushioned it with the shirt, then stared helplessly at her. There was absolutely nothing else he could do until help arrived. She moaned again, moving her head from side to side, and he carefully cupped her chin once more to still it.

"Shhhhh, Wendi," he soothed. "It's going to be all right. I won't let anything else happen to you. Help's on the way."

He didn't know whether she lost consciousness or his words soothed her, but she stilled. The hound walked over to the other side of her and sat down, whining in its throat and drawing Nick's attention. Reaching out, he snared a piece of white cloth caught on a burr in the dog's coat.

He rubbed the cloth between his fingers. Coarse, it felt like the material used to sew everyday shirts, the ones the plantation owners and their sons wore when supervising the various chores on the plantation. He spread it out on his palm, noticing the irregular shape. Evidently the hound had caught part of the shirt of whomever it had chased in the woods, proving the noise had been made by a human.

And proving it had to be someone of the upper class. None of the workers wore white shirts. If they wore any at all, they were blue broadcloth.

Wendi moaned again, and Nick stuffed the piece of material into his pocket. He didn't dare pick Wendi up, as he longed to do, fearing he would do more damage. But God, how he wanted to pull her into his arms and comfort her.

He satisfied himself with lifting her hand and holding it for the seemingly unending period of time it took before he heard the wagon coming down the trail.

When he glanced over his shoulder, he was half thankful, half worried to see Cecile beside Lucian on the seat. The woman looked as ravaged as though it had been her injured instead of Wendi.

Eighteen

"I don't give a good goddamn what people think!" Nick roared at Cecile in the hallway. Glancing through the open door to where Wendi lay on the bed, with the doctor examining her, he lowered his voice. "I still own this damned plantation, and my word is law. I want a cot set up in that room beside the bed, and I'll be staying in there until Wendi wakes up. If there's one available, get one of the workers' wives who knows something about nursing to come and stay with her, also."

"I doubt very much any of the women on the plantation will agree to nurse Wendi if you continue to stay in the room, Nick," Cecile said. "For heaven's sake, think of propriety. Think what you're doing."

"Propriety be damned. I'll care for her myself if no one else will." No way in hell was he going to leave her until she came to. Until he could tell her what he could barely make himself believe. How he felt as soon as he saw her lying injured and as pale as death on the trail.

Cecile sighed tiredly, and for an instant guilt stabbed Nick. Deep circles darkened the skin beneath the woman's brown eyes, and she had aged physically way more than the ten years since he'd last seen her called for. She looked far too old to have a twelve-year-old son, but Lucian had told him his age on the ride from New Orleans to Belle Chene.

Funny. Nick didn't recall Lucian's birth two years before he left New Orleans. Usually word of the birth of a bastard son to someone like Cecile would have filtered through society's circles in town, whispered behind raised palms in judgmental tones. Especially given the supposition of the boy's sire. The rumormongers had sure as hell spread the other scandal fast enough.

"What if I try to get one or two of the workers' wives to come in and at least do the cooking and cleaning?" Cecile asked. "That way I can help you care for Wendi. But it will cost you extra for the wives' pay."

"Do whatever you want," Nick conceded, "as long as you forget about trying to make me leave her." The doctor turned to the black bag on the bedside table, taking his stethoscope from it. Nick asked Cecile in a tortured voice, "How badly do you think she's hurt?"

She followed his gaze to the bed. "Badly, Nick. I think you need to send someone into New Orleans and have them find Sybilla. Tell her what's happened and that she should come back out here."

Her words and somber tone sent a coldness laced with terror through him. Swaying, he put out a hand to steady himself against the door frame. She meant Sybilla had a right to see her niece while she was still alive.

"I won't let her go," he said with aching yearning. "I can't."

Cecile touched his arm. "Perhaps you'd be more useful if you tried to find out who did this to Wendi, instead of intruding on her care."

"I'll find out," he told her grimly. "And when I do, he'll pay. He'll pay for a long, long time—before I kill him."

Cecile clenched her mouth and frowned as though trying to decide whether or not to say something else. But Cecile would never speak without considering her words. He'd known her most of his life, so well he had no doubt the ravages on her face and her loss of weight were due to her deep grief over Jacques's death. No one allowed to glimpse them together could have doubted their devotion to each other.

"Why didn't he ever marry you?" he wondered aloud.

Cecile shuttered her eyes and turned away, heading for the rear stairwell. "I'm going to see what I can do about finding someone to help out. And I'll heat some more water. I'll need to bathe Wendi after the doctor is through. An injured person rests better during the healing if she's clean."

"Cecile?"

She paused and looked over her shoulder.

"You said during the healing. Do you think there's a chance she will recover?"

"There's always a chance, Nickie, love," she said, reminding him of his childhood and the endearing term she'd called him until he got too old for it. "Just have faith."

The doctor appeared at the bedroom door, and Nick's heart sank when he saw the man's grim expression. Stepping over to him, the doctor took Nick's arm, nodding his head at the front stairwell, indicating for them to go downstairs.

Nick balked. "I'm not leaving her."

The doctor looked at him in surprise, then contemplation, but Nick didn't give a damn. He could spread the news all over New Orleans that it appeared Nick Bardou was involved with the daughter of his father's mistress. The daughter of the woman Nick would probably have been convicted of killing, had there been just a shred more evidence. Nick didn't give a shit what he said. All he cared about right now was the man's report on Wendi.

"How is she?" he demanded.

Once again the doctor shook his head. "Bad," he said, echoing Cecile. "I can't make any type of prognosis at this point, but at least she's still alive. However, even if she does regain consciousness—"

"What?" Nick insisted when he broke off.

"There's an awful lot of injury to the side of her head—and to her brain inside. Whoever hit her used something meant to kill her. In cases like this, the brain swells from the injury, and her recovery depends on how her body handles that."

Nick took a deep breath, forcing out his next words. "You indicated that even if she regains consciousness, there might be permanent damage."

The doctor patted Nick's arm. "Let's don't worry about that until it happens," he soothed.

"I want the truth."

The doctor sighed. "The realm of possibilities doesn't allow me to know what the truth is, Monsieur Bardou. I've practiced medicine for thirty years, and I've seen other injuries like this. She can wake up or she can't. If she does, she could be herself after a recovery period, or she could have sustained damage that could leave her with anything from permanent physical injury to permanent brain injury. There's just no way to tell."

"Oh, God."

"He's the only one who can foretell what will happen, Monsieur," the doctor said. "Do you have someone available here to nurse her?"

"Yes."

"Then I'll be going. But I'll come back tomorrow, and every day until we see something happen. One way or the other."

Shoulders slumping, Nick nodded, unable to find the strength to detain the doctor any longer. Unable to find the strength to listen to any more macabre pronouncements of what might be. He'd asked for what he heard, but now wished he had left himself a small window of hope.

He couldn't even bring himself to do as Cecile asked—start an investigation to find the man who had done this to Wendi. Seek vengeance. Even vengeance wouldn't fill the hole left behind if Wendi died.

The sound of the doctor's footsteps faded down the stairwell, and Nick walked over to the bed. Flashes of the portrait back at the St. Charles Avenue manor house superimposed themselves on Wendi's face as she lay there. The old scandal rose up in his mind, then disappeared. Somehow he felt cleansed and totally empty.

The cleansing came from knowing he didn't care any longer about the scandal and what it had done to his life. Wendi being so near death set the priorities straight in his mind.

The emptiness came from the future yawning before him with the possibility of Wendi not sharing it. The possibility that her lovely body would lie in an above-ground tomb, at peace, but leaving him to suffer after the light of her in his life had been snuffed out.

He visualized her when he first saw her, when he disembarked from the ship so recently.

No, no that wasn't the first time. Once in a while he'd seen her as a child on Canal Street—been nudged by a friend who snickered and pointed her out. Pointed out the child of his father's mistress. The witch's daughter.

Even though it had been common knowledge that Wendi hadn't been fathered by Dominic, the sly innuendos came Nick's way anyway. God, how many times had Wendi lived through similar snide remarks? Or even been taunted to her face by other children in the neighborhood, trying to raise their own stature by lowering hers?

She'd been a vivacious child from what he remembered, never still whenever he chanced to see her skipping down the street. Usually she'd been at Sybilla's side, not Sabine's, he reflected. Strawberry braids bobbed on her back, and her dresses were always neat and clean. Once, though, he'd come upon her suddenly, kneeling beside a water-filled ditch as she swept a net around, a bucket of crawfish at her side.

She'd gazed up at him, blue eyes dancing with mischief and life. So much life. So much life now hidden behind those closed eyelids of unconsciousness. So much life hanging there behind the soft, delicate shields to her soul, waiting to either pass into the darkness or brighten into a flame of mischief again.

That child was a woman now. Last night had proved that to him beyond doubt. Though he hadn't been her first, he had no qualms that she'd never experienced anything like what happened between them. Their lovemaking had been the sort of joining each person dreams of finding one precious time in his life. The shattering, overwhelming blending of both body and soul that only happens with one certain person. The lucky ones nurtured that gift to their lives, cherished it, and revered it for the rest of their lives.

Instead, he'd left her in his bed as though she were a passing fancy. Stifled his feelings and kept the barriers around his emotions intact.

For a priceless flicker in time, he allowed himself to believe that, were he given the chance, he could tell her how he felt. Tell her he loved her. Ask her if she would have him. If she would forgive him.

She looked so peaceful there, her breasts barely rising and falling as she breathed. But at least they moved. Cecile had cleaned her face prior to the doctor arriving and helped the doctor wash out the wound to examine it further. Now a white bandage hid it from view, but the dark, ugly bruise had spread over her delicate features on the left side of her face.

His fault. His fault.

No, he could never tell her how he felt. It would be better for him to get the hell out of her life again. Hadn't his relationships with everybody he touched turned to disaster for what seemed like eons?

Pulling a straight chair in the room closer to the bed, he sank down into it and buried his face in his hands. This, too, was his fault. He should never have brought her out here to Belle Chene. Even worse was he had no idea why her presence had threatened someone. Why someone had tried to kill her.

For there was no doubt this was a deliberate attempt to murder her. To get her away from Belle Chene before she uncovered something that would damage someone else. That was the only thing that made sense.

Nick stifled a moan of agony, very near a sob. It was a two-edged sword. If someone was afraid of what would be uncovered, perhaps it meant he himself wasn't responsible for Sabine's death. But the woman lying near death in the bed had paid the price for this revelation.

He sensed rather than heard anything, raising his head to see Sybilla in the corner of the room, as though she had appeared there. Which she probably had. He couldn't find the fortitude to berate her, either, for her leaving and hurt-

ing her niece with her desertion or for using her magical
powers to show up here in the bedroom.

Sybilla walked over to the bed, reaching out a hand to
touch Wendi's face.

"I sent someone in to find you," Nick said. "But they
haven't had time to get there yet."

"I knew she was injured. I felt it. I—I had something to
do before I could come out here."

"Something more important than being with Wendi
when she was conceivably on the verge of dying?"

Sybilla didn't deny his indication of Wendi's possible
death, plummeting Nick's hopes even deeper. Suddenly he
didn't care whether what he was about to say made him
appear a fool or not.

"I want you to look into the future and see what happens
to her," he pleaded. "I have to know."

She gazed at him solemnly and sadly. "I can't. I've already tried."

He lunged from the chair and gripped her shoulders,
shoving her away from the bed and against the nightstand.

"Try again! Now! I'll pay you whatever you charge to
read for me. I'll pay you a hundred times that amount."

Sybilla dissolved in his hands, and when Nick whirled
around, she stood behind his chair, as solid as she'd been
when he held her.

"My powers have strengthened considerably once again,
since I arrived on Belle Chene property," she said. "You'll
not touch me if I decree it otherwise."

He gaped at her, clenching and unclenching his fists, then
slowly wilting to the floor. Gazing up at her, he whispered,
"I have to know. I'll give you all I own."

She watched him quietly for a few seconds, almost as
though she felt some compassion for his heartbreak. As

though she wanted to help him in some way. But then she shook her head.

"It's not about money, Nick. It's about karma and Fate and free will, all mixed together. Even the magic won't work if the potential results are counter to what's meant to be. But I don't guess you'll believe me unless you see for yourself."

Reaching into her skirt pocket, she pulled out a small crystal ball. Motioning to him, she went over to the lady's desk beside the window and placed the ball on the surface, then took the chair.

"This is my scrying speculum," she said when he limped over to join her. "Wendi uses a different type of speculum, an old glass fishing lure she found on the beach one day. But you saw that the first day you came to our house. Each witch uses what feels right to her."

She glanced over her shoulder when the bed clothing rustled, but it didn't appear that Wendi had moved. When he followed her gaze, Nick frowned. He'd thought the sheets were a little lower on Wendi's breasts a moment ago. Sybilla turned back to her speculum and cupped it with her hands, and he turned his attention back to her. Surely she would have sensed it had any other entity been in the room.

Sybilla whispered words he couldn't make out as they both gazed at the speculum. He wasn't exactly sure what it was supposed to do, but recalling the lure Wendi used and what had happened to it that day, he assumed it should at least emit a glow. But it stayed dead and dull.

He caught himself concentrating on the round crystal, fervent pleas voicing themselves in his mind but not passing his lips. The atmosphere in the room leaned toward oppressive, even with the windows wide open. A breeze filtered in, then died as though something had shut it off, the curtains fluttering to a dead stillness against the wall.

Yet the crystal remained cloudy and dull, unglowing.

At last Sybilla leaned back in the chair, pushing a strand of hair from her forehead. "It's no use. One of us isn't supposed to know, and it's obvious we would share with each other if we did see anything. Try to relieve the other person's distress, because we each care so deeply for her."

When he didn't answer, she continued, "You do love her, don't you Nick?"

"Yes," he barely breathed. "More than my own life."

"One thing I can tell you," she said, holding up a cautioning hand when he felt a stir of hope. "No, not about whether or not she will live. But part of the problem is, and will continue to be, the disruption of the karma. The unsettled threads of what is supposed to be. Until that's taken care of, even if Wendi wakes, the two of you won't be able to be together. You're star-crossed lovers, Nick, and you've evidently found and lost each other before."

"I never even knew her before," he denied, suddenly realizing what she meant. "You mean, in a previous life. I don't believe in that, Sybilla."

"You didn't believe in magic, either, Nick. Not before you returned to New Orleans and saw it happen for yourself."

Nick looked over at the bed, but Wendi hadn't moved. Cecile would probably return any minute, but he didn't care if she wondered how Sybilla had gained entrance.

"What about Miz Thibedeau?" he asked. "Wendi claims she's a powerful witch, and she's been living with me all this time without revealing herself."

"Thalia has a part in this. We're not sure exactly what, but the signs we were able to interpret told us she was to go to you and stay there until it was time for you to return to New Orleans."

"I feel like I've been manipulated."

"Fate manipulates all of us, Nick."

Confused and frustrated as he tried to understand her words, he glared at her. She'd been at this magic stuff lots longer than he'd been around it, and you'd think she could explain things in simpler terms.

This time she did read his mind.

"There aren't any simple terms, Nick. Nothing's clear until it happens. Sometimes the predictions aren't open to interpretation, but most of the time they are. It's like your religion, if you'll recall. There are various interpretations for a single verse in your Bible."

"Are you trying to tell me that Wendi's being injured like this was foreordained? That it's all a part of Fate's plan?"

"No." Sybilla stood. "Free will often throws a kink in Fate's plans for us, and no one can say that's not what happened here. Someone had a choice as to whether or not to hurt Wendi, or risk her uncovering something this person didn't want known."

Nick studied her carefully. That was the same conclusion he'd come to earlier, but unless Sybilla had been inside his mind, she couldn't have known that.

"I didn't read your mind that time," Sybilla said with a small smile. "Not even right now. It's not always necessary to use my magic. I could tell by looking at your face what you were thinking. Evidently, you believe our coming to Belle Chene is what set this into motion, also."

Nick reluctantly nodded.

"Wendi told you that day at our house that you might not have killed Sabine," Sybilla mused. "I believe the killer is here on the plantation. He . . . or she, as the case might be . . . has felt safe all these years. But your returning to New Orleans, your remaining here, now threatens him or her."

"As soon as she's able—I refuse to believe she will die," Nick said quietly. "As soon as she's able, I want you to take her back to New Orleans. I'll deed the St. Charles Street house over to you both and go back to California."

"Fate might have other plans, Nick. We'll see."

Nineteen

~~

"How is she?"

Julian's figure wavered in front of Nick's bleary-eyed gaze. After rubbing his face and refocusing, he saw his cousin had already bathed and redressed for the evening after his day in the fields supervising the work at Belle Chene. He supposed Julian was on his way over to Candlemas to see his fiancée. A vague thought passed through Nick's mind that Julian hadn't bothered to check on Wendi since she'd been brought back to the plantation in the wagon bed. To give him the benefit of a doubt, he probably assumed his place was keeping the plantation running smoothly, which it was.

"No change," Nick said.

"I hate to bother you," Julian said, nevertheless sounding determined to do exactly that.

Nick rose, shushing him until he left the room as quietly as he could and joined Julian in the hallway. Even then, he had scant attention for whatever problem he was about to hear. The entire goddamned plantation could burn down right now, and all he'd worry about would be rescuing Wendi in time.

He blew out an exhausted breath. That wasn't exactly true, but it had better be some huge clog in the wheels running the plantation to take him away from that high-poster bed behind him. Never could he recall caring this much about another person.

Julian cleared his throat, indiscreetly, it seemed to Nick. But the sound made Nick concentrate. "What is it?"

"Five of our workers quit this evening," Julian said bluntly. "They were all single men, who stayed in the community house together. But I think the only thing keeping some of the others here is the fact they have families and aren't ready to give up the cabins we provide as part of their salaries."

Hearing Cecile coming back up the rear stairwell, Nick motioned for Julian to go down the hallway. "I'll meet you in the study. We can talk there, where the noise won't disturb Wendi."

A brief hint of displeasure flickered in the twist of Julian's lips before he grunted an agreement and left. Cecile opened the rear stairwell door, balancing a small tray with a teacup on it. Her eyes slid past where Nick stood to the other end of the hallway where Julian had gone, then came back to him. She paused before going into the room, but didn't speak.

"I need to discuss some plantation business with Julian," Nick said. "But I won't be gone long."

She nodded, and Nick cast one lingering look into the room before he turned and went after Julian, following him to the study. Julian had two glasses of bourbon poured, and he handed Nick one when he entered.

"You look like you need this," Julian said.

"Thanks." Nick took a long swallow, then rounded the desk to sit in the padded chair. As before, a petulant look crossed Julian's face, but he settled across from Nick.

It was late evening, and the drapes were drawn and wall sconces lit. Any other time the masculine atmosphere of comfort would have soothed Nick, but now he ran a hand across the stubble on his face and sighed. He'd always had to shave twice a day, especially if he had an evening engagement, and he felt grubby and unkept, not at all in the mood to deal with what he had a feeling was coming.

Didn't matter. It wasn't going to go away. Hell, sometimes it didn't pay to be an adult.

Julian cleared his throat again.

"All right," Nick said. "Did the workers give a reason for quitting right in the middle of the season?"

Julian met his stare without blinking. "If you'll think a minute, you'll know why."

"I'm too goddamned tired and worried to think, Julian. Tell me what the hell they said when they quit."

He shrugged. "That they wouldn't work on a plantation where witches were living. I even offered to double their bonuses at the end of the season, but only one of them took that offer. The other five left anyway."

"You should've let the sixth one go without protest," Nick said, and Julian's eyes narrowed in anger at Nick questioning his judgment. "He'll just cause more problems by hanging around. And you'll have to do the same about the bonuses when he tells the rest of them what happened."

Julian gulped the rest of his drink and leaned forward, slamming the glass down on the desk. "And just where the hell do you think I'll get more workers this late in the season? Every other plantation already has its crews in place, and the rest of the men available are the dregs. Most of Belle Chene's workers have been with us since after the war, and I could depend on them. It would be more work than it was worth to hire lazy help and have to stand over them to get them to do what was needed!"

"I don't care." Nick rose to his feet, his leg protesting with a sharp stab of pain, which had gotten worse all day long. He should have taken time to drink the cup Cecile was bringing him before he joined Julian. The last cup he'd had was the one Wendi conjured up for him at noon.

Noon. God, it seemed like a week ago.

Limping over to the sideboard, he poured his own glass full of bourbon again while Julian glared at him. Damn, he barely recalled drinking the first glass, but he felt it in his belly if not in diminished pain. Picking up the decanter, he held it out toward Julian, quirking his eyebrow in question. The glower on Julian's face told Nick a thin restraint kept his cousin from attacking him.

Good. Let him. It would give Nick an excuse to vent some of his worry in rage.

"Now what the hell's wrong?" Nick prodded.

Julian's jaws clenched before he visibly relaxed, disappointing Nick while at the same time making him realize fighting wouldn't help anything. Picking up his glass, Julian walked over, waited until Nick poured him a drink, then took his seat again. His deadly silence was more clamorous than if he had shouted whatever thoughts he barricaded in his mind.

Nick took his own seat again, leaning back and drinking, letting the silence linger. If Julian had more to say, he would have to say it without further prompting. Damn, he was tired and wrung out.

At last Julian spoke. "You're forgetting something, cousin. You've got whatever businesses you've started out West to provide for you. All I've got is Belle Chene."

Nick nodded an acknowledgment. "But if I remember right, you told me that the lovely Felicite is an only child. Or is now, anyway. Her brother was killed in war. So Candlemas will be yours after the two of you are wed."

"Probably, but her father hasn't said," Julian admitted. "Felicite said more than once he's threatened to sell the place as soon as he has her wed. Travel for his remaining years with his wife on the money he gets."

"I see." Nick drained his glass, too tired to rise and get another drink. The bourbon didn't kill the pain nearly as well as the brandy used to. Or was he just used to the other medications Wendi had shown him how to use?

Wendi. Oh, God, why had he ever brought her to Belle Chene? If she died here—

"How would you feel if I said I was going to go ahead and deed Belle Chene over to you?" Nick asked Julian.

Julian quickly tempered the astonished look on his face with a skeptic grin. "Sure."

"I'm not kidding, Julian. You're the only male Bardou heir besides me, and I have no plans at all to remain in Louisiana. If I did . . ." He didn't know where those words came from, but he continued, "Even if I did, it wouldn't be here at Belle Chene. The memories would never allow me any peace. And I'd have more trouble than you keeping workers."

Julian leaned forward eagerly. "Are you serious, then? You'd give me Belle Chene?"

Nick rose. "Consider whatever operating profits you get this year your own money, without any percentage to me. As soon as Wendi's out of danger, I'll send word to my lawyer in the city, Justin Rabbonir, and have him draw up the papers. In the meantime, you can assure any other workers who give you problems that I'll be taking Wendi out of here as soon as she's able to travel."

Julian kept his seat, shuttering his eyes and taking a swallow of bourbon. "Then," he said when he lowered the glass, "you feel she'll recover."

"No," Nick admitted, wanting to get back to Wendi. He

clenched his fists and gulped back the rising dread through a tightening throat. "I mean, I don't know for sure. Even the doctor can't say. But I'll take her away from this hellhole one way or the other."

Leaving the study, he headed up the stairwell. At the top, he nearly collided with Sybilla.

"I was just coming to get you," Sybilla said, tears streaming down her face.

"No." Nick could barely force the word out. Blood roared thunderously in his mind, and pain he thought would kill him exploded in his chest. He staggered and hit the wall, covering his face with his hands.

"Nick. Nick!" Sybilla grabbed his arms and shook them. "She's not dead. She's awake, Nick."

The words penetrated the cacophony in his mind, but he couldn't make himself understand them. He stared at Sybilla in confusion.

"I can't believe it myself—not this soon," she said. "But she's awake, Nick. She's not able to say very much, and she's going to drift back to sleep any minute. But she's going to live."

Stunned, Nick couldn't move for a moment. Then a wild sort of joy filled him. Shoving past Sybilla, he raced down the hallway. Cecile blocked the doorway, holding up her hand but with a slight smile on her face.

"Don't scare her to death, Nickie," she said. "She's still very, very ill."

Nick nodded, head bobbing as though controlled by a puppet string until he thought he'd never get it to stop. He took deep breaths, all the while peering past Cecile. God, he didn't want to do anything to counteract Wendi's recovery, but he wanted to be close to her so badly he ached with yearning.

"Love means doing what's best for the one you care

for,'' Cecile said. She stepped aside. ''Go on over there, Nick, but don't tell her how awful she looks.''

He stepped forward, his boot landing with a clump on the bare floorboard before the carpet began. On the bed Wendi opened her eyes, a slight smile curving her lips when she saw him. He gulped and took another step, this one quiet, since he'd reached the carpet. Then another one. Weakly Wendi lifted one pale hand and beckoned to him. He crossed the room in two more strides, taking her hand and bringing it to his lips.

He kissed her hand. ''I love you,'' he said.

Her blue eyes smiled tolerantly at him. ''You don't have to say that,'' she whispered. ''But thank you for the thought.''

He sat down in the chair, never letting go of her hand. ''You don't understand—''

''I do,'' she interrupted. ''You thought I was going to die, so you've got a whole lot of pity and sorrow for the way you treated me built up in you. It's all right, Nick.'' She squeezed his fingers, then shut her eyes. ''It's all right.''

Her breathing softened, and Nick stared wildly at Cecile and Sybilla, who had joined him at her bedside. Cecile removed Wendi's hand from his, tucking it beneath the bedsheet.

''She needs to rest now, Nick. This time it won't be unconsciousness, but a healing rest. True sleep. It's probably better if you leave now.''

''No.''

''Yes, Nick,'' Sybilla put in. ''Your frantic worry is disturbing the healing vibrations in the room. It will be better if you get some rest yourself now.''

He rose to his feet. ''My worry didn't disturb the vibrations while I was waiting in here for her to wake up!''

"Shhhh," Sybilla said. "That was a good sort of worry, Nick. It probably even hastened her returning to consciousness. But now it can cause problems."

He looked at Cecile, hoping for assistance.

"It's for the best right now, Nick," Cecile said.

Capitulating, Nick bent over the bed and tenderly kissed Wendi's forehead. He'd talk to her later about this stupid notion that he'd only admitted his love to her out of pity. She wasn't fully cognizant yet of what she said or thought. She couldn't be. She'd feel differently when she regained full use of her faculties. When she was farther on the road to healing.

He tenderly caressed her cheek with the back of one finger, but she didn't wake again. She would wake, though, and she wouldn't have any permanent damage from the injury. She'd known him and spoken rationally. Not logically, but rationally. He could hardly contain his elation.

Reluctantly he left the room and Wendi's care to the women. At the bottom of the stairwell, he found Julian waiting. His cousin gave him a questioning look.

"She's going to recover," Nick told him, unable to repress a huge grin.

"Then perhaps you regret your hasty decision about Belle Chene."

Nick frowned at him, perturbed that Julian appeared more concerned about that damned plantation than Wendi's recovery. But hell, it wasn't his cousin's woman lying up there hurt. His cousin was on his way to see the woman he wanted to spend his life with, so he supposed Julian's concerns were founded.

"I'll write a note to Justin in the morning," he told Julian, "instructing him to draw up a deed transferring Belle Chene to you. Will that be soon enough?"

Julian dropped his gaze. "That will be fine, Nick.

And—'' He took a breath. ''And I'm happy Miss Chastain will recover, for your sake. I assume you'll have some tidings yourself for us soon?''

Understanding immediately what he meant, Nick shook his head firmly. What on earth had given Julian the notion that he and Wendi might wed? ''No. No, of course not. As soon as we have things settled here, I'll be going back to California.''

''Without Miss Chastain?''

''Without her,'' Nick acknowledged.

''But it seemed like—''

''Without her,'' Nick said more sternly. ''But I'll see that she's taken care of.''

A near sneer lifted one corner of Julian's mouth, but he looked at Nick and evidently thought better of his words. Instead, he tilted his head in a leave-taking and walked out the front door.

Nick turned to gaze back up the stairwell. Julian's sneer was tantamount to the same type of attitude Wendi's mother had faced when word leaked out that she was his father's mistress. Could he really expect Wendi to face that type of censoring, judgmental gossip the rest of her life?

Making a slightly different decision, he headed for the study. He'd go ahead and prepare the instructions for Justin this evening, and also have him find a minister.

He'd go ahead and marry Wendi before he left. He still didn't intend to remain in Louisiana, but it would leave her more protected as his wife than just his former mistress. It would prove his love to her, negating that stupid idea in her mind that what he felt was only pity.

Twenty

Wendi was not an easy patient. And, not surprisingly after the reaction of the workers on Belle Chene to her presence, none of the wives stepped forward to help with either the nursing care or the housework. By the end of the third day of her recovery, even Nick found himself avoiding the room—or at least, asking someone to see if she was awake or asleep before he went to check on her, so he could gird himself one way or the other for the encounter.

Asleep, she was a beautiful princess, ensconced in snowy sheets and the spiderweb throw covering the bed, her hair and pink cheeks the only spots of color besides the cherry wood posts and head- and footboards. Awake, she was a petulant witch, frustrated both by her weakness and the fact Sybilla's prediction about her magic had come true. Until she healed completely, she wouldn't be able to perform even the simplest magic.

Unfortunately for herself and Cecile, Sybilla had conjured up a small bell for Wendi to use if she woke and found no one there to take care of her needs. More unfortunately, Sybilla had given the bell a tinkling quality unlike anything anyone had ever heard before. The tone, instead of a pleasant sound like wind chimes, had a flat, off pitch, which made a person grit his teeth when it reverberated against his eardrums. Nick swore the sound penetrated even the far walls of the manor house.

At least no one ever missed hearing it!

Sybilla met Nick at the bottom of the stairwell. "Cecile's turn with her," she responded with a relieved sigh to his unspoken inquiry. "And I need to ask you something."

"Should we go into the study?"

"No. No, I just want to know if you have any objections to Thalia returning. I think I can talk her into it, but not if you're going to make her feel unwelcome here."

Nick's stomach chose that moment to growl loudly, and Sybilla smiled in understanding.

"Neither Cecile nor I have had much time to cook lately, have we?" she asked.

"And what you have cooked hasn't been—uh—" Nick floundered to a stop, cheeks flushing in embarrassment, but Sybilla only laughed.

"That's one of the things Thalia can take over," she said, grinning when Nick's hand settled on his stomach. "And I'll admit, I need her vast experience here with me. Wendi's asking questions about when her magic will return, and I don't have answers for her."

Nick stared up the stairwell, shaking his head. When had his conceptions changed? A month ago, if someone had told him he would be standing there discussing magic with a witch, along with the problems some other witch was having with her magic, he would have laughed. No, he would have probably thought the other person had escaped from a loony bin. Now, he couldn't decide if he was the crazy one or if Sybilla was. Or both of them.

Sybilla's eyes twinkled when he looked at her, and he knew at once she'd been inside his mind. Rather than piss him off, he was glad he didn't have to discuss his confusion out loud.

"Bring her back if you can," he said. "And if she's coming by air, have her bring a load of crawfish with her." He winked at Sybilla, then turned to the front door when someone knocked. "I'll get it. You go ahead and contact Miz Thibedeau."

When he opened the door, Justin Rabbonir stood there, with another slighter-statured man, who glanced around apprehensively. Even without the telltale collar, Nick established the man as a minister. He quirked a brow at Justin.

"Hello, Nick," the lawyer replied. "I know you thought I might not make it out here until tomorrow, but here I am. And this is Reverend Coglin. You said you didn't care whether we had a priest or not, and the reverend is a new arrival to our city."

Not new enough not to have heard the tales of witches at Belle Chene, Nick thought, immediately gleaning the reason for the man's fearful attitude. But a newly arrived minister would need funds to prove his mettle, and he'd told Justin to pay whatever it took to get a minister here. He held out a hand to the man, although it took the reverend a few seconds to notice the outstretched palm. Finally he gave a weak response.

"I've also got the paperwork started on the transfer of the plantation, Nick, but we've run into a snag," Justin said.

Nick motioned them on into the house, closing the door behind them as Justin continued, "They haven't got the records at the courthouse updated yet, showing that your taxes are all taken care of. They did cancel the tax sale, but their clerk left without notice to head for California, and they're still trying to straighten out a mess of paperwork he left behind. A few dollars under the table put your paperwork on the top of the pile, and they're supposed to have everything ready for me tomorrow.''

"Fine, Justin. Now, does the reverend understand what he's here for?''

Nick carefully watched Reverend Coglin's face while he asked the question. To give him credit, the small man nodded and answered for himself, indicating he did. But his huge Adam's apple bobbed and his fingers twisted like snakes in the Garden of Eden around the back of the Prayer Book he held. Nick shook his head in disgust, but turned toward the stairwell.

"Let's go up and tell Wendi what's going to happen,'' he said.

Justin grabbed his arm. "Whoa, Nick. What do you mean? You haven't told your bride there's going to be a wedding today? You haven't asked her to marry you?''

Nick shook off the hold. "Don't worry, there isn't any problem. You did bring the license, didn't you?''

"Yes, but—''

Nick caught sight of Sybilla down the hallway, and motioned for her to join them. "Have you . . . uh . . .''

"She's not responding,'' she said. "What's going on here? Are you taking these men up to Wendi's room instead of speaking with them in your study?''

"Yes, and you might want to be there, also,'' Nick told her. "Come along.''

He turned, hiding his grin. He didn't know if it was possible to keep Sybilla out of his mind, but he schooled himself to think of nothing, just in case she tried one of her intrusive quests. Leading the group up the stairwell and down the hall, he went on into Wendi's room without pausing to ask for admittance.

She was actually up on the side of the bed, and she flashed him a beautiful smile at first. Then she noticed the others and hurried into the wrapper Cecile was helping her don, gripping the collar tightly.

"Nick?" she asked.

"How are you feeling, darling?" he asked.

She gave him a puzzled look at his use of the endearment.

None of the group followed him over to the bed, instead, waiting by the door as though they sensed a dangerous atmosphere in the room. Even Cecile left him and joined Sybilla. Nick heard a couple undertoned whispers, but he concentrated on Wendi, who hadn't answered him yet. In fact, she was staring past him at the group by the door.

"Nick," she repeated, this time more in a warning than questioning tone.

He lowered his voice. "Look, Wendi, I should have discussed this with you, but I wasn't sure whether Justin was coming out today or tomorrow."

"So what? For what?"

Suddenly Nick wasn't as certain he was doing the right thing. He hesitated, wishing for a moment he could read inside Wendi's mind, as she could his at times. Immediately he realized he didn't need to read more than the spark of suppressed outrage in her lovely eyes.

"Why have you brought these men into my room?" she asked when he tried to think of his next words. "Isn't that one man a minister? The one carrying the Prayer Book?"

"Oh." He glanced over his shoulder. "I'm sorry, darling. I didn't think that you might be uncomfortable with men in your bedroom. But you aren't well enough to be up and about, so I didn't want to bother asking you to dress and come downstairs. This won't take long, and we can get it over with so you can lie back down."

"Get what over with?" With gritted teeth this time.

"Wendi." He lowered his voice even further. "Maybe

you haven't thought about this, but it's possible you might be with child.''

"I'm not." Flatly.

"Well, even if not, we did spend the night together. And I've got to get back to California soon. Before I go, I'm going to deed the St. Charles Street mansion over to you, and I'll set up funds for you at the bank. As my wife, you—"

"Your what!''

Her gazed speared him, and Nick actually took a step back. He held out a cautioning hand. Had he maybe suspected this reaction from her? Was that why he'd held off discussing it with her and brought people into the room with him when he did? Hoping she might not embarrass herself in front of a group of others? Embarrass him?

If so, he was wrong. Almost dead wrong.

Injured, she shouldn't have been able to move so fast, but she did. Grabbing the pitcher on the nightstand beside the bed, she heaved it at his head. He brought his forearm up in time to deflect it, but water showered over him, drenching him. He had to wipe his eyes before he could see again.

The pitcher hit the floor behind him, shattering despite the carpet covering the floorboards. Footsteps clattered down the hallway, but he didn't dare look behind him to see if anyone at all had stayed to support him. Wendi was searching for another weapon.

"Look," he said. Then he remembered something and plunged his hand into his trouser pocket, pulling out a small box. Ducking her next missile, a vase of flowers that shattered on the bedpost he dodged behind, he quickly opened the box and held it out to her.

"Wendi, look, I even brought you a ring. It's been in my family for ages.''

"Get the hell out of here!" she shrieked. Damn, how could an injured woman have such a piercing voice? "Oh, if I only had my magic back! You'd be a toad right now! Worse than that, a snake! Yes, an ugly, slimy snake!"

"Now, listen," he said, stepping out from behind the bedpost and realizing his mistake at once. She'd hidden a candy dish beside her, just waiting for him to make a clearer target. It hit him in the chest, and when he tried to grab it, it ricocheted off his hand and hit him in the mouth.

Both the ring and the candy dish fell to the floor as he lifted a hand, pulling it away from his lip with a stain of blood on one finger. He looked at Wendi in time to catch a faint hint of worry on her face, but she quickly masked it.

"You're not hurt that badly. Not nearly as badly as you should be! Get out!"

"Fine!" he shouted in return. "When you're ready to talk about this sensibly, you let me know. Until then, I'm going to be making plans to get back to California, where the people are rational!"

"I'll talk about this again when hell freezes over," she gritted. "And you can't get back to California soon enough to suit me!"

"Fine!" he shouted again.

"Fine!" she snarled back.

Nick stormed out of the room, and Wendi sat there in the silence, her anger slowly seeping away to be replaced by an intense, abiding wound in her emotions. How could he? How could he speak of wanting to marry her as "something to get over with?"

Oh, she hated him. She'd never before in her life felt this deep, enduring hatred for another person. The moment the thought flashed in her head, she knew she was lying. It wasn't hate—it was love. Thwarted love. He didn't love her in return. All he wanted was to pay her off and leave. Pay her off in the form of giving her a house and his name, but not himself.

Thalia materialized in the corner of the room, and Wendi didn't even care that the other woman was witnessing her misery. Not bothering to remove the wrapper, she sniffed and laid back on the bed, refusing to wipe at the tears streaming down her face. She didn't feel like talking, and maybe Thalia would go away if she ignored her.

"Would you like me to help you regain your magic faster?" Thalia asked.

That got Wendi's attention. She sat up, the quick movement making her head spin, but not nearly as much as it had the last few days.

"Yes," she said. "As quickly as possible."

"You have to want it for the right reason," Thalia warned, moving closer. "Not to turn Nick Bardou into a toad or a slimy snake, but to contact your mother and right this disturbed mess of karma."

"The karma's completely tranquil as far as the relationship between Nick and me is concerned," Wendi said angrily. "I only want my magic back so I can finish up here and go home. I never want to see Nick again."

Thalia smiled enigmatically, but nodded. "Then I'll help you. Sabine's been here anyway, because you wouldn't be so chipper if she hadn't come by and already started your healing."

"You know," Wendi mused, "if that's true, I don't know if I give a darn whether I help right this disturbed karma or not. Why didn't she let me know she was here? If she was."

"I truly don't know," Thalia said with a shrug. "Spirits on the other side know more than us about when the time is right for certain things. Maybe part of the reason you can't contact her is exactly because you haven't fulfilled your duties as to doing what you can to correct the karma."

Wendi sighed and quirked her lips in disgust as she sorted through that convoluted statement. Right now she didn't much give a damn about her mother's problems. A true mother would care that her daughter's life had just been shattered. Would contact her daughter to give her what comfort she could, instead of dwelling on her own spiritual problems. Even dead, a witch had that ability.

Then she experienced a stab of selfishness, and laid her head back on the pillow. "Tell me what I have to do."

"You're not going to like it," Thalia warned.

"I haven't liked a lot of things that have happened the last month. What now?"

"You need to apologize to Nick and ask him not to leave. You need to keep him here in order to have him help you with the séance."

"No!" She sat up, crossing her arms over her chest and ignoring the swirl of vertigo. "I'll do anything else, but I won't do that!"

"Yes. Yes, you will, Wendi," Thalia refuted. "Otherwise, I won't be able to help you."

"He'll never believe me, after the scene we just had. And I refuse to tell him I'll marry him. I won't lower myself to being a liar, even though by now the rest of New Orleans probably thinks I'm as much of a whore as they thought my mother was after the tales that doctor carried out of here. And I'll *never* marry Nick Bardou!"

"You don't have to go that far. Just mollify him. He's hurting, too, you know."

"Sure," Wendi snarled. "The only thing on him hurting is his lip, where the candy dish hit him."

Thalia sighed and walked over to the bed, sitting down

in the chair Nick always used and fixing Wendi with a resigned gaze. She let the silence linger until Wendi could hear each breath of breeze flowing in the windows and each brush of the lace curtains on the windowsills.

"Nick's never fallen in love before, Wendi," she finally said. "He doesn't know how to handle it. He's scared."

"That's for sure. He's a coward," she said unthinkingly.

"He feels that way about himself, too."

Thalia's words stabbed straight into Wendi's heart. "What do you mean?"

"He's blamed himself for years for what happened here. And for not being with his mother when she committed suicide. Maybe he could have stopped her, he thinks. Taken her away and taken care of her, somewhere she wouldn't have faced the judgment of the society that was her life-blood. Do you know he also blames himself for your getting hurt?"

"He didn't have anything to do with that."

"You don't know Nick nearly as well as I do," Thalia said, "despite having made love to him. I lived with that man for five years, and I knew him and his family all their lives. Their ancestors before that. I didn't become this powerful of a witch by only living one lifetime measured in human terms."

Wendi nodded a petulant agreement. Some witches *could* live longer lives.

"I know what made Nick's parents the people they were," Thalia continued, "and what made Nick into the embittered man he became. And you, my child, are not the right woman for him yet, so don't worry about me trying to force you to marry him. That's not what it's going to take to soothe the karma."

Resentment filled Wendi, and her glare clashed with that

of the older witch. "I was enough of a woman for Colin. Enough of a woman for Nick to bed!"

"But not enough of a woman to make Nick want to stay here instead of running back to California," Thalia reminded her, mixing hurt into the resentment in Wendi's heart. "Make no mistake, Wendi Chastain. He *does* love you. More than he's able to admit now. And there's room yet for that love to grow into something better than what it is at this point."

"Let me tell you this," Wendi snapped. "I'm getting extremely tired of kowtowing to some poor man's easily injured feelings. Or his inability to understand his feelings and come to terms with them and what they mean as far as a change in his lifestyle! I'm tired of playing second fiddle to some man's desire to be nurtured and comforted at the peril of my own happiness. I let Colin talk me into getting married so he'd have someone to share his life and bed, then let him go when he realized he had made a premature decision. Realized he'd settled for liking and that love had finally walked into his life with Cassandra. I'm ready to have my own feelings be the most important for a change."

"Growing up means understanding that things don't come easy, Wendi. Things worth having are worth waiting for and worth building."

"So, if I were a mature enough woman, I could understand that, I suppose. Understand that it's worth waiting for Nick to realize he loves me enough to be a full husband to me and admit that to me."

"Not exactly, but partially. It's not totally your fault, Wendi. In fact, the scales of fault are not even balanced heavier on your side. Nick has a lot of demons to work through, and until that happens, he'll continue to be an extremely unhappy man."

She rose to her feet. "Wait a couple days, my dear. Let your body heal and your magic return. Nick's not going anywhere, even though he thinks he is. And when you talk to him again, perhaps you might try to get him to explain his resentment toward his father."

Before Wendi could ask her to explain further, Thalia faded from sight. It didn't matter. She'd given Wendi scads of information to try to comprehend. It would take her days to work through all of it in her mind.

She laid her head back, willing her mind to start the examination, but falling asleep instead.

Twenty-one

~~

Nick glanced in the mirror across the room. God, was that him? Sitting up in bed with his arms crossed, a stupid, petulant pout on his face? He looked like a child in a man's body!

He glanced at the sheet covering his lower body. And he damned sure was a man, with the evidence to prove it this morning! His dreams had been filled with a strawberry-blond witch, who appeared as solid as any woman until he tried to take her in his arms. Then she faded into mist, a high-pitched laughter sounding like that damned bell she used ringing throughout the room. His hardness was as much the result of a night of frustrated dreams as the usual morning state.

Sliding out of bed, he stomped into the washroom. Tried to stomp, anyway. More like limped, since his leg was advertising his restless night this morning. He'd barely been in the washroom more than a minute before he heard someone knocking on the door.

"Come in!" he shouted.

The door opened, and Nick continued stirring the shaving

cream in his cup into foam. The hell with it. Whoever needed to talk to him could come to the door of the washroom. He had a towel around his waist in case it was a female.

Someone cleared his throat—a male sound—and Nick saw Julian in the doorway. "You just getting in from Candlemas?"

"I brought you a carafe of coffee," his cousin said instead of answering the inquiry. "It's on your nightstand."

Nodding, Nick swiped a brushful of shaving cream across one jaw.

"Look," Julian said. "Can we talk a minute before you get involved in shaving?"

"I can talk and shave at the same time," Nick growled. "What do you want?"

When Julian remained quiet, Nick gave a resigned sigh and set the cup down. Grabbing another towel, he wiped his face and walked past Julian when his cousin stepped from the doorway. On the nightstand, he found two cups of coffee already poured, a pleasant, welcoming mist of steam rising from them. He handed one cup to Julian and drank half of his in one swallow.

"Now." He held the cup, ready to finish the coffee. "What do you need so early in the morning?"

"Do you realize that some of the workers on both Belle Chene and Candlemas share relatives?" he asked.

"So?"

"I understand there was a minister here at Belle Chene last evening."

"True." Nick finished his coffee and poured another cup.

"Are you going to tell me why he was here?" Julian asked.

"It's not important now," Nick said. "If the people are speculating, let them wonder."

"Damn it, Nick, sometimes speculation leads to trouble. It's better to nip the rumors in the bud and put out the correct information!"

"Not this time." Nick set his cup down without drinking. "I need to get dressed, Julian. If there's anything else you want to discuss with me, meet me in the study after breakfast."

Julian glared at him, but Nick knew he would never force a confrontation with the prospect of owning Belle Chene still dangling under his nose.

"By the way," Nick said. "The rumormongers should have also mentioned that Justin Rabonnir was here. He reported that there was a snag in the paperwork he needed to draw up the deed transferring Belle Chene to you. He should have it ready today, though."

Julian's jaws clenched, but he gave a curt nod. "I've already had breakfast," he said. "I'll be out in the fields if you need me for anything."

He left, and Nick stared at the doorway for a moment. He couldn't help wondering why Julian hadn't asked him to meet Felicite and her family. Of course, he knew them already, but you'd think Julian would want to renew the relationship between the two families, if nothing else than because it was considered a proper courtesy. Usually a man paraded his betrothed in front of friends and family, whether he was actually in love with her or not. Marriage was as important a part of the southern culture as the birth of an heir.

He headed back into the washroom to shave and bathe. For that matter, you'd think Felicite's family would have made a move when they learned Nick was in residence at Belle Chene, perhaps inviting him to dinner. Julian hadn't said anything about an engagement party, either, and with him spending nights sneaking in and out of Felicite's bedroom, you'd think they'd be worried she'd get with child. An early-born babe would offer some speculation of its own to the gossips.

Of course, the betrothal wasn't official at this point, so maybe that was the hold-up. Or . . . Nick frowned into the mirror. More likely, they were waiting until he left before things proceeded. Nick couldn't blame them there. The attention would probably be on him instead of the betrothed couple at any gathering he attended.

They might have to wait a while then. Even though he'd told Wendi that he was on the verge of leaving, he couldn't just up and go like that. He couldn't leave her behind without some arrangements to take care of her, so he wouldn't have to worry whether she had food and clothing on a day-to-day basis. Without giving one more try at getting her to marry him, so she would be safe.

He firmed his resolve while he dressed, heading for the manor house totally assured of his goal. He entered through the rear of the house, and at the foot of the front stairwell, he stopped as though a gate blocked the steps. Touching the small cut on his lip, he gazed upward. Wendi's room was at the rear of the second-floor hallway, too far for him to be able to hear any voices even if she had her door open.

Straightening his shoulders, Nick climbed halfway up the stairwell, then stopped. Damn, maybe he'd better give her a little more time to cool off. She'd had a pretty horrible temper tantrum yesterday evening.

Yeah, he'd let her cool off a little more. Check with Sybilla as to the state of Wendi's temper before he made an appearance in her room.

He practically ran back down the stairs and headed for the study, although his leg protested the hasty effort. He'd check to see if Julian had perhaps changed his mind and left a note about any other problem they needed to discuss, then go get breakfast—

When Nick halted in the study doorway, Wendi rose from one of the chairs in front of the desk. Ethereal and beautiful in her filmy white gown and robe, she made Nick think for just a fleeting instant she might be a ghost. Or maybe the ghost of Sabine. Instead of fading away like she did in his dreams last night, though, she remained a tangible presence.

A womanly presence. Completely. The gown and robe did more to tantalize than hide, and the part of Nick that was tantalized let him know about it. It thudded to prominent attention when Nick saw a tiny, bare set of toes peeping out from beneath the gown.

Damn, he needed to get behind the desk, especially when he realized Wendi was aware of his response. The secret smile and the catlike gleam in her eyes told him that. He wouldn't be surprised if she licked her lips in anticipation.

But she didn't. Instead, she ducked her head shyly, the innocent gesture causing a greater uproar in him than if she'd continued to remind him of a prowling feline, especially when she sneaked a peek at him through her lashes.

"Uh—aren't you supposed to be in bed?" he asked. The corner of her mouth curled in reaction to his words, and she kept her eyes on him.

"Uh—I mean—uh—in your room. Yeah, in bed, too, but—You're still recovering. Don't you need to be lying down? Resting, I mean?"

She giggled and sat down in the chair. "I need to talk to you, Nick," she said. "And I'm lots better. Even Aunt Sybilla said I needed to start getting up now and then. That moving around would hasten my recovery more than lying in bed."

Nick hurried around the desk and took his seat. When he noticed Wendi's gaze on his mouth, he touched the small cut with one finger. "It's nothing," he reassured her worried look. "It doesn't even hurt this morning."

"How's your leg?"

"It could use a massage," he said, his voice lowering of its own accord to a sensuous growl. Clenching his fists, he shook his head. What the hell was wrong with him? She was recovering from injuries of her own, and here he was hinting she needed to expend the energy to soothe his pain.

"But it's really not that bad," he said. "Really. What's important now is your regaining your health. Uh—" He stared around the room. "Uh—is your magic—Has it—?"

"I warmed the water in my pitcher this morning so I could bathe," she said, and Nick visualized her naked, with drops of water clinging to hidden, delectable places. Visible, delectable places, too.

Suddenly she placed something on the desk, getting his attention. "I wanted to give this back to you," she said. "You left it in my room."

Nick stared at the velvet ring box. His physical desire drained away, replaced by a deep, abiding emotional pain in his heart and a hollow feeling in his stomach. She could have cut his heart out and laid it beside the box and not caused him as much pain as her returning the ring did. Until that moment, he'd still had hope—hope she might overcome her anger at him and think of the repercussions of their lovemaking.

She sat there waiting for some response, but he had no idea what to say. Shit, the pain was so intense, he might cry if he tried to talk. That would be a hell of a note, wouldn't it, letting her know how deep his feelings ran. She very obviously only wanted an opportunity to explore this disrupted karma thing, and his ownership of Belle

Chene meant she had to go through him to do that. She'd made it extremely clear ever since he returned that her magic and smoothing this disrupted karma were the most important things in her life.

It would be a hell of a note to let her know he'd fallen in love with her, when she only wanted him for permission to be at Belle Chene.

Sighing as though tired of waiting, she rose to her feet. He kept his eyes on the ring box. Were he to look at her, he might make a total fool of himself. Beg her to reconsider. Tell her he wanted her to marry him because he loved her, not just because she might be carrying his child. Not just because he couldn't live in California and be worried about how she was surviving half a continent away.

Tell her maybe he'd been wrong. Maybe he should think about them having a real marriage—one where he could take care of her every day himself. Watch any child he put in her belly be born and grow up into a man or woman they could both be proud of.

Who the hell was he, though, Nick Bardou the possible murderer and destroyer of his family, to think he might have a chance at love?

Aware of every nuance of movement, he listened to Wendi turn away. Satin rustled against silken skin, and bare feet padded across the carpet, then the floor just inside the door. Then down the hallway.

He very carefully got to his feet. Leaving the ring on the desk undisturbed, he headed out the door. He had to get out of here or go crazy. He had an almost unrestrainable urge to destroy everything in the study. Start throwing things, as Wendi had the previous day.

Instead, he'd go riding. On horseback, rather than in a buggy. The pain that caused in his leg might eventually override the emotional pain he felt.

If not, so be it. What ever made him think that Nick Bardou deserved to be happy, after all the misery he left in his wake the past ten years?

He didn't come home all night. Wendi knew, because she only half slept once she finally went to bed after an endless day. Her emotions ran the gamut from hurt that he hadn't even attempted to talk her into keeping the ring to outrage at his obtuseness. Couldn't he see she wanted him to tell her that he loved her, instead of just offering her marriage in case she was with child?

The gamut peaked at fury. How could he think for one minute she'd abide a marriage where her husband lived completely across the continent from her? Damn it, she might someday find a man who actually loved her in return, find someone who was willing to build the relationship Thalia Thibedeau seemed to think there could be between a man and woman. Some man who believed love could be whispered in the same breath as commitment. And divorces weren't as easy to get in Nick's world as they were in hers.

Staring out through the misty morning predawn light, she glared at the *garçonniere*, knowing it stood empty. More correctly, the bed inside—the bed she would give practically anything to share once more with Nick—was empty of the man who made the bed so desirable. Where was he? He had no business staying out all night in this humid weather.

There was all sorts of trouble he could get into. Not that she was worried about him. But his horse could throw him. Maybe into the swamp. There, a huge alligator could slide into the murky water and attack him before he could get out. She'd seen alligators in the bayous in the city huge enough to be extremely dangerous, and hadn't she heard tales of them eating stray dogs that wandered too close to the banks?

Realizing how childish she was acting and thinking, she turned from the window and went back to her bed. Climbing the footstool, she laid on the mattress and stared at the overhead canopy. She let her mind roam again, but couldn't make contact with even one person. By noon the previous day, she'd known her magic was returning, but slowly. She'd also become aware that Sybilla had deserted her again, and probably taken her hound and that pup with her. This morning she'd get dressed and go see for sure, but she didn't think her aunt would leave the hound and pup behind.

Her stomach growled and she sat up. She hadn't gone out to the kitchen house to fix her anything to eat the previous evening, making do with the leftovers from a lunch tray Sybilla had brought her just before she disappeared. Granted, she'd given her aunt cause to avoid her vile temper. She'd taken out her frustration over Nick's total nonresponse at her returning the ring on Aunt Sybilla when she brought the breakfast tray. By noon, after seeing Nick ride off and not return, she had been in a fine fury.

But Aunt Sybilla didn't have to treat her like a child.

Like a child banned to its room until it finished pouting. That thought flashing into her mind told Wendi that her aunt was at least checking on her now and then.

"I'm sorry, Aunt Sybilla," she whispered. Sybilla had closed the communications between them again, though, as she had kept it all day and night.

Both her aunt and Thalia Thibedeau were right. She was acting like a pouting child instead of a woman grown. She slid from the bed and went over to the mirror. Sybilla had removed the bandage on her head yesterday morning, telling her the wound was healing nicely and the swelling nearly gone. Today she pushed her hair back and probed, finding a slight tenderness but that was all. She hadn't had any dizzy spells recently, either.

Her hair badly needed taming, and she picked up her brush. While she brushed, she studied her face. She didn't understand how she could consider her mother so beautiful—have everyone tell her they looked so much alike—yet feel so . . . so . . . *unpretty*. Her own blue eyes returned her confused gaze.

Pretty is as pretty does. That didn't sound like Sybilla's voice in her mind. Could it be her mother's? It had been so many years since she'd heard her. But when she probed, she met a blank.

She sighed. If anything, she supposed the voice was referring to her temper tantrum the previous evening. Sabine Chastain looked so calm and collected, she probably never gave in to the personality trait their hair signified and allowed anger to take control. Wendi frowned as a vague hint of a voice similar to her own but raised in anger fleeted through her mind.

Finishing with her hair, she gathered it up off her neck and bound it loosely, being careful not to pull on her tender wound. After she bathed and dressed, she tested her magic by making the bed and straightening up the room. Satisfied the magic was working once again, at least somewhat, she headed for the kitchen house, going down the back stairwell. On the kitchen house porch she paused, hearing voices inside and peering through the window.

Nick. Nick and Cecile. She couldn't believe she hadn't been aware of Nick returning.

Both of them looked up, as though something told them she stood at the window. Without speaking further, Cecile rose and went up the stairway to her living quarters. Nick motioned for Wendi to enter, but she couldn't make herself open the door. She'd wondered off and on all night what she would say to him when she saw him again, but achieved nothing conclusive. And the sight of him so solid and substantial right there in front of her blew any tentative thoughts out of her mind.

She walked back to the top of the porch steps, but instead of leaving, sat down. Propping her elbows on her knees and chin on her hands, she gazed out at the garden, concentrating on the morning smells she hadn't paid any attention to on her walk out here.

Roses. She smelled lots of roses. They grew in profusion despite the lack of care in the garden. She'd never been one to enjoy gardening and plants, although she helped Sybilla around their yard at times. It did seem a shame for the garden here to be reverting to wild when it had probably been carefully tended for over a hundred years.

A board creaked on the porch, but she'd known Nick was coming up behind her without that telltale sound. He sat down beside her, close enough that she could feel his heat but not close enough for her to lean against him, as she longed to do. He laid something between them, and she glanced down to see two biscuits on a snowy linen napkin. Butter oozed from their middles, and her stomach chose that moment to utter a loud growl.

She silently chastised her belly, telling it that it could have at least made a more subdued sound. Nick picked up one of the biscuits and broke off a bite, holding it in front of her lips.

Oh, she wanted so badly to take that piece of biscuit from him with her lips. Kiss his fingers while she did. Maybe lick off that little drip of butter on his thumb—

She took the biscuit from him with her fingers and put it into her mouth. Before he could break off another piece, she picked up the other biscuit herself and started nibbling on it. He sat beside her silently until she finished.

"There's coffee and milk in the kitchen," he finally said. "Can I get you one or the other?"

"I can go in there myself."

She started to rise, and he put a hand on her arm. When she looked at him, he said, "I'd like to stay out here where it's a little cooler and talk for a while, if you don't mind. Or do you think you need to get back to your room and rest?"

"I need fresh air more than I need rest right now." She dropped her gaze. "And I need us to talk, too. There are things that need said."

"Yes," he agreed. "Do you feel like going for a buggy ride? I know a pretty spot where we won't be disturbed. I can pack something to take with us to eat."

"That would be nice."

She could feel his eyes on her for a long moment, then he heaved a resigned sigh and rose. She stood, too, and said, "Why don't I go on out and tell your stable hand to get the buggy ready?"

She moved on down the steps without waiting for his acquiescence and walked to the back garden gate. He must have watched her during the time it took her to get down the path—she knew he did—and she didn't hear the kitchen door squeal until the same moment she opened the gate and went through. She walked on to the barn, went inside, and took a moment to close her eyes and feel before she searched for the stable hand.

It was no use. She heard little scurryings and the "meowrrr" of a mother cat calling its kittens. A flutter of wings as a barn swallow sailed out a window. The stomp of a horse's hoof, somewhat muffled in the straw on the floor of its stall.

She smelled hay and dust. The sharp tang of leather and

horse sweat. Even the odor of the manure pile drifting in the door, which counteracted the overall sense of cleanliness inside.

Something caressed her face, and her eyes flew open.

Mother?

But no, a stray sunbeam had filtered through a tiny clear spot on a windowpane high on the wall beside the barn loft. She'd felt it when it hit her cheek. Funny that it had managed the exact angle to make her think her mother's fingers had touched her.

From her position, she could see more than just hay stored up on that loft. There were boxes and crates, shadowy things she couldn't make out but which could have been old plows and what looked like a rusty iron wagon wheel. Something white gleamed for a brief second in the sunbeam, then died into the dimness.

A ladder led up to the loft, and another loft bisected, holding hay for the animals. Wendi turned away and went looking for the stable hand. She would have to handle the coming talk with Nick without any guidance from another woman—alive or dead.

Twenty-two

Damn it, he couldn't believe how nervous he was! Nick halted the horse beside the small pond where he and his brother had spent so many pleasant summer hours swimming. Their grandfather had shown it to them as soon as they were old enough to learn to dog-paddle, explaining the pond was there because of their grandmother. She'd refused to allow them to dig out the clay they needed for bricks close to the house, adamant that she wouldn't allow a pool of water there that might spawn mosquitoes. This area was the nearest they could find with the appropriate type of clay soil, and Grandfather had conceded to his wife, even though it meant more work transporting the bricks for building purposes. It even had the requisite vine—an old, gnarled grape vine—to swing out over the water and fall with a gleeful splash.

He'd thought one day that sons of his own might . . .

Wendi smiled, so she must like his choice of a picnic spot. There was a slight breeze today, so he hoped the bugs wouldn't bother them. Nick got down and tied the horse, then held up his hands to Wendi. As much as he longed to let his touch linger on her, he removed his hands from her waist as soon as he set her on the ground.

Did he imagine it, or did her touch on his shoulders linger an instant longer than necessary?

She moved away from him, though, leaving him to bring the blanket and picnic basket. Carrying them to the grassy bank of the pond, he set them beneath a large live oak and spread the blanket. Wendi had gone down the bank to the edge of the pond.

"Are you tired?" he asked, firmly refusing to join her down there. "You can sit down and rest up here."

She came back up the bank. "I'm not tired, but I would like to sit down. Only if you join me, though."

She sat on the blanket, folding her legs to the side and arranging her skirts. Funny. He hardly ever noticed what she wore, but today he did. The dress was neat and clean, but long out of fashion, and the faded material had probably gone through hundreds of washings. Still, on Wendi it was more than just a faded rag—at least in his eyes.

Pink. Hadn't he heard somewhere that women with reddish hair couldn't wear pink? It suited Wendi, and her blue eyes stood out delightfully, the long golden lashes and arched brows clearly defined.

He'd never seen her wear anything other than capped sleeves in the heat, and the neckline draped low, still covering her breasts. Because he knew what the material covered, it was more enticing that way than if she'd bared the curves of her breasts. The skirt draped past hips a perfect fit to a man's hands and on down slender legs.

"Have you changed your mind about talking?" she asked, making him realize how he'd been standing there staring at her, eyes hooded to near slits. "Would you like to return to the manor house?"

"No. No, please." He joined her on the blanket, glad

he'd brought one large enough for both of them to sit on without touching—wishing immediately that he hadn't.

"I'd normally allow a lady to have her say first," he said, interrupting Wendi when he realized she was going to speak. "But I'd like to say something. If you'll listen."

"That's what we're here for, isn't it, Nick? To talk to each other?"

She avoided his gaze, and he noticed a handkerchief she must have taken from her skirt pocket in her hands. When she twisted it around her fingers, the knuckles whitened with strain.

"Would you rather talk before me?" he offered.

Anger flashed in her eyes, but she gripped the handkerchief even tighter and took a deep breath. "This is ridiculous! We can't even decide who will speak first."

Before he could stop her, she got to her feet and headed for the buggy. Over her shoulder, she said, "I want to go back. There's no use pursuing this."

"No!" He scrambled up and limped after her, grabbing her arm and turning her to face him. "Damn it, you're not the only one who's got a temper! You sit your ass back down over there and let's get on with this!"

If he thought he'd see fear in her eyes, he was wrong. The small tilt to her lips indicated he'd walked right into whatever manipulation she had in mind for him.

"And if I don't?"

He didn't answer in words. Instead, he swooped her into his arms and headed back to the blanket. His leg protested even her slight extra weight, but he gritted his teeth and made it to the blanket. Still, he was glad he'd caught her before she'd gone very far. Trying to cover up his relief, he put her down, then loomed over her.

"Don't you even think about trying to leave again until I have my say," he warned.

"My magic's back, you know," she said, slipping a calculating look from beneath her lashes. "I could just disappear on you."

He groaned and sat down. "Please don't," he whispered.

Her face changed, and she looked at him fully for the first time that morning. "I won't," she said. "And I'm sorry I'm acting like such a child again. I promised myself this morning that I wouldn't do that again, but when I get around you, I act very foolishly at times."

"Me, too," he admitted.

"I tried to make you lose your temper a minute ago," she said. "You're always so stoic and cold, Nick. I know you're fighting pain, but—"

"The last time I lost my temper," he said in a flat voice, "your mother died."

Wendi gasped, then reached out a hand, laying it on his arm. "I wasn't sure what I believed, even after what my scrying speculum said that day. I know you now, though, Nick. There's no way you could have killed my mother, either in a calculating way or in a fit or rage."

"Sure," he snarled. "And pigs fly."

"I can make them do that."

It took a minute for her words to sneak through his guarded mind, but then a laugh exploded. Full-blown and belly-shaking. God, it felt good.

She smiled tolerantly until his laughter died and he shook his head. Reaching out, he pulled her into his arms, where she snuggled against his chest. But when he tried to lie down, taking her with him, he winced in pain.

Wendi pushed back. "You lie down," she said. "Let me give you a massage while we talk."

The brief protest was gone before it even had a chance to put down a tentative root in his mind. "Could you conjure up some of that liniment and salve to use?"

Eyes twinkling, she held out one palm and snapped her fingers on the other hand, murmuring something about love and pain and healing. He was more interested in the way her lips moved than the actual words. With a little poof, two jars appeared on her palm, one small and round and the other one taller and filled with liquid.

"Lie down on your stomach," she ordered, "but first pull your trousers down."

His mouth went dry, but hell, what had he expected? He'd known he'd need to bare the area of the wound for the massage. Or . . . maybe that had been his intention all along.

"We *will* talk while I work, Nick," she said in a mixed tone of warning and mischievousness. "Only talk."

He shrugged in feigned nonchalance. "Of course. If you can do it, so can I."

His barb hit home, and she giggled, the delight dancing in her eyes and warming him as much as the liniment soon would. Keeping his gazed fixed on hers, he reached for his trouser buttons and started opening the fly by touch alone. To give her credit, her eyes only flickered downward briefly at one point, then quickly back to his face.

Shifting, he leaned a little toward the side of his good leg in order to slide his trousers down, and Wendi swallowed audibly. But she kept a bright, waiting look on her face. He wondered—

He licked his lips very slowly, an action which on her could turn him to mush. Her blue eyes went from sparkling to a dark and stormy pre-thunder shower indigo, and a flush stained her neck. He dropped his gaze in time to see her nipples peak and harden.

"Only talk, that's all," he reminded her in a voice he hardly recognized as his own. Deep and gravelly, it crawled through him like a prelude to sex.

She did herself proud. The only other sign of her tension was when the two jars on her palm trembled and hit together, the glass tinkling. She didn't answer him, so maybe her throat was as tight around words as his, but she clenched her fingers and the tinkling died. The resulting silence only enhanced the lack of noise.

"Lie down now?" he asked, quirking an eyebrow and trying to force her to speak.

She only nodded.

"Do I need to remove my underdrawers, too, or can you work around them?"

She shook her head negatively in response that time, and he said, "Which? Remove them or let you work around them?"

She flicked an index finger in a circular motion, and suddenly Nick found himself facedown on the blanket. Rather than anger him, he laughed again, knowing the action was a defense on her part. He pillowed his cheek on his arm and waited.

"You know," he said as she set the salve jar down and poured some liniment into one palm, "that was sort of fun—when you tossed me around like that. Think maybe you could take me flying some day? I've always wanted to know what the world looked like from up in the air."

She rubbed her palms together, then placed them on his thigh. Good thing he was lying on his stomach—well, maybe not. His erection was as uncomfortable to lie on as a rock.

". . . do that yet," Wendi said.

"Hmmmmm?" he asked. "Sorry, I wasn't listening."

She worked magic in another way right now, with her palms and fingers and the warmth of the liniment. The massage soothed the pain into nothingness—or maybe it was the masseuse.

". . . yet."

"Hmmmmm? Sorry, I wasn't listening again."

She leaned over and spoke in his ear, her breast pressing against his arm and her warm breath sending a cascade of longing through him. No, not speak. She shouted.

"My magic's not developed enough to take someone with me when I fly yet!" she yelled.

Nick flinched, then roared with laughter. He'd asked for that by being too distracted to listen to her words. She sat up, a smirk on those pretty lips, which beckoned him to kiss it away. She reached for his thigh again—

He flipped over and captured her, pulling her onto his stomach. Although he hadn't actually planned that part of it, she ended up situated exactly right over his erection, her skirt being the only thing separating that part of him from what it wanted. The material didn't keep the heat of their need from penetrating, though.

If he thought she would be embarrassed, he quickly realized he had lots to learn yet about Wendi Chastain. Placing her hands on his chest, she pushed her upper body away from him, which snuggled her lower body more tightly against his. Then she stretched languidly, as though trying to find a more comfortable position.

Nick groaned, deep and needy. "You win," he managed. "Do with me what you will."

She wiggled those delectable hips, is what she did. Oh, God, he was going to explode like a randy teen. She ceased just in time, and he opened eyes he hadn't even realized were shut. He shouldn't have. The sensual, you're-in-my-power look on her face was nearly his undoing again.

"Say something," he pleaded.

"Ummmmm," she replied, licking her lips and lowering her head to his.

When he tried to grab her, she jerked back and shook

her finger at him. That finger that shot fire in more ways
than one.

"No, no, no." She twitched the index finger back and
forth like a pendulum. "Hands at your side and no touching
on your part. I'm supposed to be giving you a massage,
remember?"

He laid his hands down, clenching his fists to resist ignoring her orders. "You're supposed to be massaging my
wound."

"If that's what you want—" She started to roll off him.

"No!" She quirked a brow, secret satisfaction in her
eyes and the tilt of her lips. Damn it, he didn't care if she
was the one in control right now.

"Witch," he whispered. "Have your way."

She kissed him, softly and lingeringly at first, then responding to the unspoken plea of his lips—hard, deep, and
with all the lip and tongue he could ask for. That quickly,
they both caught fire and the wanting need changed to ir-
resistible longing. She didn't protest when he started pulling on her dress, getting it over her head somehow at about
the same time she got his shirt open. Her palms rubbed his
muscles, leaving behind a highly erotic tingle from the
traces of liniment still on them.

God, he hoped she didn't reach downward with her
hands. Liniment wasn't something he particularly wanted
on that part of him, burning that sensitive skin. But he
couldn't have stopped her if she tried. He was too busy
yanking on her chemise in between the kisses she laved on
his nipples.

When he got the chemise off, he gathered her breasts
between his hands and pushed them together, close enough
so he could suckle one nipple, then the other, with the least
wasted motion.

"Nick!" she cried.

She opened her legs and straddled him, and he had just enough sense left to grab her thrashing hand when she reached to put him inside her himself. She moaned in frustration, but it turned to a purr when he slid in her, sheathing himself in the place that fulfilled his need for more than just sex. Filled his need for love—a home—a refuge from all the pain in his life. Fulfilled his need for this woman, who was all that to him.

His need for Wendi.

They reached that nirvana they'd found before in seconds, and Nick held her tight as he emptied himself inside her, never, ever wanting it to end.

Twenty-three

~

"We were going to talk."

"So, talk," Nick said, rubbing his chin against the top of her hair.

"I'm all sweaty. Would you like to wash off with me?"

"Only if you'll let me do the honors."

"Of course," she agreed.

He kissed her lightly, heaved a sigh, and loosened his arms. Without shame—he'd seen and touched every bit of her since the first time they made love—she stood and waited for him to join her, carefully checking his face for pain. He winced, but only a little, and she unfocused her eyes to check his aura. No blackness today, only a light blue of healing and harmony.

And brown. She giggled.

"What?" he asked. "What are you laughing at?"

"Not laughing," she denied. "Snickering. I was looking at your aura, and there's brown there."

"And?"

"Brown means, among other things, sensuality. I have to say I agree with that reflection."

He blushed. He actually blushed, and she giggled again.

"I'd think red would be for sensuality," he growled.

"No. No, red's anger and frustration. You're a long way from frustrated right now."

She read his movement in his eyes a second before he lunged, slipping away and half-stumbling down the bank to the water. She ran full tilt into it, high-stepping and sending geysers of water flinging into the air with her feet. She didn't turn to see if he was behind her until after she plunged deeper and pushed off, swimming toward the middle. When she did turn, she screamed. He was right there, a wicked gleam in his eyes.

"I want you to know that my wound doesn't bother me the least little bit when I'm in the water," he said, curling his lip in a mock threatening gesture. "I can swim and dive like a porpoise."

And he showed her how true that was by upending and diving right in front of her. She gaped for a second, barely having time to shut her mouth, let alone take a breath, when he grabbed her feet and dragged her down with him. They drifted back to the surface amid cascades of bubbles, and Nick pulled her into his arms and kissed her. They floated downward again.

Once back on the surface, Nick guided them toward the shallower water, halting where he could touch the bottom but she couldn't. She wrapped her arms around his neck, and he growled when her breasts bobbed in the water right in front of his mouth. Then did what any normal man would—what any normal woman would want him to do. He sucked one nipple into his mouth.

Wendi gasped, desire so strong she vaguely wondered why the water didn't turn to steam. She wrapped her legs around Nick's waist, rubbing against the hardness there waiting for her. He guided the tip right to her entrance, then paused and looked into her eyes.

"Are you brown now?" he asked.

"I'm damned near as dark as mud," she replied, catching her heels behind his back and taking care of the rest of it herself. When they both reached their peaks together, Nick managed to stand steady for only a couple seconds before he fell backward. Laughing wildly, the two of them scrambled nearer shore and collapsed on their backs, bodies still in the water but heads on the sandy bank. Their hands reached for each others as they got their strength back.

Nick turned his head to look at her. "Will you believe me this time when I tell you I love you?"

With a quicksilver twist of emotion, tears filled Wendi's eyes. She blinked them back and sniffed. "I want to," she admitted. "But we haven't had that talk yet."

His eyes darkened in disappointment, and Wendi explained, "To me, love is special. When you find it, it means sharing your life with that person."

"I offered you marriage," he said in a puzzled voice.

Anger flashed. At times he was so darned obtuse. But Wendi reminded herself that an argument wouldn't help them work things out—in fact, would muddle them worse. Sighing, she sat up and pulled her knees to her, laying her chin on them and gazing out over the water.

"Nick, why are you so afraid of commitment? When I say sharing, I mean living together. I don't want a husband who's clear across the continent." She let herself look at him to gauge his reaction to her next comment. "Love not nurtured can die. And I might find someone else down the road, someone who wasn't afraid to live with me."

He wrenched his gaze from hers, but not before she saw the deep pain of jealousy there.

"You're damned sure right about love dying," he

growled. "I'm sure at one time my father loved my mother. At least from what I remember from my younger years, he did. But I wasn't very old at all when I saw things changing. So who the hell can promise another person that their love will last forever?"

"Dominic loved your mother desperately, Nick." This time she was the perplexed one. "That's how all this started."

"What the hell are you talking about?"

Sucking in her bottom lip, Wendi chewed on it contemplatively. She wasn't afraid of Nick—really, she wasn't. But they were out here alone—far from any help should she need it. With a convenient pond there, and no one to know whether or not she could swim.

"Goddamn it, Wendi, get that scared look off your face! Do you think I'm going to kill you, like I did your mother?"

Anger won this time, chasing away any fear from her mind. "Well, goddamn you, too, Nick Bardou!" she snarled. "How many times do I have to tell you that I don't believe you killed my mother?"

He got to his feet and headed for the blanket without answering. By the time she joined him, he was putting on his trousers over wet legs, tugging and muttering in frustration. She picked up her chemise and saw it was beyond repair, although she didn't remember him tearing it. Throwing it on top of the picnic basket, she pulled on her underdrawers and slipped her dress over her head.

Barely a minute later, they were in the buggy, heading back to Belle Chene, the unopened picnic basket on the floorboards between their feet. There was plenty of room for it. She and Nick sat as far away from each other as they could get. Wendi refused to try to force further conversation. For once in his life, Nick Bardou could sort out his feelings on his own. Discuss things maturely—like she was trying to do—or bury himself in pouting petulism for all eternity as far as she was concerned.

She finger-combed her hair, hoping she could get herself into some sort of presentable mode before they reached the stable. She needn't have bothered, because she didn't see a stable hand around when they drove into the barn. Nick halted the buggy inside the door, and she climbed down without waiting for him to assist her.

Shrugging, he climbed down himself, then led the horse toward the stalls farther back in the barn.

She gave up the struggle to let him figure out his own emotions. Some men obviously remained little boys all their lives, needing to be mothered and guided.

"Nick."

He stopped and looked back at her.

"Will you do one thing for me?"

His shoulders slumped, and he said in a low voice, "I'd do lots for you if you'd let me, Wendi. But it's like everything else that's happened to me in this godforsaken state. I always end up hurting people instead of—"

She flew toward him, shaking her head wildly and guilt filling her at how deeply she'd misread him. He barely managed to drop the reins before she threw her arms around his neck.

"No. No, Nick, no!" she cried. "Oh, how could I be so wrong? Listen, we need to work this out together, instead of misreading each other so unjustly."

Pulling her closer, he kissed her. Tenderly, softly, and lingeringly. Then he pushed her away.

"You're not misreading the situation, darling," he said. "You're judging it correctly. Whether it's this karma stuff you keep talking about or something else, there's no future for the two of us together."

"You just said you'd do anything for me, Nick. Please. Please read my mother's last Book of Shadows before you make any final decision. The last one I have anyway. If, after you read that, you don't want to talk about this any longer, I'll let you leave without protest."

He shook his head. "It won't do any good. But if that's all you're asking of me, I'll do it. Go get it and bring it to the *garçonniere*. I'll read it right now."

"Thank you," she breathed.

Whirling, she raced out of the barn and down the path to the manor house. She glimpsed Cecile talking to Lucian as she hurried by the kitchen house, but she only lifted a hand in greeting and passed on by. In her room she went to the armoire and opened the doors, reaching in for the portmanteau she'd used to carry her clothing.

For a second, she thought it was gone, and she turned the satchel up and shook it. Then she remembered reading it while she recovered from her head injury, dropped the portmanteau, and went to the bed. She found the book stuffed down between the mattress and sideboard, and reached for it gratefully. By the time she got to the *garçonniere*, Nick was waiting for her.

"Do you want to come in while I read it?" he asked as she handed the book to him.

"No. No, I'll wait in the house."

He glanced down at the journal in distaste, almost as though he were touching her mother instead. Briefly she wondered whether she'd done the right thing, then blew out a resigned breath, chasing a curl from her forehead. What would be, would be. If she couldn't work out the disrupted karma in this life, she'd have to worry about it again in the next one.

Dredging up an effort of will she thought for a minute she wouldn't be able to find, Wendi turned and left Nick standing at the door of the *garçonniere* alone. Her stomach grumbled, reminding her she hadn't eaten anything except a couple bites of biscuit today, and now it was well past noon. Changing direction, she headed for the kitchen house to see if Cecile could find her something to eat.

Cecile fixed her some cold chicken, cheese, and warm bread, making innocuous conversation and shelling peas as Wendi ate. There were many things Wendi would have liked to talk to Cecile about, since the woman had known Nick both as a child and young man, but she couldn't concentrate right now. The other woman didn't seem to want to talk about anything serious any more than she did.

Wendi knew the Book of Shadows by heart, and she was fairly certain it would raise more questions in Nick's mind than give him answers.

The problem was, would he care whether or not he got those new questions answered?

For the rest of the day Wendi alternately paced her room and tried to mentally contact Sybilla. She refused to peer into Nick's mind and see what his feelings were, knowing he would resent it if she did. Sybilla never answered her, and after the sun went down, Wendi stood in front of her bedroom window. Not one light shown in the *garçonniere*, and she imagined Nick sitting in there in the dark, pondering what he'd read.

He had to have finished the book by now. He couldn't read without a light. But had he even read it?

Of course he had. He'd surely been too curious not to, even though he'd handled it with distaste.

Maybe he was just humoring her.

Darn it! She could be spending her time a heck of a lot more productively than trying to form an opinion of something she had no way of knowing about until Nick came to talk to her again. She could be practicing her magic, although that didn't appeal to her at all, especially since her magic was still one of the barriers between her and Nick.

She could be looking for her mother's last Book of Shadows. After all, that's what they'd come to Belle Chene to do, and she hadn't done her part. Instead, she'd taken Aunt Sybilla's word that she and Thalia Thibedeau had looked every possible place while they were supposedly only doing housework. If anything, she had probably hindered the search, with her getting hurt and her turmoil with Nick. Even her attempt to perform a ceremony and contact her mother had fallen apart.

Her need to perform a séance had been thwarted time and time again, although she had no doubt in her mind her mother had been making attempts to contact her. Thalia Thibedeau had assured her that her mother had visited while she recovered—had helped hasten her recovery. She'd been here in the room then, not in the barn. Maybe a ceremony here would make contact.

Wendi wrinkled her brow. At least it would help pass the time. She crossed to the small chest of drawers in the corner of the room and pulled out the drawer where she'd stored the candles and other supplies she'd brought with her from New Orleans. After gathering what she wanted, she laid them on top of the chest, closed her eyes, and breathed deeply, murmuring and chanting the proper words to show her respect for the rite she would perform.

When she felt the changed atmosphere, she took each candle and held it while she dipped her finger into the jar of jasmine oil and rubbed it around the wick, up and down the sides. After walking over to the mantel, she placed each candle in the appropriate spot and arranged her bowls of water and salt. She set her incense burner at the last of the

four corners. Continuing to murmur respectfully, she lit the
candles and incense, then moved over and sat on the window seat while they burned, filling the room with pleasant
odors. She would—

Nick. Nick was outside the door.

He opened it without knocking and came in. When she
dropped her legs from the window seat and patted it invitingly, he moved over and sat down beside her.

She bit her lip, completely undecided as to what she
should say, if anything. Avoiding her gaze, he bent and
placed his forearms on his knees, staring at the floor. He
sat that way for a good five minutes before he said anything.

"I didn't know your father was Laurent Chastain."

"We lived in the family mansion on Royal Street for a
while," Wendi told him. "Until shortly after my grandparents died."

"That's what the book says. But it ends there."

Wendi let the silence stretch for a while, wanting Nick
to ask for more information rather than have her offer it.
Finally he did.

"I need to know the rest of it."

Relieved, Wendi said, "I was hoping so badly you
would. Shall I light the sconces?"

"No. No, let's just let the candles burn. It seems appropriate somehow."

"All right." There was enough room on the window seat
for her to get comfortable—this discussion would take a
while—and she drew her legs up again. Settling sideways,
her back against the deep wall, she wrapped her arms
around her knees, hesitating. What was to come would
change things, and she had no idea whether what she was
doing was right or wrong.

A brief touch flittered on her cheek, and she quickly

turned her head, closing her lips before she could utter the one word that might send Nick out of here without listening. *Mother*. That touch was enough. She was doing the right thing.

Nick shifted restlessly, and Wendi began with a question. "Did you know the Chastains well?"

"No," Nick said. "After my mother's health began failing, we didn't entertain much."

"There was another son, my uncle, Louis. My father's twin. He was the second born, and over the years, I think that was what caused all the problems. For my mother and me, anyway."

Nick nodded. "I've seen situations like that before. It's hard enough being a second son, but being younger by only a few minutes—knowing you missed being the heir by a twist of time in the womb—it could make a person resentful."

"It made him vicious," Wendi said. "No one realized that until after he inherited everything, though, except I found out later my mother had her suspicions. My father was killed in a buggy accident, and it wasn't long after that that my grandparents died in a yellow fever epidemic. I don't remember all this, because I was only four years old when we left the Chastain mansion. But my mother told me the story as soon as I was old enough to understand."

She watched Nick closely. "She told me after I was old enough to realize Dominic Bardou was her lover."

Nick stiffened, and she waited for him to react.

"Go on," he said at last.

The candles flickered brightly, then settled into a warm backdrop glow.

Twenty-four

~

Sabine and Dominic met in the park one afternoon, Wendi told Nick. Met again, really, since they'd seen each other at numerous soirees and balls, at the opera during the season, at other places the cream of the Creole society mingled. Both were married, happily, and there wasn't any hint of scandal connected to either family name at the time. Dominic Bardou loved his Annabelle deeply, and Sabine and Laurent were barely past newlywed status, even though they already had one child. Laurent danced only duty-dances with any other woman besides his wife.

There had never been any hint of witchcraft connected to Sabine's side of the family. The women down through the eons had kept their secret well, knowing what would happen if they were exposed. The Inquisitions and Salem had left their mark.

They chose their mates carefully, and Laurent was aware of and accepted Sabine's practice of witchcraft. Sabine had trusted him with her secret before she would agree to marry him. Later, Dominic knew, also, but he, too, kept the secret.

Then Laurent was killed. They said—*they* being those

insufferable rumormongers—that Laurent had been drinking after an argument with his wife, whipped his horse too fast, and lost control, overturning the buggy. He'd died instantly, and everyone who saw the widow at the funeral knew she was devastated—probably from guilt, *they* sneered. There'd been no argument, however, only an unexplained loose wheel on a buggy and a man kept late at a meeting and hurrying home. A meeting arranged and delayed by his brother.

Sabine went into seclusion, and six months later, yellow fever struck. The elder Chastains were barely cold in their graves before Louis approached Sabine in her bedroom late one night. She was waiting for him, knowing this moment would come. Her magic protected her, but Louis still had the upper hand.

The next morning, he threw a small bag of gold coins at Sabine, told her it was her inheritance, and ordered her to get out. She could take nothing but the dress on her back and her child. If she refused, the child would be the one to pay, because she had to sleep sometime.

Sabine and Wendi moved in with Sybilla, because they had no one else. Their mother and father, too, had died in the epidemic, almost as though it were decreed by some karmic Fate. Fate also decreed the family home catch fire and burn a week after their parents died, with Sybilla barely escaping herself. All she'd been able to manage with the stipend left from the estate was a tiny, two-room house near where they lived now, and it was crowded beyond belief with the three of them.

Nick stirred beside Wendi. "That's enough disaster to fill several lifetimes, making that about as far-fetched a tale as I've ever heard. It's just far-fetched enough that it has to be true."

"It's true, Nick. When you come from a heritage of witchcraft and your ancestors have had eons of practice at concealing their craft, you have the ability to make do. Overcome the disasters life throws at you. Experience tells you, and you listen to the voices of those who have gone before you."

"It's well known now that you and Sybilla are witches."

"By necessity. We had to make a living somehow after my mother died and your father was killed in the war. I guess Dominic was too desolate after he lost both Annabelle and my mother to think of what would happen to Sybilla and me. By the time he did, if he did, he was already gone from here. You know how it was at first. The South thought it would only take them a few months to send the Yankees home with their tails between their legs, but the war lasted five years. I like to think that Dominic assumed he'd be home soon to take care of his concerns."

"I was in the war myself, through most of it. Not in the same regiment as my father, though."

"I know. Now, let me tell you the other side of the story—the one about Dominic."

The day they met in the park, Dominic had just come from Annabelle's doctor. The man had sent word to him to meet with him alone, and the visit confirmed Dominic's suspicions. The last three miscarriages had weakened his wife; another pregnancy would kill her.

Nick jerked upright to look at Wendi, but he didn't interrupt her. She continued with her tale in a soft voice.

Both Dominic and Sabine had gone to an isolated spot in the park, to wander the more private paths and try to come to grips with their individual situations. Sabine's money was nearly gone, and one of the basic rules of witchcraft, if a witch wanted to find karmic harmony, was that they didn't use their magic to build a fortune for themselves. They were to make their way in life as best they could.

Sabine knew what Wendi would face growing up if she and Sybilla set up shop as witches—the only way it looked like they were going to be able to make a living. Of course, Wendi and Sybilla had done exactly that later, but they'd had no choice. No one offered them another way, like Dominic was getting ready to offer Sabine then.

Sabine didn't even realize at first that Dominic was there beside her. She sat on the bench, her face buried in her hands, sobbing. Dominic sat beside her, recognizing her when she lifted her tear-streaked face.

They told each other their stories honestly—there hadn't appeared to be any reason not to. And Dominic made Sabine an offer. He would care for her, buy her a house, and provide for her, as well as her daughter and sister. In return, she would give him a bed when he could no longer suppress his masculine urges.

"Over the years," Wendi admitted, "they came to care deeply for each other. But Dominic never once gave leaving Annabelle a thought. Mother said she presumed Annabelle was well aware that Dominic was satisfying his urges elsewhere, but they took care to keep their liaison a well-guarded secret. It all came out, though, when my mother was killed at Belle Chene."

"No," Nick denied. "There were whispers before that. But since my mother never seemed aware of them, as far as I knew, no one ever told her about it."

Wendi shrugged. "Down through history, it's been accepted that men will take mistresses. That they can't control their urges. But make no mistake, Nick. Your father loved his wife dearly, and that's why this entire situation came about. He didn't want her dying from another pregnancy, and he already had two heirs. What happened was a mutually beneficial situation for them both at the beginning.''

''Until the murder.''

''Until the murder,'' Wendi agreed.

Nick got to his feet to pace the room. ''I—'' He shook his head. ''I don't remember what happened, but I do know I'd been drinking. Heavily. And I was so damned angry with my father, it wouldn't have surprised me a bit to have woken up with him dead beside me. But it wasn't him. It was your mother.''

''How long had you known they were lovers?''

''Why does it matter?''

''It doesn't, I guess.''

He hesitated for a few seconds, then said, ''It seems like I'd always known. But that's not true. I was coming out from . . .'' He looked at Wendi. ''From one of the brothels over near where you live on St. Charles Avenue.''

''They built the house there by agreement,'' Wendi explained. ''They thought even if Dominic were seen in the neighborhood, people would think he was visiting one of those houses, too. It was a fairly good cover.''

''Well, it didn't work. This was early one morning, just after dawn. About a year or so before Sabine's death. I was with a friend, Chet Emilie, and we both had a hell of a hangover. Maybe we were still drunk, too, because I doubt Chet would have said what he did otherwise. We rode past your house, and he nudged me. Said something about he wished there were girls in the house we'd just left half as pretty as my father's mistress. The one he kept in that house there.''

''I'm sorry you found out that way, Nick. It must have hurt you terribly.''

''I loved my mother deeply. She'd always been there for

me, as well as my brother.'' He headed for the door, motioning Wendi to keep her seat when she started to rise. "I need to be alone for a while now."

He paused. "But this doesn't mean I won't be back to talk about this some more, darling," he said. "And I won't run away this time. Maybe—" He hesitated, then said, "Maybe we can even work things out so you can do that séance you want. In the barn. I—"

He dropped his head, then looked back at her. "It's selfish, but I need to know myself what happened."

"It's not selfish, Nick. Finding out the truth affects more than just you."

He nodded and left, and Wendi buried her face on her knees, tightening her hold around her legs—wishing it were Nick she was holding instead of herself. She could only imagine how confused he was at the moment. She'd had years to take in the story of Dominic and her mother— years to accept it. And she'd known both the participants. Nick had never known her mother. Couldn't have known how much Sabine longed to be Dominic's wife after she fell in love with him down through the years.

Couldn't have known how Dominic suffered, too, loving two women and being unable to have a complete life with either one of them. Perhaps that star-crossed relationship, as much as the murder, began the karmic disruption.

Was it possible Nick might learn something from their story? Might decide there really was such a thing as lasting love?

She saw movement in the yard and glanced at the *garçonniere* as Nick opened the door and walked in. Even though he knew she was in the window, he didn't look up. She sighed and laid her chin on her knees again.

No, Nick would probably take the tale as another piece

of evidence that happiness was an elusive animal—forbidden to Bardou men.

Her eyes drifted shut, and sometime in the dark of the night, Wendi woke, stiff and uncomfortable in the window seat. She looked down at the *garçonniere*, but it was as dark as ever. Standing, she made her way over to the bed, removed her dress, and slipped into her nightgown. Usually she brushed her hair the requisite one hundred strokes, but her heavy-lidded eyes and a huge yawn decided her. Climbing into bed, she pulled only the sheet up in the heat, and fell back asleep.

When she woke the next morning, Nick was sitting in the window seat. The predawn light outlined him, the dark stubble on his face an indication he hadn't shaved yet. Probably hadn't slept, either, from the looks of his tousled hair and wrinkled, half-open shirt and trousers, the ones he'd worn the day before.

As soon as he saw she was awake, he said, "I didn't tell you about the curse Sabine spoke."

She sat up in bed with a start. "A curse? Oh, no."

"I never told anyone, and I assume even if you find that journal you're looking for, it won't be in there. She died before she had time to write down whatever the fight she was having that night was about. Or name whoever it was she was fighting with."

Twenty-five

"Whoever? You mean you heard them fighting, but couldn't tell who was with her?"

"No." He kept his voice low. Vicious, but low. "All I'm sure about is that it was a man."

"But then you know you weren't the one to kill her!"

"No." Nick stood and shoved his hands into his trousers. "No, I'm still not sure. They were both alive at the end of the argument, and I sat down back in the shadows of the barn. Fell down, really. Like I said, I was drunk."

He chuckled sardonically. "Falling-down drunk. Sabine was still alive then, because I could hear her crying. But I was angry—violently angry. And I had a knife in my hand—the one I carried in my boot whenever I went to the seedy end of town."

"The same knife—"

"Yes," he interrupted abruptly. "The same one she was killed with. It was in my hand when I woke up again. Beside her, after she was dead. It was covered with blood, and so was I."

"Nick," Wendi said softly. "Come over here."

He stared at her for a moment, as though her request took him by surprise. As though he couldn't believe she'd want anything to do with him at this point. It tore her heart out to see the flicker of hope crowd out the confusion and desperation in his eyes.

"Please," she whispered.

He hesitantly approached the bed, and she scooted over, patting the space beside her. He was tall enough not to need the footstool, and he settled back against the headboard, keeping a distance between them. She sighed and moved over to him, cuddling against his chest.

"Now," she said. "Tell me what the curse was. The exact words, if you can remember them."

"You still don't believe I killed her?" he asked in a wondering voice. "After what I just told you?"

"I know you now, Nick. I love you." He grunted and his muscles moved as though he were shaking his head, but she continued, "I know you wouldn't deliberately kill anyone, unless you had no choice. Even drunk, I don't believe you could do something like that."

He remained silent for a moment, tense beneath her cheek on his chest. Finally he said, "I talked to one of the doctors at the hospital after I was wounded. I told him that I didn't even remember getting hit. I remembered the hell of battle, the smoke and smells. The screams around me of the dying—both horses and men. But that was the last thing I recalled until I woke up several days later in that hospital."

"And?" Wendi asked.

"He said it happens like that most of the time. We block out the pain and even the actual occurrence. It's . . . a sort of self-preservation and defense mechanism for our minds. He said that a lot of times, those who don't block it out end up in a hospital for crazies."

"So you believe you killed her, but blocked it out."

"Yes."

Wendi sat up again and scooted around to face him. "Then I guess we're going to have to prove you didn't. By finding out who did kill her."

"Even if it's to confirm that it was me?" Nick asked.

"Tell me honestly that you believe you did it."

He smiled wryly. "Honestly? To tell the truth, I thought about more than just that journal and what it said—and didn't say—last night. I thought about what this had done to so many people."

He paused, then said, "Honestly, I just want you to tell me one more time you *don't* believe it. No one's believed in me for a long, long time. Or"—he lowered his voice to a whisper—"or told me they loved me."

"Oh, Nick!" She flung her arms around his neck and clung to him. When she felt him nudging her hair, she turned her face up and kissed him. Tried to show him with the kiss how sincerely she loved him and how much she wanted to ease his pain.

He groaned a sound of mixed wonder and desire, tightening his arms around her until she could barely breathe. Then he loosened his hold, but kept her firmly in his grasp, returning her kiss with a desperation that elated her, as though the last barriers between them had fallen, unable to withstand the power of their love. It was a different type of kiss than the ones they shared in lovemaking; those were preludes to desire overcoming them. As urgent as this kiss was, it was a meeting of souls rather than bodies. A blending of the two of them much deeper than a physical joining.

Tahlia Thibedeau had been right. There was more to love they both needed to discover. More than the physical.

When Nick finally broke the kiss, he cupped her cheek in his hand. "I love you," he said in a husky voice. "Whatever happens—whatever this crazy Fate you keep calling karma has in mind for us, know that. Know I'll die loving you. Nothing can ever make me stop.''

Tears trembled on her lashes, and one spilled down her cheek. Nick caught it with his tongue, then kissed her again, sharing the salty taste of her own emotion with her.

''But—'' he said when he ended the kiss.

She slapped a none-too-gentle hand over his mouth. ''Damn it, don't you dare! Don't you dare say something stupid about how you love me too much to ask me to share your blighted life.''

He took her hand in his and removed it from his mouth, kissing her palm tenderly. ''All right, I won't. We won't talk about that part of it right now.''

She supposed that would have to do, but she wasn't about to take that for his final answer. Hadn't someone somewhere said that love worth having was love worth fighting for? If not, they should have said it.

Nick tried to pull her against him once more, but she found the strength to resist him, and he settled for curling his arms around her waist.

''Tell me what the curse was,'' she insisted.

He shifted his gaze and his brow furrowed. ''You want the exact words, right?''

''Yes. That's important.''

''Well, you don't have to worry that I've forgotten,'' he told her with a distasteful grimace. ''Those words were burned into my mind, and they even survived my drunkenness.''

He closed his eyes as though he couldn't bear to watch her face while he said,

''Your presence fouls the spirit air.
Your blood's a demon's curse evil and free.

The hell you cause will turn on you,
Three times three, no heirs to be.
So mote it be.''

He opened his eyes and said, ''She screamed the last sentence. And over the years, it all came true, even the fact that I never had any desire for heirs after that.''

''But she was cursing whoever was threatening her,'' Wendi said, ''not you. Telling them their despicable deeds would return to them, three times three.''

''She was cursing whoever killed her. And everything that happened after that—if a person believes curses can come true—confirmed that. My family didn't want anything to do with me, and it was my own fault. I caused the hell our lives turned into.''

''But love *hasn't* forsaken you.''

''The culmination of what love should be has,'' Nick said, tenderly cupping her cheek. ''If I can't accept it. And I can't. I won't let someone else—you—share the hell that my life is.''

A burst of exasperation sparked her temper, but she quickly clamped down on it. She couldn't look at his haggard face, listen to that tender, tortured voice, and not know he believed every word he said—every emotion he felt. She felt more depth in his love by him withholding the final portion of it than if he'd given it freely, not caring what it would do to her life.

She bent forward and kissed him, but the moment seemed too precious for them to seal it even with love-making. She curled against his chest again, feeling a different type of oneness with him now that he had shared his deepest feelings with her.

He rubbed his chin back and forth across her hair. ''We have to get up and start searching for that other journal, you know. Perhaps we can find it without resorting to a séance.''

"Maybe," she agreed, running a finger up and down his corded forearm. "You know Belle Chene lots better than either Aunt Sybilla or I do. You'd know places we should look that we wouldn't think of."

"But the problem with that is your mother wouldn't have known the places I would think of, either. She wasn't out here that often. Or at least, not as far as I knew."

"Hmmmm. But she was, Nick. At least the last year or so before she died. Or she was somewhere, and I assumed it was here with your father. She said she was, and she was even gone for—"

Wendi sat up, staring around the room. "Did you hear that?"

Nick shook his head. "I didn't hear anything."

"It was a sound, sort of like a cry of gladness. It almost made me feel like someone was cheering me on. Like whatever I was saying was getting close to unraveling this puzzle."

She hesitated, watching his face closely for his reaction when she said, "It . . . almost sounded like Mother."

"Then go back over what you were just saying," Nick insisted without reluctance. "Something about your mother was gone a lot. You said it was the period right before she died."

"Yes. Yes, the last year before that. Maybe even the last two years. In fact—" She looked closely at Nick. "I need to ask you something that will probably really bother you, Nick."

"We're beyond that by now, aren't we, sweetheart? If you think it will help us figure this out, ask me anything you want."

Still, Wendi took a preparatory breath for courage before

she forced out, "Did your father go somewhere for a period of about four or five months a couple of years or so before my mother died?"

"He said he needed to go to England, to check out one of the brokers there who was handling our cotton and cane," Nick said with a frown. "He'd always left that to his underlings, but he said it was serious enough this time that he felt he needed to go himself."

"Mother had been rather ill for a while," Wendi said contemplatively. "Not completely bedridden, but having bouts of weakness and even nausea. She said the doctor recommended a sea voyage, and Dominic was going to pay for it, so she could get her health back. When she came home, she looked fine physically, but she was even more of an emotional wreck. So she'd spend time out here at Belle Chene, and she said she had become friends with Cecile. Was visiting her."

"Let's go talk to Cecile."

Nick casually pushed her off the bed, grabbing her with a laugh and a mumbled "sorry" when she staggered after the drop to the floor. She smacked him on the shoulder, her laughter joining his and too happy to see his gaiety even amid their search for the truth to be perturbed at him. Like an excited child, Nick swooped her up and circled her around, then dropped her back to her feet and took her hand.

"Let's go," he said, starting for the door.

Shaking her head, Wendi pointed her finger and slammed the door shut in his face. Nick halted, then turned to face her.

"Oh," he said with another laugh. "You probably want to get dressed first, huh?"

"It might be a good idea," she replied, grabbing the

neck of her gown before it slid on past her nipple, which was the only thing holding it in place.

Nick's eyes nearly burned the material off anyway, but she pulled her hand free and started toward the armoire. From the corner of her gaze, she saw him shove his hands into his trouser pockets, as though to keep them confined.

"How do you do that?" he asked while she searched through her meager wardrobe.

"What?" She glanced over her shoulder, and he nodded at the door she'd slammed in his face. "Oh, that. Well, some magic I've practiced so many times that it just comes naturally. You already know that a witch's magic develops over the years. She's not born with it at full blast."

Nick nodded, and she continued, "Some other things take preparation. Sometimes just murmuring a brief spell we've memorized will work to accomplish what we want done, but sometimes a full-blown ritual is necessary. Depends on what we want to do. The spells for things that are harder to do work better during a time of ceremony or celebration, when we know the spirits are more attainable and amenable to helping our magic."

Without thinking, she shrugged her gown off her shoulders and stepped out of it.

"That's it!" Nick snapped.

He was across the room before she could think of a spell to halt him. Not that she even wanted to try when he grabbed her in his arms and headed for the bed. Tossing her onto the high, firm mattress, where she bounced once, then settled against the stacked pillows, he reached for his shirt buttons.

"That's what?" she asked in a low growl around sensually pursed lips, lowering her eyelids to match the tone. "I thought you wanted to go talk to Cecile."

"I've got a few more things to say to you first," Nick

said, finishing his shirt and starting on his trousers. "Like how beautiful your skin glows in the morning light—like pearls. Like how your hair tumbles around your face, reminding me it feels like silk in my fingers. And how it makes you look even more desirable when it's my lovemaking that's tousled it instead of your sleeping alone. Like how I'm going to kiss that pouty look off your lips and eat it."

He shrugged off the shirt and stepped out of his trousers.

Wendi ran the tip of her tongue around her lips. "I'll get them ready for you," she murmured.

His erection actually bounced as it hardened in reaction to her words, and she laughed lightheartedly when Nick blushed like a ten-year-old. But the man who growled and lowered his eyes, his gaze raking over her exposed body, was way past ten years old. Had many secrets to show her. Many more years of experience to have practiced his secrets in.

She hadn't really seen him in the daylight before, and when he took a step toward her, she whispered, "Wait. Please. Just for a moment."

His cheeks heated again, but he nodded. "Not long, though."

She smiled at him, and let her eyes roam. The scars on his thigh only heightened his masculinity, an indication of exactly that—his being wounded in a war fought by men in what they considered an attempt to keep the comfortable lives for their women. That it was a life made that way at the expense of another race of human beings made no difference to their deep dedication and stubborn belief they were right.

His thighs were still corded and strong, the legs below them as shapely as a man's legs could be called, and covered with fine, dark hair. Above his thighs, ridges of muscles corded a flat, washboard stomach, the width almost too narrow to support what came above—a broad chest and shoulders, rippling with planes and valleys that made a woman's palms tingle, her mouth go dry with the desire to touch them.

A strong neck, a handsome, rugged face, with lips a perfect match for hers and eyes changing color to a deep, velvet azure when they made love—or prepared to make love, as now. He called her hair silky more than once, but she thought the word applied to his, too. Black, blacker than a starless midnight, it would silver rather than gray as he aged.

Heat pooled in the various erotic areas of her body, and she crooked her finger at him. "You can come here now."

He did.

Twenty-six

~

"Mama said she was going out into the woods to gather some herbs she needed to cook with," Lucian told Wendi and Nick when they checked at the kitchen house a long two hours later. "She seems lots better now."

Wendi couldn't help but notice he eyed her warily and kept a kitchen chair between them. No doubt he thought any moment she might turn one of the flies buzzing around the kitchen into a huge bird of prey, which would swoop down on him and peck his eyes out.

"I'm glad," she told him, vowing to come back later and talk to him. "Would you tell her that Nick and I need to see her when she returns?"

"Sure. Where will you be?"

"Around the grounds somewhere," Nick said. "Not far, so we won't be hard to find."

Nick turned and left the kitchen, and Wendi followed him without thought. Her mind was on something totally different. Black hair, black as a starless midnight—no, it couldn't be. Could it? Surely her mother would have said something to someone. Maybe Aunt Sybilla?

Nick paused in the garden. "Tell me again what your aunt said about her vision."

Wendi vaguely acknowledged his words. "Yes. Yes, that's what she had. A vision."

"Wendi." Nick tipped her face up with a finger beneath her chin. "Wendi, where are you? I asked you something and you answered something entirely different."

"Huh? Oh, I'm sorry, Nick." His finger slipped away and she looked back toward the kitchen house. "I was thinking. What did you say?"

"I wanted you to explain about Sybilla's vision again."

"Oh. Well, she said she saw a statue of Aphrodite, and she was sure right when the vision began that it had something to do with my mother's Book of Shadows. That happens sometimes with visions—you realize right away, as soon as the vision starts, what it means. It's rare, though. Most of the time, the vision is a riddle and it takes thought to even decide if it's something from the past or in the future."

"I see. And the statue vision?"

"Aunt Sybilla said she was sure it was a clue to where we could find the book. In other words, a vision of the future, if we could figure out where it was. There was a cat in front of the statue, hissing at her, though, keeping her from the statue. When she peered closer, she saw a book in Aphrodite's hands, and it looked exactly like my mother's last Book of Shadows."

"A cat?"

"Yes. Aunt Sybilla is deathly afraid of cats, although I have no idea why."

"A cat?" Nick repeated, chewing on his bottom lip as though holding back the laughter sparkling in his eyes. "A witch who's afraid of cats?"

"Yes, she—"

Suddenly Nick broke into guffaws. Deep, chest heaving guffaws, which rang in the air. He rocked back, laughing and pointing a finger at her.

"A—cat?" More snickers. "A witch? Afraid of a cat? Oh, God, tell me it's not true so I can quit laughing."

"Well!" Wendi heaved an indignant breath and stuck her hands on her hips. "I don't appreciate your laughing at my aunt, Nick Bardou. Just because we're witches, doesn't mean we aren't human beings."

He closed his mouth tightly, but still a few snickers escaped. "What are you going to do to me if I don't quit laughing?" His eyes twinkled with mischief. "Turn me into that toad, like you've been threatening to do ever since we met?"

She lifted one hand and held up her index finger as though contemplating it. Sneaking a peek, she saw he'd stopped laughing and had a look on his face rivaling Lucian's boyish apprehensiveness.

"Hmmmm. That has possibilities," she mused. "But I think I like you too much the way your are." She sighed. "Way too much."

He reached for her, but she pointed her finger at him and he froze. "But don't push me too far," she warned, then broke into her own laughter when he nodded a cautious agreement.

She flew into his arms. "Oh, Nick," she said when he held her rather loosely. "Any witch worth her salt wouldn't use her magic on people she loves. And I love you very desperately."

He closed his arms around her like she wanted him to and breathed a sigh into her hair. "Whew, I'm glad to know that." Pushing her back so he could see her face, he said solemnly, "And I'm glad you don't use magic on those you love. That means you didn't cast a spell on me to make me love you. I'm glad that's all my own idea."

"Why, I wouldn't—" She sensed something and noticed him clamp his cheek between his teeth as though holding back new laughter. "You're teasing me! Dark and mysterious Nick Bardou is actually teasing me."

"Yep," he said. "And it feels damned good." He took her hand and led her deeper into the gardens. "Now, let's look for Aphrodite. Although I don't remember a statue like that out here, I guess it could have been added after I left. And remember, Aphrodite is the goddess of love. We might have to show our love in front of her before she gives up her treasure."

"Gladly," Wendi agreed.

But although they covered every square inch of the overgrown garden, even pushing back weeds along the fence and braving tangles of thorn-ridden rosebushes, they found no marble statue of the Greek goddess. Giving up in defeat, they left the garden and made a joint search of the house, even the hot, airless attic. No goddess. Nothing at all unusual. Finally they retired to Nick's study for a brief respite before they each went to wash up.

"Are there any hidden rooms or passages in Belle Chene?" Wendi asked Nick.

"Nothing at all that romantic," he assured her. "Believe me, Pierre and I would have found them if there were. And your mother definitely would not have known about them."

"Then I don't know what to do. There's only two of us, and I don't see how we can search this entire plantation. And why would someone put a marble statue off somewhere that it would be hard to find anyway?"

"You got me. There's some stuff stored in the barn, you know."

"My aunt assured me that she and Thalia searched there the very first thing. We've already gone over everywhere they previously investigated without finding anything they missed. No, I think we're just going to have to figure out a way to have the séance without all your workers finding out about it and leaving because there's witchcraft being practiced at Belle Chene.''

He quirked an eyebrow, and she said, ''Yes, I know what happened before. Word gets around through the servants' grapevine, you know.''

''You're right. Look, the only thing I can think of is to give the workers a holiday, even the stable hands. If I gave one group a day off and not the rest, there would be talk. And it's not unprecedented, even during the growing season, for the workers at Belle Chene to be given an extra day off when they've done a good job. We usually give them a Saturday to go along with their Sunday, so they'll have two days in a row. Today's Thursday. How about my telling Julian to give the workers the day after tomorrow off as a reward, and we can do the séance Saturday night? I'd hate to try it on Friday. Although I'm fairly sure the workers will leave the premises that evening, one or two might not.''

''That would be perfect, Nick! By the way, where is Julian? He avoids me very astutely, but I usually get a glimpse of him now and then. There wasn't any sign of him this morning, though. Most mornings I at least hear his room door open and close if he's here.''

''He's been spending a lot of his nights with Felicite Debeau, at Candlemas, the next plantation over. He thinks she's going to be willing to let him announce their betrothal very soon.''

''I see.'' She stood up from the deep armchair and started for the doorway. ''Well, I'm going up and at least wash off. Then maybe we should go see what's happened to Cecile. Don't you think she should have returned by now?''

"Ummmmm," Nick said noncommittally. "Wendi, wait a minute. There's something I'd like to ask you."

She turned, but didn't sit back down. "Yes?"

"Why were you so interested in Lucian this morning? And—" He took a deep breath. "And do you think he could possibly be our half-brother?"

She was barely able to stumble back to the chair and sit before she collapsed. "How long have you been thinking this?" she asked.

"Just recently. Ummmm, since we came here to Belle Chene." He rose and went to the sideboard, poured her a glass of reddish liquid from one of the bottles, and carried it over to her. "Here. This is sherry, and you look like you need it."

She nodded and accepted the glass, taking a healthy swallow, then grimacing at the sticky sweetness. After a few seconds, she felt a relaxing warmth. Nick leaned on the edge of the desk and nodded for her to take another swallow before he said anything else.

"Lucian looks like me, don't you think?"

"Yes, yes, he does. But what made you notice? I only made that connection this morning."

"We've had other things on our minds. And at first, it wasn't so much the fact he looked like me that made me start thinking about it. I thought he reminded me a whole lot of my brother Pierre. Then I remembered people always saying how much Pierre and I favored each other."

"He died in the war, didn't he?"

"Yeah. Same battle I got wounded in."

"I'm sorry."

"Thank you." He straightened and returned to the sideboard, opening one of the doors covering the shelves above it. Pulling out a leather-bound book, he came back and handed it to her.

"I hunted this up after I started having my suspicions. There are pictures of Pierre and me in there, and there's a marked resemblance in the Bardou line of men to Lucian in some of them."

"Couldn't he be your uncle's child?"

"Possibly," Nick admitted. "But I have this feeling he's not. Don't ask me why."

"So do I," she replied, laying the album on her lap to look at later. "It all fits with what we discussed and my own suspicions. The time my mother was away on her supposed voyage. She sent a couple letters to us, but Dominic could have arranged for that. Had them delivered to one of his factors in England and remailed from there."

"And her deep interest in Belle Chene after she returned," Nick said. "She was coming out here to see her son. Her son, whom Cecile was raising."

"It's true," said a voice from the doorway. They both turned to see Cecile standing there. "It's true, but I love him as my own. I've raised him as my own. What I haven't been able to do, however, is help him develop his magic."

Nick looked stunned. "His magic?"

"Of course," Wendi put in. "He's my mother's son, and he'd have magical powers. But warlocks have to develop their magic like witches do. And—" She gave Cecile a cautious look. "Please don't take this the wrong way, Cecile, but it's rather dangerous for a witch or warlock to have magical abilities and not develop them properly. Lots of things can happen."

Cecile knotted her hands inside her apron. "Dominic always said he'd take care of his son, but then he went away to the war and was killed. I think that was just his physical death, though. He truly died the day they buried Annabelle and Sabine."

She slowly crossed to the chair opposite Wendi and sank

into it. "Oh, he loved Sabine, too. What I mean is that it was losing both the women he loved like that. It devastated him, because he felt he was responsible for their deaths. He didn't protect Sabine, and he wasn't there for Annabelle when the scandal drove her to suicide."

"That was my guilt," Nick said in a sorrow-laced voice. "Father wasn't nearly as much at fault as me. If I hadn't started digging around, trying to find some way to make him give up Sabine and start being faithful to my mother again, none of it would have happened."

"You're wrong, Nick," Cecile assured him before Wendi could speak. "The forces for what happened had been put into place long before you found out what had been going on. They'd been building for years. As to Dominic, he came out here before he left for the war. He stayed two days with Lucian, although the boy was still way too young to remember it now. But he knew him then. He knew him as a man who loved him, although he was never allowed to call him poppa."

"What was my father going to do about him in the future?" Nick asked in a tortured voice.

Wendi rose and went to him, and he wrapped one arm around her, as Cecile said, "Other than his assurance that he'd take care of him, I don't know. It wasn't my place to ask. I think I would have, after a time, but he never came home."

She faced them defiantly. "Have no doubt I've come to love the boy as my own," she said. "And he cares for me as his mother. I won't let you take him from me. He loves Belle Chene, but he's mentioned wanting to see other places—places he reads about in the books he takes from this study here. I want that for him, but I hope he will always come back here."

"Did Jacques know?" Nick asked.

"Yes," she replied. "Yes, he knew. How could he not? And yes, yes, we were lovers. Not at first, but over the years we fell in love."

"Why didn't you marry?" Wendi wanted to know.

"He wanted to," Cecile admitted. "But I thought the scandal if we did that would hurt Lucian. If we'd fallen in love and gotten married during the time Sabine was carrying the child, we could have passed him off as our own. The way things were, our love happened later on. I was sure if we made it known by getting married, there would be a lot of talk about whether Lucian was Jacques's or Dominic's son. Do you see?"

"I see," Wendi said. She left Nick and knelt beside Cecile, taking the woman's hand in hers. "What do you want for Lucian now?"

"He's older now," she said. "Before, he would have been cut to ribbons by the children's vicious tongues. Things they heard from their parents. I believe he's old enough now to understand when I explain things to him."

"He's still pretty much of a little boy," Wendi said. "He was in my room the other day, hiding in the armoire while I performed some magic. I'm afraid it frightened him pretty badly."

"His own magic is starting to scare him, although he's not even sure what's going on," Cecile admitted. "He needs to learn to handle it."

Wendi stood. "Yes, he does. You realize, with him being my mother's son, his magic will have problems developing, too, until we find the book."

"The book?"

Wendi explained to the woman about a witch's Book of Shadows and the reason they had come to Belle Chene in the first place. She watched Cecile closely, hoping against hope the explanation would trigger something. That Cecile might have an idea as to where the book was hidden. Disappointment filled her when Cecile did speak.

"I don't recall a statue of Aphrodite anywhere around Belle Chene," she said. "I taught Lucian the best I could. We read some of the books together after I taught him to read, and one of them was on the Greek gods and goddesses. We studied the statues that are around the garden and identified them. Ceres and her daughter, Persephone. Narcissus. Circe. There was no Aphrodite among them."

"We're planning a séance in the barn," Nick told her.

Cecile gasped and laid a hand on her chest. "Please. Please don't involve Lucian in that. He's too young."

"He's definitely too young," Wendi agreed. "And his magic is unformed. No, we wouldn't want him there, because he might cause some real damage by not being able to control his magic. Do you have somewhere you can take him until after this is over?"

"My sister's," Cecile said with a nod. "She's the housekeeper for Tall Oaks, about two hours' north of us. I go visit her at times, and she has two boys close to Lucian's age."

"Take one of the buggies," Nick told her. "We'll send word when you can return."

Twenty-seven

~~~

The next day passed with agonizing slowness for Wendi. Nick assured her that Julian had given the workers the following day off. Several times Wendi tried to contact Sybilla, not only failing to get a response, but meeting a brick wall of resistance even when she tried to sense where Sybilla was. Finally she resorted to going in her room and lighting every color candle she had with her, then pleading with Sybilla to contact her. At first, it seemed useless, then she saw her aunt in the corner of the room.

When she started toward her, Sybilla held up a warning hand. "No." Her face was creased with worry and her hand trembled. "This is about the hardest thing I've ever done in my life, Wendi, darling," she said. "I'm not even supposed to be here. You have to do this alone, and neither Thalia nor I can help. We've been adamantly cautioned by the Goddess not to lend you a hand or interfere."

"Interfere? Aunt, am I placing Nick and this plantation in danger by pursuing this?"

"I—" A loud wind filled the room, drowning Sybilla's words and blowing her clothing around her. Her aunt raised an arm toward the ceiling. "Please. Please, just let me—"

Light flashed, stunning Wendi into closing her eyes. When she opened them, the room was silent and still. Sybilla was gone.

"Tell me!" she insisted. "Who's in danger?"

No one answered. She'd never felt so alone in her life, even when she heard Nick's footsteps in the hallway. He entered the room, a troubled look on his face.

"Did you hear or see anything right before you came in here?" she asked before he said anything.

"Hmmmm? No, nothing. Should I have?"

"I guess not. Are you ready for me to fix you some supper?"

"Wendi." He took her hand. "Wendi, we might have to postpone this séance. I need to go back into New Orleans. Justin Rabbonir sent word the house has been vandalized. Someone even set fire to it, but they were able to get it out before it damaged more than just the study. I need to go in there and take an inventory—see if anything's missing. If there is, it might give us a clue to who did the vandalism."

"I understand. But you can go and still get back by tomorrow night. I won't start until you get here."

"I'm not leaving you here alone!"

She pulled her hand free. "And I'm not leaving here until after the séance, Nick. There are things to do—preparations to make. This isn't just a normal reading like I'd do over on Canal Street. This is too important for me to take lightly and not make the proper preparations."

"I don't like it. Look, I'm not leaving until morning, anyway. If we go very early, we can stop by your house in town and ask Sybilla to come back out here with you. I'll hire a hack for the two of you at one of the stables."

"You can't force me to go with you, Nick."

When she first met him, he probably would have roared

and blustered—threatened her, as he had indeed at times. Now he looked at her quietly.

"No, but I can ask you to please come with me."

She stepped into his arms. He'd learned how to get his way without worrying about her magic all too well, she thought with a smile.

"I'll go," she agreed. "But let's get started early."

"I said we would." He kissed her, and she heard his stomach rumble, recalling that she hadn't fixed much lunch for them, just some cornbread and beans Cecile had left. She took his hand and led him out of the room.

"Let's see what we can find in the kitchen house for a nice, romantic meal."

"Right now, I'd settle for filling rather than romantic."

She whirled on him, and Nick backed away, holding up his hands. "I'm teasing," he said with a chuckle. "Please don't turn me into a toad!"

Laughing, she raced down the hallway ahead of him. "Last one to the kitchen house is a toad!"

They met Julian at the bottom of the stairwell, and Nick informed him of the fire and that he and Wendi would leave in the morning. He nodded, then told Nick that he'd left the weekly report from the overseer on the desk in the study, asking him to look it over so they could discuss it after dinner. Apologizing to Wendi, Nick headed for the study, but instead of joining him, Julian went the opposite way, toward the back veranda. With a shrug, Wendi decided to go with Nick and wait until he could walk out to the kitchen house with her.

The evening mysteriously cooled far below normal temperatures for the season, and a pleasant breeze filtered through the kitchen house later while they ate. Wendi hadn't lit the stove, since she found some melons, cheese, and bread in the cooling room. And pie. Cecile had left them several pies to tide them over until she returned.

Leaning back in her chair, Wendi stifled a yawn. Across the table, the candle flames showed Nick's eyes with heavy lids, and when he looked at her, he raised a hand to cover his own yawn.

"Sorry," he said. "It's not the company. I'm just suddenly very tired."

He pushed his dessert plate aside with his pie only half-eaten. She'd wrinkled her nose when he chose rhubarb to her apple as she named off the flavors of pies in the cooling room, but cut him a generous piece anyway when he assured her it really was his favorite. Cecile had evidently remembered that while she was preparing food to last them until she returned.

"I have a nice, stuffed feeling," she said, "but my yawn wasn't from tiredness. I was hoping we might go for a walk in this cool air. I doubt we'll have weather like this again before November or December. I can't get over how there's no humidity, either."

"Oh," Nick said with a groan. "I guess I might manage a short walk. Not far, though." He started to rise, and suddenly a strange look came over his face.

"What is it, Nick?"

"I . . . don't know if it's my wound or what, but I can't seem to get my legs to work."

"Nick!"

He surged upward, as though determined to gain his feet, then toppled sideways onto the floor with a crash, pulling the tablecloth and dishes with him. By the time Wendi rounded the table and knelt by his side, he was unconscious.

"Nick! Nick!" She shook him frantically, but he failed to respond. Suddenly Sybilla's face, tense with worry as it was in her bedroom earlier, flashed through her mind. With an obstinate effort, Wendi gained control of her emotions. She was in this alone, and she'd never figure out what was going on if she didn't keep her wits about her.

Leaning closer to Nick, she heaved a sigh of relief when his breath feathered against her face. She placed a hand on his chest, feeling his heart beating strongly. That was it, then. He'd been drugged. Someone had put something in the rhubarb pie, knowing that would be what Nick chose. Someone who knew his favorites.

Could it be Cecile—who knew different herbs from using them in her cooking? But what had she used? How dangerous was whatever he'd eaten?

Forcing herself to her feet, with his broken china plate and the remains of the pie in her hand, Wendi stared at the half-eaten pie in dismay. Finally she sniffed it, catching a very faint odor beneath the tangy rhubarb.

Henbane! Devil's Eye, as some of the healers called it. A form of the deadly nightshade. She could barely smell it, but there was no doubt in her mind it was there, almost covered up by the rhubarb's strong odor. Anyone not familiar with the various aromas of the healing herbs—or the dangerous ones—would have missed it, as Nick had.

If left untreated, he would die. She needed bitterroot to counteract the poison. There was bitterroot in her room, among the ceremonial supplies she carried.

Wendi started for the door, then stopped when she heard a step on the stairway leading to Cecile's living quarters. Whirling, she faced Julian, who was standing just far enough down on the stairs for her to be able to see his face, which had a demonic look on it. He held a deep-bladed knife in his right hand.

"You!" Wendi cried. "It's been you all along, not Nick."

"You should have insisted he let you stay behind when he went in to investigate the fire I paid to have set. Then I wouldn't have had to poison him."

"You killed my mother."

"And you're next," Julian hissed. "They'll think Nick went berserk over your resemblance to his father's whore. Killed you, too."

"You drugged the pie."

A maniacal laugh erupted from his throat. "That's the least of what I'm going to do this night! Wasn't it nice of my cousin to get rid of everyone, so I don't have to worry about someone interfering with me? And this time I won't leave him alive to take the blame. He can take it just as well dead. The henbane will take care of that."

"Nooooo!" Wendi raised her hand, but nothing happened. Her magic was failing her.

Please, she pled of the Goddess. *Don't make me handle this without magic!*

She'd heard of things like this. She should have seen it coming when her magic began giving her trouble. When Sybilla and Thalia set this up, then deserted her. As Sybilla had warned, she was deemed to right the karma with her wits alone. She hadn't realized that meant without the aid of her magic.

"What's the matter?" Julian sneered, moving down the stairwell. "Sabine couldn't protect herself that night, either. I asked the old voodoo woman, who I got the henbane from in case I needed it, what the deal was. It had bothered me for ten years. Sabine was a witch. Why couldn't she protect herself from me?"

Wendi edged toward the door. She hated desperately to leave Nick, but the part of her mind separate from the almost debilitating fear allowed her to rationalize that her only chance would be to draw Julian away before he used the knife on Nick. Escape, then come back and administer the antidote to the henbane. She had a little while. Henbane worked effectively, but slowly.

"Even magic can't work against karmic intentions," she said, trying to keep Julian's mind off Nick.

"That's what she told me." He snickered. "Right before I killed her so she couldn't tell anyone I'd bought the henbane from her."

As he stepped off the last step, making his move toward Wendi, he caught his toe on a rag rug at the foot of the stairs and staggered.

Since this might be her only chance, Wendi fled. Out the door. Across the porch. She heard him cursing behind her. Close. Too close. He had to have regained his balance almost immediately.

She tried to turn toward the house, but the words *no, barn* flashed into her thoughts, and she quickly changed direction. Racing toward the back gate, her mind worked frantically. The words she'd heard confirmed there *was* some magic here. If not hers, someone's. And the barn was where it would all come together.

Her heart beat frantically and she fought the dread filling her. The barn would also be silent and empty. There would be no one there to help her. No one to see her die. No one to find her body until the stable hands came back in two days.

If her death was the karmic intention, it would happen there. Where her mother had died.

Nick. She couldn't let Nick die. If she died, Nick died. No one would be able to administer the antidote in time.

Aunt Sybilla! she screamed in her mind. No one answered.

She flew through the gate and raced onward. The night was silent and still. Overhead, a bright, orange moon floated. From the corners of her eyes, she saw tree trunks and bushes blurring past as she ran. No matter how fast she was running, she felt as though she were running in quicksand, and the barn door never seemed to get any closer.

Suddenly it was there. She went through, ducking immediately to the side as though someone had whispered that's what she should do.

Julian barreled past her, but immediately plowed to a stop and whirled. Knife in his hand, he threw back his head and laughed.

"Did you really think I wouldn't see you duck over there?" he said after a second. "That goddamned white dress is the same color Sabine wore that night. And believe me—" He lowered his voice to a growl. "Believe me, it made the blood stand out like a crimson river. A crimson river running from her throat."

He curled his lip as he stared at his knife and gloated, then cocked his head to one side, worrying Wendi when he didn't move toward her immediately. What was he thinking about? What should she try next?

Surely she was far enough back in the shadows that he couldn't see her move her eyes. Without turning her head, she slid her eyes sideways to measure the distance to the barn door. Not that far, if she could distract him. But if she led him outside, he might go back and kill Nick.

"It's almost as though it's happening all over again," Julian mused. "Do you feel it? It was cool that night, too. It was late November, though, not June. The moon was full. Do you remember?"

Throat closed in fear, she couldn't answer him, and he snarled, "Do you! Answer me, bitch!"

"Why?" Wendi managed. "There was no reason for you to kill her."

"No reason?" he said in a puzzled voice. "No reason? There was *every* reason."

Wendi lunged for the pitchfork by her side, throwing it at him in the same motion. He tried to deflect it, but one tine pierced his arm, and he howled in pain. She leaped for the ladder to the loft beside her and scrambled up it. Plunging over the top, she peered back down to see him watching her, not attempting to follow.

He threw back his head again, demonic laughter filling the air as he plucked the pitchfork tine out of his arm and dropped the pitchfork as though he felt no pain. Probably he didn't, in his demented state.

"How do you think that's going to help you?" he asked. "Are you going to fly out the loft window? Leave here without one last attempt to help your lover, dying on the floor in there?"

He wasn't completely insane, Wendi realized. He could still think rationally. She wouldn't leave Nick. She couldn't.

At that moment she heard a sound at the barn door. Aware Julian had heard it, too, and turned his head, she froze in fear.

Nick. Nick was clutching the side of the doorway, barely able to maintain his feet.

"Nick!" she yelled. "Get out of here!"

He kept his drugged gaze on Julian, not saying a word.

"Well, well, well," Julian mused. "Looks like I didn't give you enough of the henbane to do its job. But that's all right. Now you'll be here while I kill your little witch, like I got rid of the one Uncle Dominic had before she could ruin everything. At least all the players are here. Maybe we'll just reenact the little drama that took place ten years ago."

Twenty-eight

~~~

"By the Goddess, you won't kill him!" Wendi screamed.

Her answer from Julian was another maniacal laugh, which mingled with the echoes of her shout and bounced off the barn rafters. The noise startled a flock of pigeons roosting for the night, and they flew out through the loft window, their coos and throaty chuckle-warbles an idiotic counteraction to the drama taking place below.

Wendi ducked when one white bird flew close to her face, a wingtip brushing her cheek as it whooshed past. Off balance, she fell to her knees, quickly scrambling to the side of the loft to peer down again.

Julian didn't seem in any hurry to kill Nick. He tossed the knife back and forth from one palm to the other, carefully keeping his gaze trained on the other man. Nick tried to stagger forward a step, but had to clutch the doorframe again before he fell.

"Let her go," Nick gasped. "There's no reason for you to kill her."

Julian shook his head slowly from side to side. "You know that's not true, cousin. Or haven't the two of you figured it out that far?"

"I've already deeded Belle Chene over to you," Nick said with a gasp. "Justin sent someone out yesterday and I signed the deed. The courier took it back to town to file for record."

"Too late," Julian said. "What good's all this to me without someone to share it with?"

"No one need ever know!" Nick insisted. He took a step away from the doorway and stood swaying on his feet. "Whatever you want, we'll do. I'll take Wendi back to California with me."

One of the pigeons had landed in the corner of the loft, and it fluttered its wings. Wendi ignored it while she desperately searched the loft for some sort of weapon. She saw only crates too big for her to move, and none of them were open so she might find something inside to use.

Just then, a small kitten stumbled into view near the pigeon. The bird flapped its wings again, startled, and a mother cat snarled nearby. The cat weaved out of a pile of hay, where the rest of the kittens were probably burrowed, and the hay shifted. For a moment Wendi thought there was another white pigeon there, but then she realized what she saw.

Down below, Julian said, "It's time to get this over with."

His voice was amazingly calm and flat. He took a step toward Nick, and Wendi screamed at him.

"Don't! Julian, Nick's right. We'll do anything you want!"

He didn't even look up at her. Gripping the knife in his right hand, he advanced another cautious step toward Nick. Nick straightened and shook his head as though clearing it of the vestiges of the drug, and Julian stopped to study him.

"You'll never be able to fight me, Nick," Wendi heard Julian say as she got to her feet. "Even if you didn't take enough to kill you, henbane doesn't leave your system that fast."

The hay cushioned Wendi's silent steps as she raced to the corner of the loft and grabbed the statue. Smaller than most of the other statues she and Nick had found in the garden, she easily lifted it and headed back to the edge of the loft.

Julian was shaking his head at Nick, who had taken another step back. Standing in the barn doorway, Nick swayed dangerously, and Julian feinted a jab at him, too far away to connect but close enough to make Nick jerk in reaction.

Wendi sent a brief prayer to the Goddess and threw the statue at Julian. It fell soundlessly, crashing into Julian's right arm—knocking the knife free and sending Julian to the floor.

Nick got to the knife while Julian pushed the statue aside and stumbled to his feet. Wendi scrambled over to the loft ladder, grabbing her skirts in one hand and stepping onto it. She tried to watch what was happening below as she started down the ladder.

"Get back up there!" Nick ordered as he and Julian faced each other.

Wendi ignored him and took another step downward.

Shaking his head at Nick, Julian then threw back his head. This demonic laugh was worse than any other, a mixture of howls and anger, which sent chills up Wendi's spine. Right in the middle of it, Julian lunged for the statue on the floor beside him.

He grabbed it, swinging it back and then throwing it at Nick. Suddenly Julian's face changed to terror, and it was as though the statue had attached itself to him. He staggered behind it, stumbling into Nick as the statue released itself and whizzed past Nick's head. Both men fell to the floor, and Wendi scrambled down the rest of the ladder, staring horror-stricken at where the two of them lay on the floor.

For what seemed like forever, neither man moved, and Wendi took a hesitant step forward. She couldn't tell which one of them groaned, but it was Nick who slowly shifted and stood. Blood dripped from the knife blade in his hand.

"I saw it, but I can't believe it," Nick whispered. "His shirt caught on the statue, and it jerked him forward, into me. It wasn't as much that I killed him as that he fell right onto the knife blade."

Wendi raced over to him, and Nick tossed the knife aside when she reached him, pulling her into his arms. They stood wrapped in each other's embrace for a long, quiet moment before the atmosphere in the barn changed so dramatically that they pulled apart and stared at each other.

"What's going on?" Nick asked.

"I think I know," she replied. "Just wait and watch."

She pulled him back from Julian's body, over by the ladder, where they halted. The air chilled even more, and the silence in the barn became almost deafening. To their left, in the spot where Sabine had died, a white light began to glow. At the same moment, a darker, more grayish light engulfed Julian's body.

The grayish light shifted like a pool of water, then began forming into a tall sphere. When Wendi tore her attention from Julian's light, she saw her mother standing where the white light had been.

"Mother," she whispered.

"Yes," Sabine replied. "I'm here, darling. I'm here to let my killer know he has finally received his punishment for my death."

The grayish light never formed into a recognizable shape, but Sabine talked to it anyway.

"You thought only of yourself, Julian. You didn't care that Lucian, your own cousin, would be deprived of his rightful inheritance by your killing me. You would have killed Dominic if he'd come back from the war, so no one would know another Bardou heir was more rightful than you. You even killed your own father when he wouldn't agree to keep Lucian a secret from Nick.''

She glided forward, and the gray shape appeared to cringe. ''When Nick returned, it wasn't enough for you to have him deed Belle Chene over to you, was it? You knew if the truth of Lucian's parentage ever came out, no family of blue-blood lineage, including Felicite's family, would have anything to do with you. The other scandal had died, but a new one was brewing, wasn't it? The scandal you would face when it was revealed you were the cousin of a warlock.''

A howl of rage escaped from the gray shape, and it suddenly narrowed and grew taller, filtering into the air and across the loft. Out the loft window. When Wendi drew her attention back to Sabine, her mother was shadowy rather than fully formed.

''Mother!'' She held out her hand. ''Please don't go yet.''

''I must, daughter,'' she said. ''But I'll always be with you, as I have been all this time. You'll realize now what it was all about—that the karma had to be corrected by Nick saving your life, so he wouldn't blame himself any longer for my death.''

Her gaze fell on Nick. ''You understand now, don't you?''

''I think so,'' he replied, but he gripped Wendi's hand so tightly she thought her fingers would break. ''I just can't believe I'm standing here talking to a ghost.''

Sabine laughed merrily. ''If you try to insist later it was only the henbane, Nick, you'll be lying to yourself. You need to accept her as she is, you know. But you will. Dominic and I were star-crossed, but yours and Wendi's path is now free of obstacles. However, you have to crawl out from under all your guilt, or you'll never make a proper father."

Sabine faded in a twinkling of the eye, and Wendi whispered goodbye. She heard a faint answering acknowledgment.

"Bye," Nick put in, and Wendi finally managed to free her hand from his.

"Nick, the next time we talk to spirits, please don't try to break my fingers. I might need them for something."

"I'm sorry. I still can't believe it."

He wobbled, then sat down on the ground, and Wendi hastily knelt beside him. "I still need to get the bitterroot for you," she said worriedly. "Will you be all right while I get it from my room?"

"It's not that," he denied. "I think I've overcome the drug. It's—" Suddenly he looked at her in apprehension. "What do you mean, the *next* time we talk to spirits?"

"I—"

"And what did Sabine mean about me being a father? Wendi, are you—?"

He got to his feet and took her hand. "I'll take you back into the house and you can rest while I take care of things out here. A woman with child needs to rest all she can. I at least know that much about it, although—"

"Nick, hush and listen to me." She tugged her hand free. "Nick, as far as I know, I'm not with child. But even if I were, I can't leave you here to deal with things alone. I think there's one more deed that needs handled."

"What? I'll take care of it." He pulled her into his arms. "Oh, I know what you mean. But I'm not about to ask you to marry me here. We'll do it right. Go back to New Orleans and have dinner at one of the finest restaurants. I want to see you all dressed up and with candlelight shining in your beautiful eyes. Candlelight that looks like reflected moonlight.''

She threw her arms around her neck. ''You better be sure you want me to say yes this time, Nick. I love you.''

''I love you, Wendi. I want you for my wife forever.''

''Even with my magic?''

''Even with your magic.''

Thalia Thibedeau's voice broke into the dreamy atmosphere surrounding her and Nick, and Wendi immediately bristled.

''I can't believe you don't recognize her, Sybilla,'' Thalia said. ''Why, it's plain as day.''

Wendi stared over Nick's shoulder to where Thalia and Sybilla stood, holding the statue between them. She didn't see Julian's body anywhere.

''What are you two doing here now?'' Wendi demanded.

''We just dropped in to help you clean up,'' Thalia said with a nonchalant wave of her free hand. ''I put Julian's body outside, in a coffin in a wagon.''

''Aunt Sybilla?'' Wendi said.

Her aunt shoved the statue at Thalia and rushed toward Wendi. Nick refused to relinquish his hold totally, but Sybilla wrapped her arms around Wendi and held her close.

''I'm sorry, my darling,'' she said. ''You don't know how hard it was for me to let you handle this alone. But you had to do it. It meant your happiness for the rest of this life if you accomplished righting the karma.''

''I know, Aunt,'' Wendi said, patting her on the shoulder. ''But what are you going to do about the part you still have left to play?''

Sybilla stepped back, her face white and strained. ''I suppose the book's up there wherever you found the statue.''

Wendi nodded. ''Yes, the statue of Psyche, the Roman goddess Cupid fell in love with. Not Aphrodite.''

Sybilla studied her warily, and Wendi inclined her head toward the loft. "It's up there, beneath some hay. I assume you didn't find it because there was a litter of kittens protecting it, and you didn't search in that corner."

Sybilla looked over at Thalia, who had moved closer to them. "Can't you—?"

"I can't get it for you, Sybilla," Thalia interrupted. "This is something you have to do yourself, if you want your own magic back at full power. That's why we couldn't get your dog to come with us. He isn't supposed to help you."

Sybilla gulped audibly, clenching her fists at her sides and staring at the loft ladder. Very slowly, one hesitant step after another, she walked over to the ladder. Gathering her skirts, she ascended the ladder in the same manner—one step, a hesitation, then another. Finally she disappeared over the top, into the loft.

They couldn't hear her footsteps, but here and there particles of hay filtered down between the cracks in the boards, marking her progress. Then they heard the hiss of a cat, silence, then laughter.

"Go on with you!" Sybilla said. "Your babies are beautiful, and I want to hold one of them. Oh, they're soooo cute!" She raised her voice and called, "Wendi! Wendi, there's a kitten up here that's the same strawberry color as your hair. Do you think we could take it home with us?"

"What about Alphie?" Wendi responded with a laugh. "He's not overly fond of cats."

"Oh, we'll teach him to tolerate them," Sybilla called. "Oh. Oh, look. There's Sabine's Book of Shadows. Right there beside the kittens' nest."

There was silence for a few seconds, then the hay particles tracked Sybilla's return to the edge of the loft. She peered down, holding a small kitten in one arm and a leather-bound volume in the other.

"Catch!" she called, tossing the book to Wendi.

Nick reached out and grabbed it, and they watched Sybilla carefully descend the ladder, carrying the kitten with her. When she reached the floor, she turned to face them. Chucking the kitten under the chin, she said, "Because I hated cats so much, I never saw any baby kittens before. I didn't realize they were this cute."

"They grow into cats," Wendi cautioned her.

"Pooh. By then, I'll love it so much it won't matter."

Thalia moved over to admire the kitten with Sybilla, and Nick slipped his arm around Wendi. He led her out of the barn and down the path toward the gardens. Overhead, the moon had changed from orange to the soft, silvery light so similar to candlelight. He didn't speak until they went through the gate and settled on a marble bench.

Picking up Wendi's hands, he gazed at her as though they were the only two people in the universe.

"She's right, you know. You can come to love someone so much nothing else matters. I've been so steeped in guilt, it didn't occur to me that others were suffering, too. And my own half-brother was one of them."

"You didn't know, Nick. Instead of feeling more guilt over that, you should be glad you know the truth now. That you're in a position to make things right for Lucian."

"I will," he promised. "What do you think of us staying in New Orleans? Cecile said Lucian loves Belle Chene, and I can make sure he's trained to take it over when he's of age."

"What about your businesses in California?"

"There's nothing there I can't either sell or run just as well from here."

Wendi hesitated, turning her gaze away from him. "I don't know."

"It's time you came to terms with your own problems, Wendi," Nick said quietly. "The way I have."

She rose to her feet and paced back and forth in front of him. "You don't understand. Everyone here knows now, and it's not just me who will be affected. It's you. And our children. They'll be called children of a witch, and it will keep reminding you of everything over and over again."

"You don't trust me then. This has all been for nothing."

"Trust you?" She whirled, shaking her head and not understanding how he could be so dense. "It's not about trust."

"It is," he said. "You tried to avoid love once by marrying Colin, but you set him free when you realized he loved someone else. Then Charles tried to use you. Now you think I'll never be able to overcome all that's happened and stand by your side. That your magic and your being a witch will ruin our marriage if we stay here in New Orleans. You don't trust me enough to believe I mean it when I say I love you. When I tell you how proud I will be to have you as my wife. Now and forever."

A tear trickled down Wendi's cheek, and she brushed it away.

"But—"

"No *buts*," Nick said. "All or nothing. Do you realize how much good you do with your magic? With the arts that come with it? I haven't been this pain-free in the last ten years. And you took away that woman's birthmark that day. I have no idea how many other good deeds you've done, but I'm sure there are hundreds."

He held out his arms. "Trust me, Wendi. Let's stay here and make a life for ourselves."

A beam of moonlight flowed down from the sky, outlining Nick as though a hundred candles had flickered into being. Wendi stepped inside the circle of light, into his arms.

Presenting all-new romances—featuring ghostly
heroes and heroines and the passions they inspire.

♥ *Haunting Hearts* ♥

__*A SPIRITED SEDUCTION*
    by Casey Claybourne   0-515-12066-9/$5.99

__*STARDUST OF YESTERDAY*
    by Lynn Kurland   0-515-11839-7/$5.99

__*A GHOST OF A CHANCE*
    by Casey Claybourne   0-515-11857-5/$5.99

__*ETERNAL VOWS*
    by Alice Alfonsi   0-515-12002-2/$5.99

__*ETERNAL LOVE*
    by Alice Alfonsi   0-515-12207-6/$5.99

__*ARRANGED IN HEAVEN* 0-515-12275-0/$5.99
    by Sara Jarrod
Prices slightly higher in Canada

TIME PASSAGES

_CRYSTAL MEMORIES Ginny Aiken   0-515-12159-2
_A DANCE THROUGH TIME Lynn Kurland
                                       0-515-11927-X
_ECHOES OF TOMORROW Jenny Lykins   0-515-12079-0
_LOST YESTERDAY Jenny Lykins   0-515-12013-8
_MY LADY IN TIME Angie Ray   0-515-12227-0
_NICK OF TIME Casey Claybourne   0-515-12189-4
_REMEMBER LOVE Susan Plunkett   0-515-11980-6
_SILVER TOMORROWS Susan Plunkett   0-515-12047-2
_THIS TIME TOGETHER Susan Leslie Liepitz
                                       0-515-11981-4
_WAITING FOR YESTERDAY Jenny Lykins
                                       0-515-12129-0
_HEAVEN'S TIME Susan Plunkett   0-515-12287-4
_THE LAST HIGHLANDER Claire Cross 0-515-12337-4
_A TIME FOR US Christine Holden   0-515-12375-7

Prices slightly higher in Canada   All books $5.99

Payable in U.S. funds only. No cash/COD accepted. Postage & handling: U.S./CAN. $2.75 for one book, $1.00 for each additional, not to exceed $6.75; Int'l $5.00 for one book, $1.00 each additional. We accept Visa, Amex, MC ($10.00 min.), checks ($15.00 fee for returned checks) and money orders. Call 800-788-6262 or 201-933-9292, fax 201-896-8569; refer to ad # 680

Penguin Putnam Inc.   Bill my: ☐Visa ☐MasterCard ☐Amex_____(expires)
P.O. Box 12289, Dept. B   Card#_____
Newark, NJ 07101-5289
Please allow 4-6 weeks for delivery.   Signature_____

Foreign and Canadian delivery 6-8 weeks.

Bill to:

Name_____
Address_____City_____
State/ZIP_____
Daytime Phone #_____

Ship to:

Name_____ Book Total $_____
Address_____ Applicable Sales Tax $_____
City_____ Postage & Handling $_____
State/ZIP_____ Total Amount Due $_____

This offer subject to change without notice.